Carl Hiaasen is a native of Florida with an outstanding reputation as an investigative journalist exposing local scandals. He now writes a thrice-weekly column for the *Miami Herald* and has been nominated twice for the Pulitzer Prize. William D. Montalbano is one of America's senior foreign correspondents. His reporting from more than seventy countries on five continents has won a dozen national awards. Currently Rome Bureau Chief for the *Los Angeles Times*, Montalbano is at work on his fifth novel.

Also by Carl Hiaasen and William D. Montalbano in Pan Books

Powder Burn

Also by Carl Hiaasen

Tourist Season
Double Whammy
Skin Tight
Native Tongue

TRAP LINE

Carl Hiaasen and
William D. Montalbano

PAN BOOKS
LONDON, SYDNEY AND AUCKLAND

First published 1982 by Atheneum, New York
and simultaneously in Canada by McClelland and Stewart Ltd

First published in Great Britain 1992 by Pan Books Ltd,
Cavaye Place, London SW10 9PG

9 8 7 6 5 4 3

© Carl Hiaasen and William D. Montalbano 1982

ISBN 0 330 32666 X

Printed and bound in Great Britain by
Cox & Wyman Ltd, Reading, Berkshire

FOR PATRICIA HIAASEN
AND VINCENT F. MONTALBANO

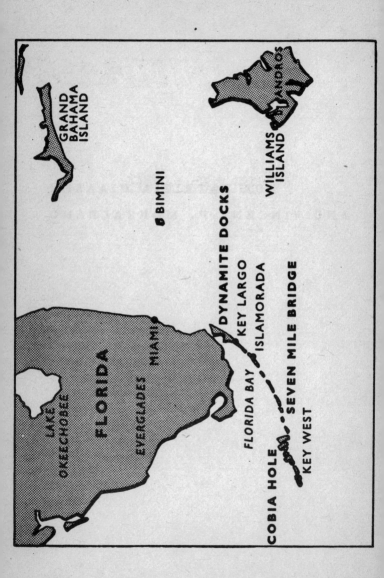

TRAP LINE

PROLOGUE

Miami, Florida

THEY HAD AGREED to meet at the Omni Hotel, a double obelisk that rises on Biscayne Boulevard near the bay. The businessman had booked a suite for two weeks; bayside, as always.

Manolo flew up from Key West. He had been told to come alone, so he had. He took a Yellow Cab from the airport. It overheated twice on the short trip.

Inside the hotel complex, Manolo wandered like a rat in a maze for ten minutes before locating the right elevator. He stepped out on the eleventh floor and strode across a thick amber carpet to the businessman's suite. Manolo knocked twice, then shifted the briefcase to his right hand.

The Colombian, lithe and bronzed, answered in bare feet and white shorts with a royal blue stripe. The two men shook hands and exchanged greetings in Spanish, their accents as distinct as Boston and Biloxi.

Manolo followed the businessman along a trail of scuffed sneakers and sweaty socks to a chilled bucket of champagne. He lay the briefcase on a marble coffee table. The Colombian poured two glasses. Manolo, who hated champagne, paid no attention to the extravagant label.

He noticed four new graphite tennis rackets on a toffee-colored sofa.

"For my backhand," the Colombian explained. "If I improve my backhand, I am unbeatable, I assure you. I have a lesson in one hour."

Manolo glanced at four large boxes piled haphazardly in a corner.

"*Por Dios,* Jorge, more Betamaxes? Didn't you buy three the last time you were here?"

"A primitive model. These are truly sophisticated." Jorge set his glass on the coffee table next to the briefcase. "Everything is here, no?"

Manolo nodded. The briefcase contained exactly one million two hundred thousand dollars in neatly stacked twenties and one hundreds, nonsequential.

"Good. There are no problems?" The question was rhetorical. The Colombian would have known about problems.

"Things are going smoothly," Manolo answered, gesturing toward the city's infant skyline. "The market continues to be magnificent."

"Did you have a good flight from Key West?"

"Ah, twenty minutes: nothing."

The Colombian slipped into a canary yellow pullover and attached a gold Piaget to his left wrist. A young woman with coffee-colored eyes and small breasts appeared briefly, nude, in the doorway to an adjoining room. The Colombian waved her away.

"I need a favor," he said, sipping slowly.

Manolo knew there were no favors, only debts. He also knew that his side of the ledger was perpetually red.

"I have some friends," the Colombian continued, "who will be needing some reliable transportation."

"Oh?"

"In about two weeks they will be on an island in the Bahamas. They will need a boat to the mainland. Key Largo will do . . ."

Already Manolo was shaking his head. "It's no good, Jorge. My people won't run aliens."

"You mean Colombians, don't you? Your people won't run Colombians. Not long ago, if I recall, *your people* brought a hundred thousand aliens into this country from a port in Cuba. Mariel, wasn't it?"

"That was different," Manolo said, reddening.

"Oh, no, my friend. A lot of your people did that purely for money, not out of decency or love of family. Is that not so?"

"That was different."

The Colombian picked up one of the tennis rackets and ran strong fingers across the strings.

"Think of this as a family mission, Manny. Like Mariel, but perhaps a bit less heroic, more private. These friends are important to me. I need them here, and, therefore, you need them, too."

"But . . ."

"They will help assure that we do not lose any of this *magnificent* market."

Manolo squirmed. The hotel room suddenly seemed small, terribly hot.

"You don't understand. The boat captains who work for me will not do it, no matter what I offer them. Grass, pills, coke—anytime, by the box or the ton. Even guns, if you like. But not people."

"But I do not understand. And I dismiss the distinction as irrelevant."

"Look. People are not bales or boxes. You can't heave them

over the side when the Coast Guard shows up and turns on the blue light."

The Colombian slammed the racket against the edge of the coffee table.

"Basta!" he commanded. "I need one man for one run. That is all. We will take precautions to see that there are no questions afterwards."

"No!" Manolo urged. "This isn't the Guajira. Key West is a small town where dead people still attract a certain amount of attention."

The Colombian shrugged. It had been an uneven struggle, and it was over. He reached for the champagne.

"Handle it however you must. Go home and get me a captain. The best one you can find. Persuade him, if necessary."

"I will try."

The Colombian smiled, and his new American teeth gleamed like perfect ivory tiles. "You will try, my friend, and you will be successful. You are an honorable man, a valuable man."

Manolo forced an appreciative sigh.

"It has been a good month for us, no?" the Colombian said brightly. "I'm not even going to count what's in the briefcase. That is how much I trust you."

The preposterous lie amused Manolo. The cash, he knew, would be sifting through an electronic counting machine within the hour.

"Call me soon," the Colombian ordered at the door.

"Of course," Manolo replied. "Good luck with your backhand."

In the lobby, he patted his jacket to make sure the airline ticket was in his pocket, then walked out into the suffocating heat to hunt for an air-conditioned taxi.

CHAPTER 1

THE *Diamond Cutter*, a forty-three-foot Crusader, Key West-built with an 892 GMC diesel, cleared Stock Island twenty minutes after dawn. Albury, splay-legged at the helm, drank bitter coffee from a chipped white mug. Jimmy ran a rag across the wheelhouse windshield.

"Engine sounds good, Breeze. Real good."

"After five days' work, it ought to," Albury said. The parts alone had set him back a thousand dollars.

"Well, it sounds fine," Jimmy insisted. "Gonna be a good day."

"I hope so. Anybody needs a good day, it's us. Won't be long until the end of the month."

Jimmy laughed through the new gold beard that dwelt like peach down on his sunburned face. Reflexively, Albury turned the *Diamond Cutter* to the southeast, where the first line of crawfish traps rested on a shelf of coral. He could have found it blindfolded. The fine porcelain sky, the rising white sun, the hot and cool sea hues of the Florida Straits; these were Albury's birthright. He had first made the trip in another era, with his granddaddy sitting on a sun-bleached whiskey crate steering an old one-lunger with no winch and hardly a wheelhouse. And, since that morning, how many times, in how many boats? And how long since the excitement had died? Too long.

The end of the month. Surely it had not weighed so heavily on his granddaddy, like the massive, unsheddable shell of a loggerhead. Albury could not imagine the old man fretting in his pine cabin, neatly stacking the bills as they piled up like driftwood.

But now, with his boat cutting a clean vector toward the crawfish waters, Breeze Albury mentally riffled the accounts due that awaited him in the sagging trailer that his granddaddy would have rightfully spurned as a chicken coop. Boat payment, dockage, fuel, parts; then there was the rent—pure robbery—car payments, the electric, and, of course, the installment on the TV.

Against these he weighed the account of Albury, William Clifford. This month it came out worse than usual. Fishing had been good, until the engine quit. The parts had taken cash, plus he still owed for the cypress on two hundred new traps.

And spikes. He had promised Ricky a new pair. Pitching was hell on spikes. His mind held the image of Ricky's arm flashing, the streaking ball a white pea as it flew to the plate, the foot slamming down hard in a balanced follow-through.

Albury smiled. He leaned back from the waist and let his belly steady the wheel, gentling the lobster boat through the quiet morning sea. He would buy the new spikes, pay on the boat and whatever else he could, then let the unpaids chase him. Wouldn't be the first time. Let them take back the color television if they wanted it bad enough.

Albury lit a cigarette and nudged the *Diamond Cutter* on

a course that would intersect up-current with the first trail of orange-and-white buoys that marked his trap line.

"Hey, Jimmy," he called down to the deck where the young mate was coiling rope. "The captain needs a cold beer."

A few minutes later, Albury jockeyed the boat with unthinking precision as Jimmy hauled the traps. He would snare the pumpkin-sized buoy with a swoop of long practice, fix it to the winch, and watch expectantly as the cypress trap spun to the surface. Albury only half-heard Jimmy's running count as he stripped the traps, rebaited them with a strip of cowhide, and sorted the catch.

"Breeze," Jimmy said, "what say we keep a few of these shorts today?"

"No shorts. Toss 'em back."

Shorts were the undersized crawfish that measured less than five and one-half inches from bony carapace to tail. Get caught with them and it could cost a couple hundred dollars, except that no self-respecting crawfisherman would get caught. If the Marine Patrol happened by, all you had to do was cut the weighted sack from a line on the stern and let the delicious evidence sink. There weren't many Key West captains who could resist the shorts now and then; easy to sell and good to eat. Albury could have gotten away with it, but Laurie would have lectured him for sins against the ecology. Risk was another factor. A fine was the last thing he needed, especially with the end of the month coming. You could never tell about the Marine Patrol. One morning they wave hello, next morning they get nasty and board you.

"Hey, Breeze, you been to Miami a lot." Jimmy had climbed into the wheelhouse with two fresh cans of Bud. Albury drank deeply as the *Diamond Cutter* plodded dutifully, like a milkman's horse, toward the second line of traps.

"Sure, I spent some time in Miami. Why?"

"I just wanna know if it's safe up there."

"Safe for what? Christ, don't tell me you never been." Albury was incredulous.

"Sure, with my dad, a few times. But it's been a couple years. I want to know is it safe for Kathy, if I take her up there with me. You read about all these murders anad crazy shit . . ."

"How old is Kathy?"

"Almost seventeen."

"And you've been married . . ."

"About three months. She wants to go up there and do some shopping."

Albury laughed. "Sure. It'll be fun."

"Well, I asked her what's wrong with shopping on the island, but she says everything's too ugly or too expensive down here."

"Sounds like she wants to see Miami."

Jimmy ran a calloused hand through his bleached-out hair. "Maybe so," he said.

Albury drained the beer, squashed the can, and tossed it neatly into a broken lobster trap on deck. He gestured toward the windshield. "Trap line comin' up."

Jimmy turned for the deck, but Albury stopped him with a question. "You got enough money for a shopping trip to the city?"

"No, I ain't, Breeze. Not yet. But I figure you and me gonna pull us some fat fucking crawfish out of the Cobia Hole this morning, and I'll be fixed just fine."

"OK," Albury said. "You got it."

The second line of traps bore decent fruit. With Jimmy happily babbling a soon-to-be-rich aria for the very young, Albury aimed the *Diamond Cutter* out to sea, toward the final trap line, the new and private one he and Jimmy called the Cobia Hole.

Albury had discovered the improbable underwater ridge two years earlier. It was four hours southeast of Key West, further than lobstermen normally ventured on a one-day trip. If you believed the charts, the water in this area was too deep, but a good hard look at the color told Albury there was a ledge below. Intrigued, he had investigated, patiently tracking a long and narrow ridge where none should have been. Jimmy, who was new on the boat then, spotted a huge school of cobia churning crazily in *Diamond Cutter*'s wake. On a lark, he had tossed a couple of short crawfish into the hungry swarm of brown, half-blind game fish, which had fallen into a frenzy and milled behind the boat for more than a mile.

From then on it was the Cobia Hole. A gamble, too. Albury needed extra fuel to make the trip, longer lines for the deepwater traps. There had damn well better be crawfish, he had warned Jimmy. And there had been. The first two seasons had been bountiful, and somehow the hole had remained Albury's secret. God bless Jimmy for keeping his mouth shut.

This year it was too early to tell if the gamble would pay off. The first catches had been good, but in twenty-five years, man and boy, of crawfishing, Albury had seen more than one bonanza dry up overnight. And it was only a matter of time before other boats moved in at this hole, too, and then Albury would move on.

On the docks at Stock Island, everybody knew Breeze Albury liked to fish alone. Or not to fish at all: a few knew that, too, the ones who had gone to school with him and watched over the decades as he had dulled from a rakehell all-state fullback into a thickening, middle-aged fisherman who rolled with life's punches. It was easy to surrender to the potbellied, parboiled ennui of the island.

If you were a Conch, you were a Conch. Simple as that. You could run a bulldozer in Georgia, fell trees in Oregon, drive an eighteen-wheeler cross-country, fix fancy foreign cars in Atlanta . . . even work for a year in a New York brokerage house, management trainee, for Christ's sake, suit-and-tie, sorry-you-are-leaving, Mr. Albury . . . do it all until the Conch called you home in excitement and dismay to the broiling rock where your granddaddy hauled crawfish and ran rum; where your daddy died drunk in his hardware store, slumped across the counter clutching a ball of brown twine at forty-three; and where those goddamned motherfucking orange-and-white lobster buoys danced with false promise in the morning sun.

Eighteen years Albury had been back. Eighteen years: three boats, all owned by the bank; one wife, a slut pickled in alcohol long since; two kids, one nightmare and one dream; and Laurie, sometimes.

At least the boats had served him well. He had had this one—what?—nearly nine years now. She rolled a bit and skittered in a bad following sea, but *Diamond Cutter* was a hell of a crawfish boat. Albury had commissioned her the *Peggy*, and she had fished with that name until one night he had walked into the trailer to find the old lady in bed beside an empty bottle and a bald stringbean who drove tourists around on the Conch Train.

Probably it was just as well Albury had been half-lit himself. At first he had resolved to burn down the trailer with the two of them inside, but all he had had was a disposable lighter, and, lying there green on his belly in the musty living room, he couldn't get the carpet to catch. So he had stormed out, fallen asleep on the boat. In the morning, he got a can of red paint and changed the name of the boat. For two years Albury had fished as captain of the *Peggy Sucks,* mocking her every time he had motored out of the harbor. Everybody had understood.

The boat had stayed that way, its crooked name in red and black, until Albury had repainted her in a fit of off-season energy. *Diamond Cutter* was a perfect name. Even then, Ricky was just getting out of Little League, but you could tell he was going somewhere. Boog Powell made it off the Rock. So would Ricky. Good size, a blazing fastball, and good stuff to wrap around it. He pitched smart, picking at batters the way a heron speared glass minnows.

A good kid, too. Last summer he'd hung around the boat constantly, wanting to help. Albury had refused, although he had been more tempted than he'd ever let on.

"Look, champ, let's make a deal. I fish, you pitch. Fishing is for bums, and you're going to the majors. If you don't make it, then I'll teach you how to catch crawfish. In the meantime, if I catch you pullin' traps, I'll break your fucking arm—the pitching arm."

Ricky had laughed and found himself a job at the Burger King down on Roosevelt Boulevard.

An internal clock snapped Albury's reverie. He looked at his watch, then at the sea. He could feel the ridge. The boat had to be over it now. So where—? His eyes narrowed, his jaw muscles tensed. He checked the compass by flicking it with an index finger. He turned on the fathometer, and in moments the Cobia Hole rose in graphic relief on the screen. With fists like claws, Albury spun the wheel until *Diamond Cutter* turned south-southwest to follow the ridge.

The motion awakened Jimmy.

"Hey, Breeze," he called without rising, "ain't we there yet?"

"We're there."

Jimmy unfolded and stood up. "Jesus, why didn't you tell me?" he said groggily, peering out across the bow. "Where are the traps?"

"No traps."

Jimmy either didn't hear or misunderstood. He stretched luxuriously, hands high above his naked chest, staring ahead where he knew the orange-and-white buoys would soon be bobbing. He stood like that for what seemed a long time, and then he knew.

Jimmy leaned over the side. "Breeze?" he cried. "Breeze, we're over the ridge. Where are the fucking traps?"

Albury's voice snagged somewhere in his throat.

"Breeze?"

"No traps, Jimmy. Not one."

Jimmy ran to the bow and pressed himself against the rail. "The whole line's been cut!" His voice cracked. His eyes fanned the water. Under the noon sun, the secret ledge sketched a faint indigo seam, eighty feet down. Albury idled the engine and climbed down to the deck.

"Who?" Jimmy asked. "Marine Patrol?"

Albury shook his head. "This was a legal line. Besides, they'll just bust the slats out of a few traps, as a lesson. They won't cut your pots off like this."

Albury felt sick. Mentally he cataloged a list of his enemies. Nobody hated him bad enough to cut his traps. He couldn't take his eyes off the water.

"Shrimper," Jimmy murmured. "Motherfucker probably did it last night. Never looked, just dragged the goddamned nets over the traps."

Albury slowly guided *Diamond Cutter* in a wide arc around the ridge, then began tacking back, against the tide, to the north. A shrimp boat is sloppy. The odds of one raking all fifty-five traps was remote. A few of the severed markers should be floating loose, Albury thought. A copper taste rose in his mouth as he scanned the bridge.

"Breeze?"

"It was no shrimper, Jimmy."

"Shit." Jimmy sagged back onto the ice chest. "Who? What for?"

"I don't know."

They checked four more trap lines on the way back to Key West, all sabotaged. By the time they reached the reef where the last one should have been, Albury had figured out the marauder's course. He was not surprised to see whitecaps where he should have seen the buoys; he watched unblinking as Jimmy retrieved a single orange-and-white buoy, examined the limp tail of rope, and pronounced it hand-cut with a fishing knife.

"What did you do, Breeze?" Jimmy asked wanly. "Are you screwin' somebody's wife?"

Albury shook his head sourly. Jimmy palmed the orphaned buoy like a basketball. "This ever happened before?"

"Years ago when I was fighting with one of the Cubans. He

got mine. I got his. But that was only a dozen traps, not three hundred."

"Three hundred and twenty," Jimmy said. He hurled the marker as far as he could. A gust of wind caught the styrofoam ball and slapped it gently into the ocean.

They rode home in heavy silence, Albury nipping liberally from a bottle of Wild Turkey he kept on board for times when beer would not do. Was it the twenty-second or twenty-first? he wondered. Didn't matter, really, the end of the month was now.

Fifteen minutes out of Stock Island, Jimmy could no longer contain himself. "Breeze, I'm scared," he blurted.

"Well, I'm pissed, but I'm not scared."

"It's Kathy," Jimmy said, embarrassed, fighting tears. Albury stared out the windshield. The island was taking shape on the horizon.

It came with a rush. "She's pregnant. It wasn't supposed to happen with the pills, but it did anyway. We can't have no baby, not livin' with her folks. Not on what I make. Shit, Breeze, she ain't old enough. I needed the money from today to take care of it. From the Cobia Hole."

Albury ran a half-numb hand across the stubble of his cheek. "That was your shopping trip to Miami."

"Yeah, I got the name of a doctor up there who does the whole thing in his office one afternoon and you go home the next day."

"That's the most sensible way to handle it," Albury agreed.

"But I got no money."

"That makes two of us, son."

Jimmy whined, "What am I gonna do?"

"Let me think on it."

At the fish house, Jimmy cleaned the boat and hauled the iced crawfish onto the scales. Only about two hundred pounds, a quarter of what it should have been. In disgust, Albury joined a small group of fishermen drinking outside the small commissary. There was a tribal likeness among them: faded baseball caps above lined and sunburned faces, slick white fishermen's boots, powerful legs and muscled torsos betrayed by bellies swollen from too much beer.

"See you got your eight ninety-two fixed," said a fisherman named Spider.

"Finally," Albury said with a grimace that told what it cost.

"Do any good today?"

"Started out real good," Albury replied, popping a Budweiser. "Then it got real bad. I lost five trap lines way down south."

"Robbed?"

"Cut."

The fishermen clustered around to question Albury closer.

"How many traps?" demanded a crawfisherman named Leech.

"More than three hundred. Cut by hand." Albury's voice was rising. The agony of the day finally was settling in his stomach.

"We got to find out who," Leech said.

"Little Eddie," Spider declared. "Didn't you get in a fight with him over at the West Key Bar?"

"A year ago," Albury said. "He wouldn't have waited a year. Shit, he loaned me some tools last week."

"Then who?"

"I don't know."

The men fell quiet. The mental arithmetic was familiar; three hundred traps at thirty bucks apiece, not to mention the loss in crawfish catch. By the time Albury spoke, each of the men had figured out in dollars how badly he was hit.

"Well, I better go help Jimmy."

"How you fixed, Breeze?" Spider asked as gently as he could. A couple of the fishermen looked away, pretending to watch another crawfish boat unload three slips away.

Albury said, "I'll be OK."

"I got some old traps at the house. Maybe a hundred," Spider offered. "A couple need slats, but that's all."

"Thanks. I might take you up on it." Albury slapped Spider on the shoulder. He lobbed his empty beer can into a garbage dumpster.

"If you hear anything about this . . . I'd appreciate it."

"For sure, bubba," Leech said. "Somebody's bound to talk."

His friends watched Breeze Albury leave in silence. They were Conchs and they were fishermen. They knew how bad off he was, and they understood his dilemma. They knew he would die before he let the bank or the fish house take his boat. You could usually hold them off for a couple months, especially if it was a Conch you owed. Everybody got behind; that was life on the Rock.

How far behind was Albury? his friends wondered. Not one of them could have survived such a catastrophe, to have nearly half your traps cut in one day. Something terrible had happened, and it was only the beginning. The fishermen understood this. They watched Albury clump to the end of the dock, chat quietly with Jimmy, then wind up his perforated old Pontiac.

The headlights snared the brown men in their white boots and glinted off upraised beer cans. Albury decided he had done the prudent thing by not mentioning the phone call of two days before. He honked at the fishermen sitting in the white penumbra. He wondered how many of them had paid everything off. In one bundle. Wearily, he thought: it must feel so damn good to get it off your shoulders. Too bad there was only one way.

17 »

CHAPTER 2

"ANGLER'S HAVEN," announced the peeling wooden sign above the gravel drive. Only a few clumps of Australian pines and the occasional tang of the sea made the trailer park bearable. Years ago it had been mapped out as an inexpensive colony for winter tourists, but the trailers had gone to hell and the tourists never came anymore. Albury's neighbors were servicemen from the Navy base, fishermen, bartenders, store clerks, and newlyweds. Albury's trailer, as far as he knew, had been sitting on the same set of concrete blocks for twelve years; it was largish, for a mobile home, and in its own way comfortable, like a dusty old coat. There were three bedrooms, separated by tissue walls of phony wood. At one end was Ricky's; the largest was where Albury and Laurie slept; and the one in the middle was a study, up for grabs. Breeze agonized over his accounts here, Ricky his homework, and, when the fancy struck, this was where Laurie laboriously pecked out the poetry she never sold.

The place was empty. Albury twisted the dial on the air conditioner and held his face to the grill until the air turned cold. He imagined a shower, but two notes on a coffee table intercepted him. Neither was signed. Neither had to be.

The first came right to the point, scrawled in big, half-forgotten schoolgirl letters on the back of an envelope: "I took them glass flowers, and that pink ashtray that was mine."

The second note, written cursively in blue felt-tip, was equally blunt: "She also took my watch and seventy-six dollars of my tips from the dresser. 'Them weren't hers.' Get them back, please.

"And for the *LAST FUCKING TIME, CHANGE THE GODDAMN LOCK!*"

Albury groaned, threw the notes away so Ricky wouldn't see them, and stormed into the tiny bathroom. He jerked three of Laurie's panties and a pair of support stockings from the shower rod and let the water run cold.

It was too early for Peg to be in the shack she shared with the Conch Train driver, so Albury went looking for her in the crowd of tourists and freaks who gathered nightly at Mallory Docks to watch the sun drip into the sea. Peg wasn't there, but Albury found her by a strip of beachfront at the island's tip that was a magnet for tourists.

When Albury had married her, she had been a good-looking woman, a little hefty maybe, but solid; blond and solid. Her family had never been much good, but—well, Albury hadn't paid much attention then. He parked the Pontiac a half-block away and walked back to where Peg sat on a three-legged campstool, fingers running idly through the coarse sand. Next to her was a canvas bag, a pile of bleached conchs, and some woebegone starfish. "Southernmost Queen Conchs $3," read the hand-scrawled sign jutting from the sand at her feet.

Time had been cruel to Peg Albury. She was only forty-three or forty-four, but sitting there alone in a shapeless house-dress, waiting for a sucker from Michigan or Pennsylvania to buy her shells, she looked twenty years older. Her eyes under the floppy straw hat were dead. Sun and whiskey, a lethal combination, and in Key West an epidemic. Albury felt sorry for her, as though for a stranger.

"Evenin', Peg," Albury called softly.

She rose to her feet, wheezing. Sand cascaded from her lap. "Don't you go beatin' on me, Breeze Albury. I only took what was mine."

Albury almost smiled. He had never beat her, even when he should have. It had been almost four years since she'd left. Now she was a sandy and pathetic stranger.

"The watch wasn't yours, Peg. Neither was the money."

"How do you know? Is that what she said, your tramp? Who do you believe, your wife or a tramp?"

"The money and the watch, Peg, now."

"Now, now, now," she snarled. "Like you were boss." Her eyes drilled him from under the brim of the hat. "What are you gonna do if I say no? Go to the cops? They'll believe me, not you, Mr. Convict."

Albury suppressed a sudden gout of anger.

"I won't go to the police, Peg. I *will* tell Ricky."

"Trash," she hollered. From somewhere in the folds of her dress she extracted Laurie's Omega and dashed it into the sand. She might have stepped on it, but Albury nudged it aside and stooped quickly to pick it up.

"Tell Ricky? Tell my baby? Why don't you tell him his daddy's a convict? Gonna tell him his daddy was in jail when his sister died? Tell him that, Breeze."

"He already knows, Peg." Just, Albury reflected, as he certainly knew what his mother had become.

"Now give me back the money."

"No!" She lurched in the sand, dislodging with one foot a near-empty bottle that had been hidden by the canvas bag. "I need the money, Breeze. Charlie's sick. Can't work."

"Drunk, you mean."

"He ain't. You think everybody's drunk, don't you? Charlie's sick. It's his heart. Doctor says he's got to go up to the VA in Miami. It's true, I swear it."

Albury knew she was probably lying, not that it mattered. To get Laurie's money he would have to wrestle her. It wasn't worth it.

"OK, Peg, you keep the money. Just keep it."

"It's for Charlie, goddamnit."

"Yeah. And stay away from the trailer. I'm changing the locks tonight, so your key's no good anymore."

Peg's hand moved tremulously to her neck, where the key hung like a charm from a rusty necklace.

"God, Peg, you're a mess," Albury said in a whisper.

She was scrabbling in the sand for her bottle as he turned away.

Albury had a couple of stops to make, one at a sporting goods store, the next at the grocery. Then he parked at Key Plaza and hurried, six-pack under arm, across to the ball park. The lights were on already, and Albury was afraid the game had started. He arrived just in time to see Ricky walk to the mound.

It was a game of no particular consequence, and it had attracted only about a hundred people, mostly parents and girl friends. Albury slid into the bleachers behind home plate next to an angular black man in sandals and a white cotton shirt.

"Evenin', Enos. How about a beer?"

"Thanks, Breeze. You cut it pretty close tonight, uh?"

"Been a poor day." Albury gave a half-embarrassed wave to Ricky, who rewarded it with a big grin and a doff of his maroon cap.

Ricky didn't look sharp. Some of his deliveries were higher than they should have been, the ball not moving as well as it might. Still, the first three batters went out weakly, and Albury felt himself beginning to relax. He leaned back, elbows propped

21 »

on the bleacher behind him, savoring a tentative breeze that had sprung up off the Gulf.

"God, that feels good."

"Yeah," Enos said. "You know, that boy of yours is some kind of pitcher."

"I think he can go all the way."

"I believe you're right."

In the second, Buddy Martin, Enos's son, stung Ricky with a sharp single off a curve nobody else on the field would have hit. Albury snorted.

"Maybe they could go all the way together. I'd rather have Buddy on the same team than hittin' against Ricky."

Enos laughed politely at the compliment.

"As long as he goes, Breeze. I don't really care if it's to baseball, to college, or to the Army. As long as he goes."

"You and your boy fightin'?"

"Hell, no. I just don't want him to grow up in this town, that's all. There's nuthin' here, Breeze. It's all the same as when we was kids, only less of it. And there wasn't nuthin' then. I don't know why you came back. You had a good job."

"Several," Albury said.

"All places change, don't they? It ain't like we were still kids, fishin' for grunts all day. You could live in this town then, Breeze. That was why I stayed. That was why you came back, too. At least you could live here, then. Now, well . . ."

"Now we got no excuse, Enos. No fucking excuse."

They watched the game while they talked. Buddy Martin stole second, but died there as Ricky got the last out on a rifling fastball.

"You're lucky, Breeze. You go out fishin' every day. That's all right. I wouldn't mind that. But if you want to know what's really happened to the island, come with me for a day, hauling the U.S. mail. Just one day. You'd see shit you wouldn't believe."

"I'm sure." Albury felt like telling Enos about his traps, but he couldn't bring himself to talk about it.

They drank another beer in companionable silence as Ricky's team, the Padres, scratched two runs off the chunky rival pitcher, a lefthander.

"You know the Fletcher place on Frances Street?"

"Near the cemetery."

"Yeah, right," Enos said. "Garrett sold it for a hundred and thirty thousand yesterday."

Albury sat up.

"Cash," Enos whispered bitterly.

"Shit. It's full of termites. They couldn't get seventeen five for it eight years ago."

"The guy that bought it was twenty-two."

Albury shook his head. "Say no more."

"I hate all this, Breeze."

"Yeah."

"I want out. If I can't leave, then my boy will. I swear."

In the fifth inning, Ricky's control deserted him briefly. He walked the leadoff batter and lost the second man to a crisp single. Then it was time to face Buddy Martin.

"Low and away," Albury yelled.

Ricky threw a fastball, letter high on the inside corner. The bat slashed forward, and Albury felt the "crack" in the fillings in his teeth. The ball rocketed into the alley in left center and smacked the Merita Bread sign on the first bounce. Both runners scored, and Buddy Martin cruised into third with a stand-up triple.

Enos beamed. "Way to stroke, Bud," he called to his son.

Ricky called time, and Albury winced in shame when he saw Ricky and his coach yoking Ricky's right spike together with a piece of friction tape.

"Damn," Albury said, "I got a new pair for him in the car. Be right back."

"I'll watch the beer," Enos said.

Albury strode across to Key Plaza, where he had parked the car. He broke into a trot when he saw the figure inside the Pontiac, stretched across the front seat, probing the glove compartment. The man never looked up until he felt the huge hands around his left leg. Albury yanked once and spilled the thief onto the pavement, his shaggy head hitting the asphalt like a brick.

Dazed, the young man foggily surveyed his attacker: sharp, angry green eyes; nut-brown face capped with short salt-and-pepper hair; the mouth a thin, icy slash; the neck thick, veined with rage.

"Easy, grandpa," said the kid. His long hair was thick, flicked with dirt and leaves. His face was milky and pocked. Albury scowled down at him.

"Where's the toolbox?" he demanded. "And the bag from the sports shop? Where'd you stash 'em?"

"Man, I don't know what you're talking about."

Albury placed a booted foot on the man's neck and shifted his weight slowly until the face turned red and a grimace bared every tooth. "You're a prick," Albury said. "And I'll snap your goddamn neck if you don't answer my question."

The thief flailed on the pavement and directed his bulging eyes across the parking lot, to where a battered red VW sat alone. Albury hauled the young man to the car. In the back seat were his toolbox and the bag containing Ricky's new spikes. He retrieved them and walked back to the Pontiac, the thief in tow.

"You gonna call the cops?"

"Where you from?"

"Atlanta." The young man began brushing off his jeans and picking the gravel off his shirt. He thought it was over.

"What are you doing down here?" Albury asked evenly.

"Visiting." The young man used his hands like a comb, straightening his hair and sweeping it out of his face.

"Visiting," Albury repeated.

The kid nodded. Albury wordlessly slammed him in the stomach with a straight right, then cracked him in the nose with an abbreviated left cross. The kid fell, blubbering, the dark blood shining in the pale lumination of the streetlights.

Albury locked the toolbox in the trunk of the Pontiac and hurried back to the ball park with the spikes. The game was already over. The Padres had won, 6–2.

"Nice game, champ," Albury said to Ricky as he came off the field.

"Yeah. You see the slider I got Buddy with in the seventh?"

"Naw, I missed it."

"So did Buddy." It was Enos, laughing. "Breeze, I got worried about you, so I polished off the six-pack."

"Some dirtbag broke into the car. I caught him before he got away. Here." Albury handed Ricky the spikes. "I should have brought 'em with me in the first place."

Ricky opened the box. Buddy Martin looked over Ricky's shoulder as he inspected the new spikes.

"Dad, these must have cost forty bucks."

"It's OK," Albury said. "Had a good catch today."

Enos gave him a doubting glance. Albury wondered, could he know about the traps already?

"Get your jacket on, champ. Let's get going before the whole car gets stolen. Enos, Buddy, we'll see you."

It took Albury ten minutes to reach Whitehead Street, after dropping Ricky at the trailer with an injunction to let his arm dangle a long time in the hot shower. Albury was supposed to pick up Laurie in an hour. Time enough.

If the Green Lantern had any distinction at all, it was as the only bar in Key West that never claimed to have fueled Ernest Hemingway. The bar was a chintzy dive of plasterboard and shadows in what was supposed to be a nautical motif.

It seemed like every time Albury went in, there was a different parrot harping in a bamboo cage over the cash register. The regulars would sometimes turn the nightly dart games on the birds, when things got loose.

Albury nursed a beer and looked quietly around. "Have you

seen Winnebago Tom?" he finally asked a bartender named Pete.

"He was here. Probably out back."

"Out back" meant upstairs in a supposedly private room reached by a stairway guarded by a tough, tattooed young Cuban. People said he had once been a commando.

Albury gestured toward the stairs with his head. The guard nodded slightly and let him pass without a word. Upstairs, about ten men formed a smoky circle on the linoleum floor, playing poker.

Winnebago Tom leaned nonchalantly against the wall, watching the action with almost scornful disinterest. Albury knew he was the house. Tom was wiry, slick, one of those savvy Key West Cubans whose family had been around so long they had all but forgotten Spanish. Tom worked for the Machine. A linkman, they said.

"Well, hey, bubba." Tom prised himself off the wall. He gestured toward the knot of men on the floor around a nucleus of dirty ten- and twenty-dollar bills. "Looking for a game?"

"Can we talk?"

Tom shrugged. "These are my friends."

Albury lit a cigarette to camouflage his dislike. "It's business," he said.

"Business!" Tom exclaimed with artificial brightness. "Why didn't you say so? Why don't you go down and wait for me in the camper? Help yourself to a drink. I won't be long."

Parked behind the bar, Tom's Winnebago was the most luxurious in all Monroe County. It was cool and quiet, the air conditioner barely audible. It smelled of wood and real leather. Albury counted eight stereo speakers inset into the walls. He poured himself a stiff scotch from one of two dozen bottles in a long cabinet behind the bar. The glass was crystal, Albury noted. Tom liked to boast that his camper had cost fifty thousand dollars.

After fifteen minutes Tom came in, humming "Help Me Make It Through the Night." He poured himself three ounces of Chivas, drank off half of it with a smack, and smiled at Albury.

"Yessir, business. What can I do for you, Breeze?"

"What do you know about my traps?"

"Orange-and-white. Everybody knows that. Family colors, always have been."

Albury stood and helped himself to another scotch.

"I heard you lost a few," Tom ventured.

"A few hundred," Albury said harshly. "Tom, you lived here your whole life. You know what this kind of thing means. You know the rules."

"I know there's a law against cutting traps."

"You know the rules. Forget the fucking law."

Tom ran a manicured finger around the edge of his glass until it squeaked.

"You called me two, three days ago," Albury said.

"Did I?"

Albury slammed down his glass.

"OK, I called you. I'm a businessman. You said no. I said OK. A man can say no," Tom said. "Even in this town, a man can still say no. I respect you for that, Breeze. Lots of fishermen woulda jumped at the chance for that kind of money. You said no. I respect that. 'Course, you weren't hurtin' then quite as badly as you are now."

Albury's eyes flashed. "Three hundred traps."

Tom whistled unctuously. "Damn! I'm really sorry, Breeze. But why you tellin' me about this?"

"Because I'm considering whether to kill you."

Tom laughed thinly. "Oh?"

Albury sat down in a leather chair that swiveled. He toyed with a set of stereo headphones. "That's right, Tom. If you had anything to do with it."

"I didn't, Breeze."

"It would have taken a boat a day and a half to cut all those traps off," Albury said. "The real mystery is how they knew about one of my spots. It's a lot of miles out, Tom. No one but me fishes there. Of course, if someone were to follow me one day, at a safe distance, they could figure it out. With radar and Loran."

"I suppose," Tom said enigmatically. "Not many crawfish boats have radar, Breeze."

"Not many *need* radar, Tom. Just a few. Fact, I can tell you the names of a half-dozen fishermen who do. And they all worked for you, one time or another."

Tom fingered a thick gold chain on his left wrist. He stared at Albury through hooded eyes. "I said it wasn't me. I got work to do now."

Tom was at the door when Albury stopped him.

"Tom, if you say you didn't, I'll accept that."

"Good."

Albury was standing now, and he had a good six inches on the taut little Cuban. "When we talked on the phone the other day, you said the offer was good for a week."

Tom's eyes narrowed. "Yes."

"I'll do it. I'll make the run."

Tom stepped back and played at fixing another drink. He said nothing for several minutes. Albury stayed by the door; he felt hot and vaguely sick to his stomach.

"One minute you threaten to murder me and the next you want to do business," Tom said reproachfully.

"It's the nature of things."

"Yeah, well, I don't know anymore."

Albury said, "Tom, your people need a boat as big and fast as mine. That's what you said the other day. More than that, you need a captain who's not going to spook or run aground. These waters are my business. What happens afterwards is yours. You're in charge of delivery." That was how Winnebago Tom had gotten his nickname. Pack the stuff in campers, five and six tons each, and send it to Miami on U.S. 1. State troopers don't often stop a Winnebago; got to be nice to the tourists. Tom was a clever man.

"I'll let you know. What's the name of your boat again? The *Peggy—Peggy* something?"

"*Diamond Cutter*," Albury corrected. "And she'll do twenty-eight knots."

"You got in trouble a few years ago, didn't you?"

"Not right away." They hadn't caught him until the stuff had been unloaded. Albury stung at the memory.

"Yeah, I remember. But if you have trouble one time, it's real easy to have trouble again."

"It was real quiet trouble, Tom." In jail he had not told them anything, and Tom knew it.

"Yeah, I remember that, too, Breeze."

Albury felt soiled, like he had wet his pants or sicked up in church.

"I'll be going now, Tom. You know where to find me."

"Right, Breeze. I'll let you know."

Wearily, Albury backtracked down Whitehead and parked the car outside the Cowrie Restaurant. When Laurie got off work just after eleven, she had to wake him up behind the wheel.

CHAPTER 3

HUNCHED CROSS-LEGGED on the rumpled bed, Laurie distractedly ran the pencil along the side of her neck. Deep in thought, she scratched the underside of her breast.

"Aha!" she exclaimed at last. "Got you. 'Russia's foe is not the land of the rising sun.' Four letters, Breeze."

"Hmmm." He was buried in the box scores.

"It's 'West.' Japan is the land of the rising sun, but the sun rises in the east; and if it isn't the east it must be the west. Russia's foe is the West. Got it?"

It looked to Albury as though the Orioles would not catch the Yanks.

Laurie swiped at his ribs with her elbow. "Breeze, pay attention. Improve your mind."

Of course, if the Red Sox could ever put their pitching together it could make a difference. That would cause some trouble.

"Goddamnit." Laurie snatched the sports page away and

levered up to sit crossways on his chest, pencil poised. His horizon shrank to one chunk of milky thigh, more Reubens than Modigliani.

"Get off, willya?"

She stared down at him sideways, not a beautiful woman—too heavy for that—but definitely not homely either.

"Now don't get cross." She tossed the paper onto the floor, jettisoned the pencil, and pivoted ninety degrees to deliver a slurpy kiss to his dong. Her knee, coming over, clipped his jaw. He saw stars for an instant, and then only an ample bottom cleft by frizzy red hair. He swatted her on the ass.

"Breakfast," Albury demanded.

"Later," she called. "Besides, we're both too fat, and anyway"—a suckling pause—"Sundays make me very sexy."

"You've already been very sexy. Twice. Once on the top, once on the bottom."

"Complaining?"

"I'm kind of hungry."

"No," Laurie said firmly, embarking on a longer, more tingling pause. "You want eat? I'll give you eat."

"What the hell," Albury said.

Later, the smell of frying bacon roused him. He lit a cigarette and assayed the sounds from the tiny kitchen. Laurie was a tolerable cook. She came in after a few minutes with a cup of fresh coffee and tweaked his nose gently.

"I'm cooking up a half-dozen eggs. With garlic," she announced. "The Sunday is young."

She was the hungriest damn woman he had ever met. Ate like a horse and fucked like a dream. She had been with him almost a year and never once let him imagine that he was the only one. Some nights she didn't come home. But then again neither did he, some nights.

Albury had met her in a bar and they'd screwed for the first time twenty minutes later in the backseat of the Pontiac. Like two horny kids.

She never talked much about herself, but as the year went

by she let more and more show, the way a hermit crab slips out of the shell to see if it's safe to dash for another. Laurie Ravenel, South Carolina girl, victim of one of those fancy New England colleges where they'd pruned her accent, straightened her hair, and filled her head with so much useless drivel that she had graduated a well-groomed zombie—poised, fashionable, and neurotic. A stockbroker had wooed her, married her, bored her, and caught her in bed with his best friend in quick succession.

She had stopped in Key West because that was where the road ended. A bright girl, but awful empty-headed sometimes. She was a sucker for causes. One week she collected petitions to build a refuge for sooty terns, as though Miss Ravenel, going on thirty and a Key West expert for all of six months, would know a sooty tern to say hello to if one nested smack between her big boobs. The gay crowd down at the Cowrie was where she picked up that kind of bullshit. It was like a virus. With each new cause—Save Fort Jefferson, Protect Our Beaches, Ban All Fishtraps—Albury seesawed between amusement and anger.

Laurie had been the first woman Albury had brought home since Peg had left. He had thought about it a long time before deciding it wouldn't hurt Ricky. He was old enough to know which end was up. And they hit it right off, Laurie and Ricky. She might not have been the mother he needed, but she did fine as kind of an older sister. She cut his hair; washed his clothes; helped him with his homework, particularly when the math was beyond Albury; and one night, when he had come home with a savage crick in his pitching arm, Laurie had spent more than an hour working on it.

Most Sundays, Albury didn't go out on the boat. Now he dozed on the black vinyl sofa. He dabbled with the newspaper, poked at a western. Laurie had appropriated the bedroom to write, so he made himself a scotch, quietly. It had been one week since his edgy conversation with Winnebago Tom. Albury had stopped by the Green Lantern a few nights before, and the arrogant asshole had waved at him and sent over a drink. A rum punch, whatever the hell that meant. Albury had left it on the bar.

The end of the month was on him. The bills were stacked up in the middle of the room, but they would keep.

Laurie emerged at one point in search of a verb. She was predictably disheveled in one of Albury's boat shirts and a pair of her favorite lime panties. Poetry really took it out of her.

"You know the word 'shirr,' like shirr eggs?"

"So?"

"Do you think I can use it as a verb, to describe time? Like time 'shirred'?"

"Sure." He pronounced it to mock her.

"Don't be stupid. I think it'll work."

Albury asked lightly, "Hey, lady, when are you going to sell one of them poems?" He rhymed poem with comb.

"Soon. Sooner than you think," Laurie said. She slammed the door so hard that the windowpanes rattled.

Albury went back to his western. He would give Tom another week to run up the flags. If not, Albury would drive up to Marathon. There was a guy up there he knew in the same business. An Anglo, too.

When Laurie next appeared, she was composed and contrite. "Breeze, what are these?"

Albury glanced at the fistful of bills. Change-up followed by a fastball. She had gone, lickety-split, from impassioned poetess to hard-eyed business manager.

"Bills," he said. "What the hell do you think?"

"Jesus, why haven't you paid them?"

"No money."

"No money?"

Christ, she was slow sometimes on the practical things. "It was a bad month. I had to overhaul the engine."

"I remember."

"And fishing was shitty," Albury said.

"Breeze, there's enough lobster around that we could serve

it for breakfast down at the restaurant and still have a full freezer. Everybody's loading up."

"Not me." It was time to find a reason for going down to the boat. He swiveled to his feet, growling.

"You haven't been gambling or anything?" Laurie asked.

Albury laughed bitterly. "No. Since you won't shut up, I'll have to tell you. I lost a couple hundred traps. Somebody cut 'em off. Brand new crawfish traps, gone just like that." He snapped his fingers in her face. She winced and took two apprehensive steps back. Her eyes began to flood.

"Oh, Breeze, I'm sorry. Baby, I'm sorry. Why didn't you tell me?"

Albury's anger evaporated. He ran a tired thumb and forefinger across his eyes. "It's just one of those things. Nothin' you can do about it. I'm just telling you so you won't ask about the money. When you're down three hundred traps, there's no way."

"Three hundred." Laurie took a deep breath. "Who would have done it?"

"I don't know. I've been trying to find out." He walked to the bar and refilled his scotch. "If Ricky finds out about any of this—any of it—"

She nodded dumbly. "He's bound to, Breeze. The kids at school are bound to be talking."

Albury grunted. She was right.

"What are you going to do?"

"Don't know."

"You act like you do."

"I'm thinking is all." Albury didn't feel like talking anymore. He told Laurie he needed to go down to the fish house. She took two Amazonian steps forward and crushed herself to him, taking his wind away and tipping three ounces of fresh scotch onto the floor.

"Oh, Breeze," she murmured against his chest. "This is terrible."

"Exactly," Albury said, taking her shoulders and moving her back so he could look at her face. "When this is settled, I'm taking off with Ricky."

"Out of Key West?" Laurie asked.

"Exactly," he said. "I'm finished with it."

The preliminaries of the run began that night, simultaneous with the start of the nine o'clock movie. Laurie had taken to bed with a yellow legal pad and three crisply sharpened number-two pencils. Ricky lay on the floor, torn between John Wayne and an English essay. On the sofa, Albury had no pangs: he had seen the movie before; he would watch it again.

Ricky answered the phone and passed it across without taking his eyes off the screen.

"Captain Albury?"

"Yeah."

"Check your mailbox." The voice hung up.

Albury lay on the sofa and tensely smoked a cigarette. He waited for the first commercial so Ricky would not link his departure to the abbreviated phone call.

"Shitty movie," Albury proclaimed at last. "Shut it down and finish your homework, OK? Get a good night's sleep."

When Ricky had wandered off, Albury slipped on his loafers and left the trailer.

Albury opened the bulky brown envelope in the dim roof light of the Pontiac. He counted the money first. A jumble of bills in two stacks, neatly banded. Used bills, tens and twenties only, not sequential. Ten thousand dollars. That would be about right. The other half would come later.

It was the Machine's way of buying loyalty and silence. If a Conch got caught with a load, which happened, he didn't talk. In return, the organization provided its own form of social security. Hadn't Peg got an anonymous envelope in the mailbox every month while he was away? Sure, they had lost the house, but that was because of the medical bills. The Machine would have paid those, too, but Albury never considered asking. Those bills were his business and nobody else's.

Albury locked the cash in the trunk and unfurled the chart that had come with it. It was the standard NOAA marine map, showing the Lower Keys all the way up to Sombrero. In pencil someone had carefully drawn a small X near Looe Key, a tiny island in the deep water off Big Pine. Albury figured that the mother ship would be another seven or eight miles out. The X designated where he was supposed to lay up with the *Diamond Cutter*. In a corner of the chart was written the date and time—Tuesday at midnight.

Albury cranked up the Pontiac and went to see Crystal.

His knock was answered promptly by a dusky girl with doe's eyes and a hook nose. She carried a baby on her hip and another in her belly.

"Breeze! *Que rico. Hace tanto tiempo.*" She bussed him chastely on the cheek.

"Well, hell!" Crystal tossed a printed circuit onto the workbench and swiveled to face Albury, a gigantic grin igniting his Zapata mustache. Propelled by oaken arms that ended improbably in delicate watchmaker's fingers, Crystal trundled down a wooden ramp and stopped at Albury's feet. They shook hands. It was a ferocious game of grip that they played, and, as usual, it was Albury who surrendered.

"You're not gettin' any weaker!" he said to Crystal.

"Hell, I'm on top of the world. See what I've been up to since you were around last?" He gestured with pride at the girl's belly. "This one's a girl, I can feel it."

Crystal was the post office. He fixed radios and he passed messages and made a good living out of both. From a console that looked to Albury like something borrowed from NASA, Crystal boasted that he could monitor every radio frequency for a hundred miles, from the Tavernier volunteer fire department to the José Martí control tower at Havana airport.

Albury believed him. Crystal was a genius. Everybody in Key West was proud of him. Ten years ago, in high school, the kid had won every science fair, even one in Miami. The Army had got him before he could get to college. In recognition of Crystal's talents, the Army had made him a combat infantryman, and nine months later it had shipped him home from Saigon with no legs.

That was back when people still believed in the war, and plenty of folks had chipped in to help Crystal get started in a repair shop. Everybody said how well Crystal had adjusted and Albury believed it, too, until one night about six years ago when he had come in late one night with a marine radio that would send but couldn't receive and had found Crystal slumped across the workbench, half-drunk, crying like a little boy, with a whiskey bottle by his head.

"Got one here not even you can fix, hotshot," Albury had said, taking a slug from the bottle but not watching the bottle or the radio or even Crystal, watching only the pistol that lay on the bench a few inches from Crystal's hand. "Probably have to send it back to the factory," Albury had said as Crystal's head came up, full of tears, Albury watching the pistol and ready to jump.

"Ain't no radio I can't fix," Crystal had blubbered.

"Not this one. Fucked up six ways from Sunday."

Then Crystal's slender hand had flashed out and caught Albury's broken radio and sent it banging down the workbench into a voltmeter. Albury, pretending to get out of the way, had let it go and eased around the other side of Crystal's chair and got himself between Crystal and the gun. They had polished off the bottle, and when Albury had pushed himself off the bench to get another, the gun had come with him. Crystal had pretended not to notice.

It was so long ago that it made Albury feel old. On the eve

of Albury's run, Crystal was a different person, high as a kite, bragging about his kids, showing off his new Bearcat scanner. Albury told him what he needed.

"Easy," Crystal said. "It'll be good to hear a familiar voice out there. Want a drink?"

They drank, and across town the Machine hummed with practiced efficiency. A weary Winnebago Tom ran down the soiled list for a final time and committed it to the flame of his lighter. Done, by God, and done well. Times like this he felt like a general, moving supplies, giving orders, summoning the troops to the right place at the right time. Smooth as silk. Tom rifled through the pile of coins on the gray metal shelf, inserted one, and made a telephone ring in a fine old Conch house on White Street.

The phone annoyed Manolo. It had been an annoying day. The Reds getting two runs in the ninth had cost him two grand. A horse in the eighth at Belmont that was supposed to have been a sure thing ran fifth. Two grand more.

Manolo laid down his book, a biography of Walt Whitman, reduced Mahler's ninth to a whisper, and waded through the wall-to-wall mauve carpet to his Ethan Allen desk.

"Yes." It was not a question.

"Everything's ready," Winnebago Tom reported on the other end.

"Details?"

"Momma's coming on schedule." He meant the big ship. It had landed in Cartagena on schedule.

"Very well."

"We have three hawks and one pigeon."

"Fine."

Tom asked, "Still sure about the pigeon? It's gonna cost us two tons."

"It is the one we discussed?"

"Yes. Of course. I went to a lot of trouble for this."

"I can appreciate that," Manolo said frostily.

« 38

"So is it too much to ask why? This is out of the ordinary. It's a big risk."

"Tom, do you get paid to worry?"

"Please . . ."

"Answer me!"

"No," Tom said, not feeling much like a general anymore.

In the house on White Street, Manolo turned up the music and resumed reading. With any luck, tomorrow would be less trying.

CHAPTER 4

T H E *Diamond Cutter* went fishing the next morning as usual.
When there were other boats nearby, Jimmy and Albury
pretended to pull traps. To be on the cautious side, they even
iced down a hundred pounds of fresh crawfish; Albury said it
would look better for them in case something went wrong.

His instincts were good. At noon the *Diamond Cutter* was
overtaken by a twenty-six-foot Cigarette boat, screaming like
a stock car. Albury had watched it coming for miles.

"This our man?" Jimmy asked nervously.

"No way." Albury suppressed a laugh.

The Cigarette was a smuggler's special that had been
seized by the Marine Patrol two years earlier. The driver
was Mark Haller, a tough old Conch, one of the grittiest
sonofabitches the patrol ever had the good sense to hire. Albury had been his friend for years, but this was the first time
it might count for something. Haller pulled up and tied to a
cleat on the *Diamond Cutter*'s stern.

"Hey, bubba," Albury said with a wave.

Haller nodded and hopped from the cockpit of the speedboat to its bow, playing the swells perfectly. He wore highway patrol-like sunglasses; Albury couldn't be sure where he was looking.

"How you doing?" Haller called.

Albury shrugged. "Lousy.'

Jimmy slipped below for a beer; the sight of a man in uniform was too much, right now.

"You want to come aboard?" Albury moved to the stern to give Haller a hand, but the chunky Marine Patrol officer motioned him off.

"That's OK," he said. "Breeze, I heard about your traps."

"I guess everybody has," Albury said with a sour laugh.

"Well, I intend to find the fuckers that did it," Haller said. "We can't have that kind of shit down here."

"I'd sure appreciate it if you did, Mark. Have you heard anything yet?"

"A little." Haller stood with his burnished hands on his hips, peering at another crawfish boat about three miles off. Albury noticed he was carrying a .357.

"Breeze," he said after a few moments, "if you find out who did it, call me. Don't try to handle it yourself."

"I can't make a promise like that. You know how it goes."

Haller wore a thin smile as he untied the Cigarette and fired the huge engines to life.

"Mark, don't suppose you're gonna tell me what you've heard?" Albury shouted.

"When I know more," Haller yelled back. "I promise." Then he was gone.

Jimmy looked up inquiringly from below deck. "Do you think he knows?"

"About tonight? Of course not," Albury said.

"Then why'd he stop us?"

"Routine. Haller stops everybody. That's what makes him Haller. Cubans can't stand him. He'll board their boats and talk for an hour, and he doesn't speak a goddamned word of Spanish. He'll do it just to make a point."

Jimmy tossed a beer to Albury. "That kind of thing makes me nervous," he said.

Albury stripped off his clothes. "Time for a swim," he declared, perching himself on the side of the boat. For a delicious instant he hung in the air, then crashed feetfirst into the blue sea. He paddled for about a minute, then floated effortlessly on his back. Albury heard the whoosh as Jimmy hit the water in a clean dive, and for an instant he felt like laughing aloud.

At dusk, they anchored off Looe Key, waiting. A northeasterly breeze carried pesky clouds of no-see-ems towards the boat from the island. Albury and Jimmy basted themselves in Cutter's insect spray.

At about nine, Crystal checked in over the VHF radio.

"Lucky Seven, this is Smilin' Jack. Your weather for the evening is clear with light winds out of the northeast. Seas three to four feet, increasing around midnight."

Albury gave him a ten-four. Midnight was the key. He lifted a hatch and pulled out two plywood boards. The words *"Elizabeth Marie* Tampa" were freshly painted on each. One went on the bow and the other on the transom; Jimmy slipped into the water to help attach them. Albury was no artist and the bogus name obviously was hand-lettered, but it covered the legend *Diamond Cutter* and the registration number. If there was a chase, and if a name was all the cops could see at night, it would give Albury an edge. It never hurt to have an edge.

He and Jimmy ate bologna and cheese sandwiches and drank two Pepsis each. Albury had abandoned the beer by nightfall. After the snack, there was nothing to do but smoke quietly and listen for engines and watch the stars announce another stunning tropical night. They had three hours to kill.

* * *

"Nobody else. No Customs, no Coast Guard, no Marine Patrol. Just us. Is that clear? We will do it alone, and we will do it right for once." One of the young patrolmen masked a snicker with a cough. Huge Barnett marked him for a month of midnights.

"*My* informant," he said for emphasis, "my informant says this is quite a haul." Barnett rocked back and forth on his three-inch cowboy boots, as though testing for spring. "He says there'll probably be a red herring, something to throw us off at just the wrong time. Captain Whitting will give you your assignments and explain how it's gonna go down. Pay attention."

Barnett lumbered to one side of the room, revealing an easel blackboard that his bulk had all but obscured. The blackboard showed a dock, a house, and converging roads. Wavy lines marked the water, crosshatches the mangroves.

Huge Barnett was a legend in his own time. He was a lawman and a tourist attraction, a Falstaffian figure equally adept with his fists and his grin. "Is This Southern 'Sheriff' the Model for Those TV Commercials?" *People* magazine once had asked. No, he was not, and not a sheriff, either, but an ole-boy chief of police who had a small genius for PR. Once, when a hotel computer threw an unaccountable fit that left peak-season tourists sleeping in cars, Huge Barnett had thrown open the doors of the Key West jail to shelter them from a cold snap. Made the network news. Once, in gun belt, Stetson, and all his chiefly finery, he had hurled himself into a shallow canal with hippopotamian zeal to save a child who might or might not have been drowning. For that, the Governor had summoned Barnett to Tallahassee and awarded him a bronze medallion.

Huge Barnett liked to boast that he knew everybody on the Rock and everything worth knowing about each of them. He had been chief so long that no one any longer remembered his real first name. Each year the city council unanimously voted an appropriation to equip their famous chief with a new white Chrysler, with special air conditioning and heavy-duty shocks to accommodate his 315 pounds.

Barnett rocked benignly, hands behind his back, jaw thrust forward purposefully, as a tall, balding captain with a dentist's stoop advanced to the blackboard with a pointer. Shorty Whitting was everything Huge Barnett was not: modern, literate, plodding, and reasonably honest.

Although he never would have revealed it—not to his wizened wife; or to his doctor, who clucked at him despairingly once a month; or to the pink-skinned tourist girls he consumed in great number—Huge Barnett was stinging. Had been for nearly a week since the night at the city council when Bobby Freed had stuck it to him about the dopers.

Freed occupied the token newcomer's seat on the Key West city council. He was a wealthy Manhattan designer who had come down about five years ago and opened the Cowrie Restaurant with his savings. Huge Barnett and the other Conchs had plenty to say at first, but over the years, Barnett had shut up about the gays. They had money, they were invariably polite, and they were far more likely to bribe than to fight if you caught them doing something illegal. But mother of God, Barnett fumed, why did they have to be so fucking earnest? The island had accepted *them;* now why couldn't they do the same?

Barnett had dropped in to the council meeting as he usually did on Monday nights: it was a good way to keep an eye on things.

He hadn't been there five minutes before Councilman Freed had badgered him about drugs and smuggling and a bad image that was keeping the tourists away. Did Chief Barnett have figures for drug arrests? No, well, perhaps he could prepare a special report for the council. Of course, they all voted for it. Turds.

Freed was like a goddamned chigger, digging his way into my skin, Barnett bridled. Faggot. He would pay for it.

". . . no smoking, no radios, and no talking. Whisper if you gotta talk," Shorty Whitting was saying.

The phone call that morning had made Huge Barnett's day.

"A crawfish boat will be coming into Ramrod Key tomorrow night about three. It's worth your time to put some men up there." The caller had not identified himself, but Barnett knew the voice. He knew, too, that the call was no coincidence; other people could read the paper about the suddenly inquisitive city council. Heat was bad for business.

Barnett was satisfied: the Machine was going to give him a boat he could wave under the noses of Freed and the city council. Barnett would unleash half the force on Ramrod. God knew what else was coming in on other boats, or where. That was part of the bargain; Barnett's prize was the decoy. Afterwards, three thousand dollars would discreetly appear in the nest-egg account he kept in the Cayman Islands. It was all so professional that it enhanced Barnett's considerable admiration for the Machine. A stupid name, but that was what people in Key West called it. The only thing Barnett couldn't understand was why an outfit so slick would use such an obvious dirtbag like Winnebago Tom.

Shorty Whitting was finished at last with his instructions to the squad of fresh-faced police. Huge Barnett returned to the center of the room for the benediction.

"*My* information is that this is a very big operation," he said momentously. "Let's try real hard not to shoot each other out there, OK?"

Jimmy talked for hours, like an excited little boy who didn't want to go to bed, filibustering his way through Christmas Eve. Albury's nerves collected in a hard knot in his belly. Jimmy's nerves jangled in his tongue. Everybody had a different reaction. It was hard, waiting in false colors on a black night at sea.

Radio traffic was light: two party boats comparing notes on the snapper fishing; a Coast Guard patrol boat looking for somebody down around the Dry Tortugas, a day sailor who sounded like a horse's ass promising all the world he'd be off the sandbank sure thing, once the tide turned. If anybody important knew about a big dope run, they weren't talking about it on the radio. The cops and the smugglers spent most of the time listening for each other, broadcasting only when necessary, and then only on little-used channels. Crystal listened to them all, and that was why he was invaluable. At quarter to midnight, he checked in with Albury with another "weather report." Everything was go. The sky was clear and star-spangled, and for the tenth time Jimmy remarked on how gorgeous it was.

Albury envied Jimmy his excitement. He had spent the previous day in methodical preparation, paying off his bills and enriching the checking account with what was left of the ten grand. Tomorrow afternoon he would drive up to Miami and look for a place.

Jimmy sat on the gunwale, hanging his legs over the side so his bare feet tickled the water. His white T-shirt seemed to glow against the indelible outdoor brownness of his arms and neck; the starlight gave his blond hair a silvery cast. To Albury, the twenty-five years that lay between him and the mate stretched out as dull and hot and halting as U.S. 1. He couldn't find a lesson anywhere that he wanted to share with the kid.

The sound of the big outboard sprang out of the mangroves on Ramrod Key. The whine grew louder, but Albury could see no boat, which meant it was running with no lights. His watch said ten minutes past twelve.

The outboard was only about a hundred yards away when the driver cut the engines. Albury went to the console and flicked his lights four times. Jimmy started to say something, but Albury shook his head sharply and put a finger to his lips.

The outboard started once, then stalled out, then started again. The driver idled toward the *Diamond Cutter,* and Albury was able to identify the boat as a twenty-one-foot T-craft. It was basically nothing but a broad hull with a flat open deck, powered by an absurdly oversized Mercury. A boat with only one function.

"Captain?" called a voice from the T-craft.

"Yeah."

"You and your mate are supposed to come with me."

Jimmy glanced apprehensively at Albury.

"What about my boat?" Albury demanded.

"I'll take good care of it, pardner." It was the voice of the second man in the T-craft.

Albury put it together quickly. He asked anyway, "Why can't I run my boat?"

The T-craft came alongside. "This ain't the *Diamond Cutter,*" muttered the second man.

"Yeah, it is. I just hung a new name on the transom."

"What for?" asked the driver.

"For looks, asshole," Albury said. "Now, why can't I run my own boat?"

"Tom said we're switching captains. Captain Smith here is gonna run your boat and you're gonna run his," the driver explained. "If either of you gets taken down, the other guy reports his boat stolen. That way Customs or the Marine Patrol can't seize the damn thing. They gotta give it back. It's for your own goddamn good, so quit complaining and hop in."

"Is that right, Breeze?"

Albury nodded, but he didn't get in the T-craft right away. "So if something happens to the *Diamond Cutter* . . ."

"Tell 'em it was stolen. Tell 'em Captain Smith must have stole it from the fish house."

Albury snorted. "Captain *Smith.* Jesus."

He and Jimmy stepped into the T-craft. Albury didn't recognize the slender man who climbed out, but the sight of the other captain in the wheelhouse of the *Diamond Cutter* stabbed him, like watching a stranger trying to fuck your girl friend.

Before Albury could issue a warning about the mortal importance of treating his boat properly, the T-craft was skimming through the chop toward Big Pine Key, its graceless hull slapping and plowing alternately. Albury and Jimmy framed the driver, each on one side of the console and he in the center, all hanging on with certitude. Albury made out the silhouette of another crawfish boat at anchor. The driver of the T-craft took one hand off the wheel and pointed. "There she is," he shouted.

As soon as he got the anchor up, Albury knew that he and the borrowed boat would not get along. The name on the stern was *Miss Alice*. It was cranky, old, and too damn slow to be a dope boat. Albury expected radar. Most of the grass boats carried the best; this one had none.

"You ever seen this boat?" Jimmy asked as Albury steered toward the coordinates provided by the T-craft's driver.

"No, I haven't," Albury said. "But it's a Marathon boat. I don't know a lot of the guys up there."

The Machine was smart. On nights of a run, it would deliberately plant false intelligence with the police, usually through a double informant at Customs. Out in the Gulf, to the west, there probably was a shrimper with a couple of lobster boats alongside, whose captains were being paid to have a raucous, suspicious-looking, but entirely innocent drink together. Albury could only hope that every cop in the Keys was watching the party.

To the east, in the Atlantic, he throttled the *Miss Alice* toward a big Texas shrimper. Another crawfish boat was ahead of him, alongside the shimper, and Albury imagined he could hear the sound of the bales dropping onto the deck, the muted rushing footsteps on the bigger boat.

"Is that the *Diamond Cutter*?" Jimmy asked.

"I don't think so," Albury replied. He hoped not. It would

be just fine with him if Tom had decided to use the *Diamond Cutter* as one of the barren decoys.

Silence enveloped the *Miss Alice*. Diesel just ticking over, Albury could now distinctly hear from the shrimper the sounds he had imagined before. Street music at sea.

Albury watched the other crawfish boat cast off, and then he guided the *Miss Alice* into place. "One o'clock," he called to the dark figure on the deck of the shrimper.

"You got it," the man answered.

The bales came fire-brigade style, with Jimmy and then Albury the final links. Each fifty-five-pound package was wrapped with black plastic over the burlap; the odor was pungent, almost sickeningly sweet. Albury stacked the bales in the hold of the *Miss Alice*. After about a half-hour, he could feel the boat settle with its new weight.

Once he looked aft to trace the sound of another boat. He saw in the shrimper's wake another crawfish boat, waiting its turn. The *Diamond Cutter*. He tugged on Jimmy's sleeve and pointed. Both of them saw two figures in the wheelhouse.

Albury figured he had loaded about two tons when the bales abruptly stopped.

"What's up?" he asked one of the crew on the shrimper, a bearded young fisherman in white rubber boots.

"That's it. See you around."

"But that's not a full load," Albury protested.

"You're the one o'clock, ain't you?"

"Yeah."

"That's all she wrote, one o'clock. Move along now, bubba. You're blocking traffic."

Puzzled, Albury steered the *Miss Alice* in a deft arc away from the shrimper and gave a backward glance to judge how smoothly the stranger docked the *Diamond Cutter*. Albury ran the crawfish boat blacked out, with only a sliver of green compass light to guide them. Jimmy sat on a stack of bales near the stern.

It didn't figure. Albury had assumed he would be hauling

at least four tons. Christ, even the Cubans could run a boat in with two tons. You had more speed, less water beneath you. Yet Tom had paid the full freight and made such a Hollywood production out of it. It made no sense.

Albury puzzled over it while the *Miss Alice* browsed through the gentle sea. He wondered if the other boats were getting the same loads; maybe the Machine was splitting the cargo among more boats to cut its losses if one got taken. *If one got taken.* He remembered what the driver of the T-craft had told him about switching boats.

Albury bickered with the radio until he was able to raise Crystal. "Smilin' Jack, this is Lucky Seven."

"For sure. You fat and sassy yet?"

"Yeah, right on schedule, but not as fat as I expected."

Crystal was silent for about twenty seconds. "You want me to see what I can find out?"

"I would appreciate it," Albury said into the hand mike. "Hey, and listen, I've got a new lady, too."

"Oh? Why?" Crystal was confused.

"I don't know, but she's old and slow, Jack, and I'm a little worried."

"Lemme call you back, Seven, OK?" Then Crystal was quiet.

By the time he reached the mouth of Niles Channel, Albury had made up his mind about one thing. He killed the engines and turned to Jimmy. *Miss Alice* drifted and turned slowly in the tide.

"You get your money?" Albury asked in a whisper.

"Yesterday, in the mailbox, where you left it."

"Good," said Albury. "Jimmy, I want you to take off. Swim to shore. I'll take her in."

"God, Breeze, what are you talking about? Who's gonna unload?"

"Shit, they got a dozen Cubans waiting there with Tom's campers. Don't worry."

Jimmy could see trouble. Albury wouldn't look at him; he was smoking furiously.

"I'll stay with you."

"You'll go!"

"Aw, Breeze," was the last thing Jimmy managed before the big man seized him under the arms and heaved him like a sack of stone crabs over the gunwale. The diesel was hacking and the *Miss Alice* was back in the channel by the time Jimmy exploded from the surface. He paddled for the mangroves and scrabbled ashore.

Within minutes, Albury was navigating the finger cut, a black ribbon of water that snaked up to the off-loading site on Ramrod Key. A short, rotting pier jutted from a clearing in the mangroves; the creek surrendered seven feet at low tide, enough for most crawfish boats. Beyond the sagging dock was a disused wooden warehouse, two junked cars, and a stack of old, broken lobster traps. At dead slow, Albury let the *Miss Alice* glide toward the dock. He had sweated off most of the bug spray, so the ravenous Keys mosquitoes were having a feast.

The accident happened five minutes too late to save Albury. Two out-of-town college kids, liquored up and 'luded out, lost it on the Stock Island Bridge. Their Camaro jumped the median and crashed head-on into a pickup driven by a black electrician on his way home from an emergency repair job at the Pier House.

The first patrol car reached the scene quickly and without sirens, the officer remembering Chief Huge Barnett's warnings about a possible red herring. He got out of the car and vomited as he inspected the wreck. Then he called for help.

"We got two or three fatalities. Get an ambulance down here and a couple more patrol units," he pleaded.

"Everybody else is up at Ramrod with the chief," blurted the dispatcher. "I think they got their radios off."

"Shit," gagged the young patrolman, "then call me a state trooper."

Crystal reacted quickly. With one hand he turned down the volume on his police scanner and with the other he nimbly adjusted his VHF to the frequency he and Breeze Albury had agreed upon. There was only one sorry reason that Barnett would be up on Ramrod.

"Lucky Seven, Lucky Seven! You got weather comin'. Hit it, man."

Albury was already running. *Miss Alice* was only a few yards from the old dock when the private alarm bells rang. Everything was wrong. There was nobody waiting, no campers or trucks. There was nothing, just Albury and a slow boat full of grass. It was an ambush.

Albury slammed the *Miss Alice* into reverse and gave her full throttle. The diesel coughed thick gray smoke and the old engine whimpered. Albury thought the boat must be aground; she didn't seem to be moving at all. He put the wheel hard over.

Huge Barnett, crouching awkwardly behind one of the abandoned cars, knew what the sound meant.

"Now!" he screamed.

Light flooded the tiny inlet. Armed men sprang from behind the lobster traps. Albury had the fleeting image of a rotund man in a Stetson, pistol waving, waddling like a bloated duck toward the water's edge. From around a bend in the inky creek two motorboats appeared like angry bees. They hummed on intersecting courses towards the turning *Miss Alice*.

Albury nearly made it. He clipped the bow of one police boat and might have successfully intimidated the second, but someone on shore, provoked no doubt by the sound and fury of Huge Barnett, loosed a cool, sharp burst of automatic weapons fire that sent Albury diving for the deck of the wheelhouse and kept him there, hands over his head, until the *Miss Alice*, undirected, backed blindly and harmlessly into the mangroves.

CHAPTER 5

ARCHIE WAS a drunk. He mewled, he hawked, he spat. His Adam's apple fluttered like a trapped moth. When he started singing, Breeze Albury rattled the bars and demanded a new cell.

He had stayed on the salty wheelhouse floor for what had seemed a long time, keeping his head down long after the gunfire had ended. Albury had noticed the thud of a small boat alongside and instantly been bathed in a police spotlight. He'd heard the wheeze of a fat man.

"Breeze Albury, goddamn," Huge Barnett had exclaimed. "We got your ass," Barnett had chuckled, gas escaping from a balloon.

"A couple of tons, at least, but nobody else on board," had come a disembodied voice.

"Where's your crew?" Barnett had demanded.

"What crew?"

"The crew that was helpin' you run this dope, shithead."

"What dope?"

They had hauled him away, lights and sirens, then fingerprints and a quick photo session, in handcuffs, for the dreary local press. By the time they had let Albury sleep, it was almost dawn.

He awoke with a hot knot in his guts. Every time he thought it through, it made less sense. Albury had made his contact with Winnebago Tom. Tom worked for the Machine. The Machine had set him up, QED. Why? Albury chewed over the question for hours. They went to a hell of a lot of trouble; they lost a boat and a couple of tons and, not insignificantly, one of the last decent Anglo boat captains on the island.

Albury had lost his ticket out. Maybe for good. A foul taste rose in his mouth. He thought about Ricky.

Neal Beeker walked out of the El Cacique restaurant at about nine-thirty and headed east on Duval Street, still savoring his wake-up orange juice. The studio was only five blocks away, and Beeker walked leisurely. The morning sun cast a dappled blanket of light over the Conch houses in Old Town. Beeker waved warmly at a young man selling shark's teeth to tourists outside Sloppy Joe's. He cut over to Simonton Street, stopping to pet a family of gaunt stray cats near a garbage bin. That was his mistake.

The three teenagers caught Beeker at Simonton and Fleming. They shoved him into an alley and clipped his legs out from under him. Two of them were fat, dull-eyed, with thick flat noses. The third was tall and black, with rust-colored hair. Beeker knew what came next. He got up and offered his leather purse. They emptied it, scrabbling for the loose change. The tall one snatched Beeker's wallet off the pavement and expertly looted it for credit cards.

"How about jewelry?" demanded one of the porcine kids.

Beeker said he wasn't wearing any. The teenager kicked him savagely in the chest. Beeker's lungs emptied in a raw wheeze.

"You faggots always have gold," said the rangy black kid, sneering.

The second fat kid seized Beeker by the scalp and wrapped a pudgy, hairless arm around his neck. Beeker gulped for air. His face was moist with sweat and tears.

"Come on, princess," the black kid taunted, "you got some gold, I *know*." He ripped Beeker's T-shirt.

"No necklace? What kind of faggot are you?"

Beeker's chest was imploding. Desperately he sank his teeth into the kid's arm and bit madly. The kid fell back, wailing. Beeker screamed.

The black kid slugged him twice, once in the gut, once in the testicles. Beeker went down again. His last image was of a Key West cop standing at the mouth of the alley, one hand on his hip, a look of thin annoyance on his ruddy young face.

Two hours after Beeker was delivered to the emergency room of Duval Memorial Hospital, Bobby Freed was in Huge Barnett's office, demanding to know how the hoodlums had gotten away. Freed's face was flushed, his neck and veins taut with rage. Neal Beeker was his lover. Huge Barnett only smiled.

Albury was not surprised by the Machine's choice of attorneys. It was the same man who had defended him the last time, an oily creep with crooked front teeth that reminded Albury of a moray eel. Drake Boone, Jr., was his name. He showed up at the arraignment with the peremptory air of an important man on a trivial errand. The crisp gabardine suit made no concession to the heat. The colorful necktie, and probably the shirt beneath it, was silk.

Boone shook hands politely with his new client, nodded at the judge, and said absolutely nothing when bond was set at

$75,000. When Albury touched the lawyer's sleeve and whispered protests, Boone waved him off. "We'll talk later," he promised.

Boone came down to the jail in late afternoon. He and Albury were ushered to a windowless, oblong room with two scarred chairs and a Formica table. The lawyer opened his black briefcase with a click and withdrew a manila file.

"I suppose the police report is accurate?" he began without introduction.

"They had to send you, huh?" Albury said, lighting a cigarette. "I guess I should feel lucky they're giving me a lawyer."

"That part is always understood. You know that."

"Why you again?"

Boone scowled. "Why not?"

"Eleven months in Raiford is why not."

"It was a locked case," Boone reminded. "They got you cold on a boat. Just like this time, apparently."

"This time was no accident," Albury said. "I was set up."

Boone made a palms-up gesture. "I wouldn't know about that, Breeze. I get a call that a boat's been taken down, I come down here to see you. That's all I know."

"Shit. Did Tom call you?"

"That I can't say." Boone studied the arrest form in the file. "A little more than two tons. And you were alone?"

Albury said nothing.

"Well," Boone said, rising, "we'll try the usual. I'll file a motion tomorrow to have the dope suppressed as evidence. We'll argue that Barnett boarded the boat illegally. Might work."

Albury rose and seized the pudgy lawyer by one arm. "What about the *Diamond Cutter?*"

Boone shook free and slammed the briefcase shut. "Safe and sound. It's over at Ming's fish house."

"Clean?" Albury demanded.

Boone nodded. "The fake name, too. It's been removed."

"What about my bond?"

"I'll post it tomorrow morning. Cash."

Albury stubbed the cigarette into the Formica. "You gonna talk to Tom?"

"Yep. Tonight."

"Find out what happened."

Boone rang for the jailer. "I'll try."

Albury snorted. "You're my lawyer, Drake. Try real hard."

The lawyer would not meet his eyes. "I'm getting you out tomorrow," he said in a reedy voice.

The jailer opened the door and Boone sidled into the hallway.

"Don't just get me out," Albury called, "get me *off!*"

Through a window, he could see Boone shaking his head disgustedly. "Hey, Breeze, you're welcome," the lawyer said acidly through the door. "Think nothing of it."

Laurie and Ricky showed up at supper time. She wore a pale blue sun dress and sandals; her hair was done back in a lush ponytail. The kid was dressed for baseball practice; he carried his glove and the new cleats. They sat at the same Formica table as Drake Boone. Laurie had brought a carton of Camels, but half of them had been skimmed off by one of the jailers. Albury smoked nervously.

"How are you doing?" Laurie asked tentatively.

"Marvelous," Albury said. He noticed sadly how Ricky was staring down at the table. "I'm sorry, buddy," Albury said. "They giving you a rough time?"

"Naw."

Albury forced a smile. "I had some rough luck with my traps," he began. "I wasn't trying to be greedy, I was just tryin' to get some of it back. you know . . . it seemed like a decent idea at the time."

Laurie said, "Ricky understands, Breeze . . ."

"I'm talking to him, honey." The words stopped her as surely as if Albury had pointed a gun at her head.

Ricky looked up. "It's OK, Dad."

"They set me up!"

Ricky nodded. "I figured that's what it had to be. You woulda never got caught in a straight race. I figured it was an ambush."

Albury smiled. "Right. You know, I think I could have got away in the *Diamond Cutter*. They gave me some old piece-of-shit Marathon boat."

Albury glanced at Laurie. She started to giggle. Ricky was perking up.

"I heard they shot at you," he said.

"Over my head is all. A grandstand act," Albury said. "That fucking Barnett."

"The paper said your rammed one of the police boats?"

"Just nicked it," Albury said. "Those kids can't drive."

"It wrecked in the mangroves," Ricky said.

"Really? No shit." Albury cackled. "That was not necessary."

"Yeah," Laurie cut in cheerily. "The driver fell out and busted his collarbone."

Ricky covered his mouth and laughed. Albury clapped his hands. "Well, damn," he exclaimed, "I gave 'em a moment or two, right?"

"I guess so," Ricky said, almost admiringly.

"I'm supposed to get my bond tomorrow. I should be out in time for the game with Tavernier."

"Good, Dad. I was hoping."

Albury squeezed Laurie's hand. "How about you? You OK?"

"Sure. Bobby made a couple remarks at the restaurant. Nothing major. He said he didn't know you ran a grass boat, too, and I said you didn't. . . ."

"Stupid fruit."

"It's all right, Breeze. He's on the council. He's got to talk like that." She kissed Albury's knuckles one by one until he pulled his hand away.

"The lawyer's due in a couple minutes," Albury lied. "You

kids go on home. We'll talk some more tomorrow." He kissed Laurie hard but not long, then cuffed his son on the shoulder. "Work on that slider tonight, OK?"

Supper was unmentionable. Breeze Albury remembered when he had been a boy. The whole sunbaked Rock seemed to live off the same unvarying diet: grits 'n grunts. Grits because they were cheap and Key West was a cracker town then. Grunts because they were plentiful and easy enough to catch that any kid could fill a bucket in a couple of hours after school. And every Sunday, Key Lime pie, made from the tangy little yellow limes that grew only in the Keys. Albury shoved the jail slop away in disgust.

"Good evening," the voice came from outside the bars. Jesus, now who? The door opened and a woman walked in.

"My name is Christine Manning. I'm a special prosecutor with the Governor's office. I'd like to talk with you a couple of minutes."

"I'm extremely tired," Albury replied. She was tallish, about thirty-five, not badly shaped beneath a white blouse and a flared skirt. A light sprinkling of gray, unmolested in a thick black mane, bespoke a certain independence.

"I'd like to talk to you about your arrest last night," she said. "I notice it's not your first time."

"What's your interest?"

"Well, as you may know, the Governor appointed a special task force to investigate drug corruption in Monroe County . . ."

Albury stopped her with a soft laugh. "That was last year. You still around?"

"The executive order gave us two years," Christine Manning said defensively.

"Miss Manning, you're a very attractive lady, but I'm not going to talk to you. Not without my lawyer here."

"I'm in an odd posture," she said gently. "I asked around about you today, and in the good Conch tradition . . ."

Albury grinned. "You said it right. Most folks can't pronounce it."

"Conch, rhymes with zonk," Manning said. "Anyway, in the upstanding tradition of this island, almost no one would say anything. Almost no one. Your ex-wife, however, was helpful."

"Mother of God," Albury groaned.

"And your girl friend."

"Shit."

"Wait a minute. She was trying to help. She thought you were in trouble. Anyway they made you seem different. I thought you might be a reasonable man."

Albury grunted.

"The first time you ran grass." Manning stopped herself. "The first time you got *caught,* I should say, had to do with Veronica, didn't it?"

Albury's smile dissipated. "That was the first time I ever ran it. I had my reasons."

"Veronica was ten at the time. To get a cancer at that age is very unusual, I know. The bills piled up, your little girl got sicker . . . Laurie said there was a hospital in Miami you were going to try."

"Go away now, Miss Manning."

"Breeze, you shouldn't have done any time for that. If only you had let your lawyer tell the judge about Veronica—God, you could have gotten probation, easy. Not eleven months."

"You don't hear very well, yourself." Albury had gone cold at the sound of his daughter's name. He squinted hard, and again Key West appeared to him as it was thirty years ago. On an afternoon like this he would have taken the skiff all the way out to the reef without a worry. The water would be like glass. You could snorkel for two hours, load the boat with Nassau grouper, and never lay eyes on another human being, much less a starched and undoubtedly dried-up emissary from the Governor's office. No one came. No one cared. It was marvelous. Now the island behaved like a dog, unpredictable and ugly in its old age, turning and biting again and again, long after the point had been made.

"What made you do it this time, captain?" Christine Manning asked. Her tone made it clear that she expected no answer. "Look, I'm going to be honest. We heard you got squeezed."

"What do you mean?"

"Pinched," Manning said. "Blackmailed. Whatever term you choose. We heard you were *conscripted* into that run last night. And if that's true . . . well, I took a chance that if that was true, you might be more of a mind to talk. I know you think the task force is a joke and that I'm a joke . . ."

"Not at all."

"Good, because I'm not. There's going to be a grand jury in a few weeks. Do you know what that means?"

"Another big payday for the Holiday Inn."

"Shit, I am wasting my time," Christine Manning said. "If something should change your mind and you feel the civic urge to testify about what you know, please call. I have an office at the courthouse." Albury craned to watch her leave along the linoleum corridor. Her walk was intriguing.

"I have a feeling you could be very helpful," she called, knowing she was being watched.

Albury felt no civic urges.

The next morning, Drake Boone arrived in a different suit and a matching briefcase. Breeze Albury thought it was hilarious, corduroy in the summer. He made up his mind not to laugh. Boone was in a serious mood.

"It's complicated, Breeze."

"Why? You gonna post my bond?"

A thin line of sweat glistened above Boone's black mustache. The fingers of his left hand rubbed anxiously against his palm. His voice crawled up an octave.

"I might as well tell you all of it. I had a chat with Tom. He and Manolo need you."

Albury's jaw set.

"They've got an important errand. They need a good boat and a good captain."

"I heard that a couple weeks ago, and look where I am. What kind of shit is this, Drake?" Albury noticed that Boone had not even bothered to open his briefcase.

"You were right. This," Boone said, motioning abstractly to the room, the jail, the whole screw job, "was no accident, Breeze."

Albury gave no conscious thought to what he did next. The lawyer struggled weakly, like a tired fish, against Albury's fists. The suit squeaked an objection. Boone's head lay pressed against the cinder-block wall, his tasseled loafers barely touching the gummy floor. Albury gave another twist to the jacket and leaned so close he almost gagged on the Brut.

"Tell me everything, son," he demanded.

"You're hurting me! Let go, damnit. I'm just a fucking messenger boy."

Albury turned him loose and sat down. He motioned to the other chair and Boone eased himself down, looking over his shoulder for some sign of the jailer. He would not be coming, Boone knew; he had slipped him a few bills to stay away for an hour. Now he wished he hadn't.

"Just listen," the lawyer said with a staged urgency. "There's a dozen Colombians hiding on a stash island off Andros. They're going to Miami. Somebody's got to bring them across. You know about the Bahamian Coast Guard? Well, so do they. So do the Cuban captains in Key West. Remember what that Bahamian gunboat did to those crawfishermen a few years back? Manolo can't find anyone to go fetch these people. Nobody wants to fuck with the Bahamians, Breeze."

"Since when is Manolo running aliens?" Albury asked.

"He's not. It's a favor for a friend down south. A business associate."

Albury nodded tiredly. "Not a favor, Boone. Repayment of a favor, right?"

Boone shrugged. "I honestly wouldn't know. Point is, Manolo needed a good captain and a big, fast boat. That would be you, and the *Diamond Cutter*."

"So they set me up?"

Boone dropped to a whisper. "They planned to give up one boat, anyway. It was . . . well, convenient for that boat to be you. Hey, I don't blame you for being hacked off. I told Tom this was a stupid way to do business."

"Did he cut my traps?"

Boone screwed up his face. "I don't know anything about your traps, Breeze. Are you listening to me?"

"Yeah." Albury stood up and stretched. "So they figure I *have* to make the Andros run now, right? They know I can't make the bond myself. They know I can't afford a lawyer, even *you*, by myself. They got me by the short hairs."

Boone summoned his best professional voice. "If you agree, I post your bond. All charges against you will be dropped."

Albury was incredulous. "How? You buying judges now?"

Boone never lost stride. "The charges will be dropped because Chief Barnett and his men have no jurisdiction on Ramrod Key, Breeze. They were twenty miles out of the city limits when they busted you the other night. They had no authority. They didn't tell the feds and they didn't tell the sheriff. It's a rather serious flaw in the case."

"For that I get off?"

"If I handle it. Don't you want to know how much Manolo is paying for the Andros thing?"

Albury clasped his hands theatrically. "God, you mean I'm getting paid on top of it? Marvelous. What generous dirtbags you work for, Drake. Yes, tell me about the money."

"Fifty thousand."

Albury stopped capering. "Jesus."

Boone smiled. "Makes a difference, doesn't it?"

"How far do I have to carry these peasants?"

"Key Largo. Dynamite Docks. You know the spot?"

"Yeah. When?"

"Day after tomorrow," Boone said. He was still smoothing his suit. "Well?"

Albury was in turmoil. "Why didn't they just ask me to do it? Why go through all this? Drake, remember last time. I never said a word. I did my time quietly. . . ."

Boone nodded and nodded. "This was an emergency, Breeze. They didn't think you'd do it without a little pressure. You got a clean reputation on Stock Island. Tom knows that. He didn't think you'd fool with Colombians. Remember, you're not talking about the Marine Patrol now. You're talking about Coast Guard and Customs. Big fucking time if you get caught. I have to warn you."

"Thanks, counselor."

"But you won't get caught," Boone said smugly. "You're too damn good."

"The money?"

Boone cleared his throat. "On delivery."

"I want half now."

"You're in no position to bargain. Manolo says you get paid in Key Largo. That's all I know. Oh, cash, of course."

Albury shoved Boone's briefcase across the table. One corner caught him in the gut, but Boone smothered an embarrassed cough.

"If this one goes bad, too, I intend to kill Winnebago Tom. Would you pass that along?" Albury said evenly.

Boone said, "Certainly. And I wouldn't blame you. The answer is yes, then?"

"The answer is what I told you."

Albury led Drake Boone to the door. Down the hall, Archie the drunk was singing again.

"Fifty grand will buy a ton of traps," the lawyer said with

such counterfeit friendliness that Albury felt like twisting Boone's neck until his greasy, fragrant head popped off. It was only after Albury was alone for an hour that the anger receded. He tried to imagine what the Colombians looked like, smelled like, after baking in the withering Bahamian sun. He had forgotten to ask Boone if any of them spoke English.

CHAPTER 6

L A U R I E H A D never seen a man so mad. She brought a red table napkin for Bobby Freed's bleeding hand. He had put his fist right through the plasterboard at the back of the restaurant.

"Easy, Bobby, easy," she implored. She wrapped the knuckles and gave her boss a hug. "The doctor says it's not that serious an operation."

"I know," Freed said. "But it's so disgusting the way it happened . . . a cop standing right there and doing nothing." Twenty-four hours later, he was still livid.

"It is disgusting," Laurie agreed. "Did Neal see his badge number?"

Freed shook his head. "He's still in shock." He took a couple of deep breaths. Laurie cleared some tables and waited. Freed popped two Valiums and poured himself a cup of hot tea. Two friends stopped by the table and told him how sorry they were; they had stories of their own.

"I will promise you this," Freed was saying when Laurie

returned, "this tidy little alliance we have maintained with Barnett and with the city fathers who indulge that fat pig is finished. The violence against innocent people will stop, and I will put it on the council's agenda every single week if I have to, until it does."

"You'll get the same bullshit," said one of the other gays. He wore a tank top that exposed firm tan biceps, thick as bread loaves. He smoked harsh Turkish cigarettes.

Freed fixed his friend with a stare. "You're right, Lee. That's why we're going to get rid of Barnett."

"Bobby, the council will never fire him. He's got dirt on everybody, their wives, their daughters . . ."

Freed said, "I don't care. He's through. I'll think of something."

He thought of all the "donations" he had made to the Key West police local; he remembered what he had been told by the bloated old Conch foot patrolman about all the catastrophic things that could befall a man's place of business without "constant, diligent police protection." A payoff, pure and simple. As a New Yorker, Freed had laughed at the quaint pretenses extended by the solicitor. A hundred bucks a month to make sure no local punks vandalized the Cowrie seemed prudent. Freed wondered how many other gay businessmen were getting shaken, while Huge Barnett got rich. He had wanted to believe the muggings were the work of 'teenage thugs, random and undirected, but the assault on Neal Beeker stank of malice.

"I think Barnett knows who's doing these things," he said to Laurie. "I think he knows who beat up Neal."

The Valium had taken an edge off his fury. "Laurie, don't you remember how pissed off Barnett was after the last council meeting? He thought I made him look foolish when I asked about the smuggling arrests. He doesn't like to look foolish in front of the locals, especially with the Governor's people sitting in the audience taking notes. I think he was mad enough to get revenge."

Laurie objected. "Surely you don't think Barnett arranged for Neal to get mugged, just because he knows . . ."

"Everybody knows Neal and I are lovers," Freed said. "I don't believe it's a coincidence, Laurie. That's all I'm going to say. I have enough friends with enough money to make the council think very hard about how dearly they value their venerable old police chief."

Albury noticed Jimmy's limp as soon as the boy entered the trailer. The mate's right foot was wrapped in dirty gauze.

"Jesus, did I do that?" Albury asked, stooping over to take a look.

"Naw. I cut it on a coral head when I went ashore," Jimmy said with a shrug.

Albury tossed him a beer and sat down on the sofa near the television. The Astros were blowing a three-run lead in the seventh.

Jimmy leafed through one of Ricky's sports magazines. Albury could tell he was trying to think of how to say it.

"I'm sorry I chucked you off the boat."

"Aw, hell," Jimmy said. "I know what you were doin', and I appreciate it. I woulda been sitting in that jail, too, if it weren't for you, Breeze. Kathy woulda left me."

"No."

"Damn right! Matter of fact, she thinks I ought to quit the boat because of what happened to you."

Albury chuckled. He could imagine Jimmy at home with his sixteen-year-old bride and her puerile lectures.

"Did you tell her the charges were dropped?"

"Yeah, it don't matter. I'm not quitting. You been good to me, and the *Diamond Cutter* is one fine boat. Besides, if it weren't for that run, we wouldn't be able to afford that doctor up in Miami."

Albury said, "I almost forgot. You goin' ahead, then?"

"I'm driving her up tomorrow," Jimmy said. "I told her the money is from crawfish, so she ought to lay off you."

Albury checked out the window for a sign of Laurie or Ricky. Outside the trailer park, on MacDonald Avenue, he noticed, was a lime-green Cadillac with the windows tinted dark blue. A typical Cuban Conchmobile; that would be one of Tom's soldiers.

"Jimmy, can you wait a couple days before going to Miami?"

The kid sat forward. "No, Breeze. We'd like to get it over with."

"Sure. I understand."

Jimmy knew when Albury was trying to smooth something over. "It's important, huh?"

Albury nodded. He told Jimmy about the Andros run and explained the deal he had cut with Winnebago Tom Cruz. Jimmy agreed that they left Albury no choices.

"I need a mate. Somebody I can trust."

"Aren't you scared? From what I hear about Colombians . . ."

"That stuff sells newspapers," Albury mumbled. "Hell, I don't think they're any different from the Cubans."

"The whole idea scares me," Jimmy declared.

"Manolo's paying fifty thousand. Ten of it's yours if you want to come." Albury heard a car pull into the gravel drive. "Think about it, Jimmy. I'll call you tonight."

"All right."

The kid passed Laurie on her way up the driveway and gave a bright hello. Albury was staring at the ball game when she walked in with a bag of groceries. She wore the same pair of jeans shorts and diaphanous top in which she had fetched him from jail that morning.

"Bobby's so mad he scares me," she announced.

"What's wrong?"

"Neal Beeker got beat up real bad yesterday. I didn't mention it when I saw you last night. Bobby thinks Barnett had something to do with it."

"Why?"

"Because of the fight they had at the last council meeting."

Albury was admiring the Astros' reliever, a lanky blond rookie who reminded him of Ricky, except that he came around from the side a little more with the slider.

"There was a cop who saw the mugging and didn't do anything," Laurie said as she arranged some Campbell soup cans in the pantry. A sideways glance told her Albury was not particularly appalled.

"Breeze, don't you think it's terrible?"

Albury grunted. Freed was probably right; the attack on Beeker simply was political fallout from Barnett. And if there was one thing that Albury made a point of ignoring year in and year out, it was the vagaries of Key West politics. His daddy had thought the city council of his day was worthless scum, and Albury saw no reason to be more charitable. Freed had gotten elected as the obligatory reform candidate, but all he ever fought for was new bike paths and rent controls for Duval Street. If he wanted to feud with Huge Barnett, the results surely would be both predictable and inconsequential.

Laurie asked, "Did you talk to Crystal?"

"Yeah. It wasn't his fault. Barnett stayed off the radio all night. Crystal didn't have a clue about him being up at Ramrod until it was too late."

"I bet he felt awful, anyway."

"Yeah," Albury said. "He also told me the three other boats made it in with a total of eleven tons. That means Tom can buy his latest mama a new Seville."

"Speaking of which, there's a guy sitting in a Caddy out on MacDonald Street," Laurie said.

"My baby-sitter."

"What for? What's he want?"

Albury had decided not to tell her the terms of his release. She would never understand the Andros trip.

"I don't know what he wants," Albury said, brushing a curtain aside and peering toward the road. "Maybe Tom's afraid that I'm still pissed off, and that I might talk."

"Tom doesn't know you very well." Laurie sat cross-legged on the sofa and pulled him toward her for a wet kiss. "I sure am glad you're out of jail."

Albury hugged her tightly and whispered, "You have a delightful neck. Did I ever tell you that?"

Laurie laughed huskily and leaned all the way back. "What time is Ricky's game?"

"Seven sharp," Albury said. "And he's going right to the ball park after work."

"Now, there's wonderful news," Laurie said, playfully shedding her blouse.

Tavernier beat Key West 4–2. Ricky Albury pitched the last three innings in relief, striking out four batters and giving up a meaningless double in the top of the seventh. Generally, he looked sharp, Albury thought. The new spikes helped on his follow-through, though the mound, as always, was too rocky.

Teal was in the bleachers, rooting for his wife's little brother, an outfielder for Tavernier.

"I didn't know you liked baseball," Albury kidded him.

"I don't. It's boring as hell," Teal said. He was a local flats guide, the best in Key West. He was the only one who ever got invited up to Islamorada for the bonefish tournaments. By and large, the Middle Keys guides thought the Key West guides were a wretched bunch. By and large, they were right.

"I'm only here because Susan's brother is playing. Ricky looks damn good."

"Thanks."

Teal looked absolutely dapper in a yellow Izod golf shirt and tan boat pants. His skin was the color of polished mahogany.

"How's fishing?" Albury asked.

"Fishing is great. Too bad there's no tourists here to enjoy it. I'm only booked two or three times a week."

"You charter guides are always bitching," Albury said.

"Yeah, well, if I had a bigger boat, I could run them square grouper like you. Pay off my house." Teal and Albury laughed together.

"Well, if you ever try it," Albury said, "I hope you have better luck than me. I swear, Teal, when things go to hell they go in a hurry."

Teal scratched at his arms. The mosquitoes were in fine form. "Breeze, there was something I meant to tell you . . . let me think . . ."

Albury was accustomed to waiting on Teal. All day in an open boat, Teal could be excused for his jumbled thoughts. The sun off the mud flats could putty your brain.

"I know what it was," Teal erupted. "Your traps!"

"They got cut."

"Right, right. But I found a bunch of markers."

"Where?"

"On a flat off Boca Grande. I was out there on a permit charter two days ago."

"How many?" Albury asked, his mind working. It was a good forty miles from the Cobia Hole to Boca Grande.

"Breeze, there must have been a couple hundred. The water was orange with them," Teal said. "It was a helluva sight. I knew they were yours."

"Whoever cut me must have dumped 'em there."

"I saw a boat leaving, too," Teal volunteered. "Now, I didn't get a name, but it was a crawfish boat, a fast one." Teal said he thought it was a Key West boat, possibly a Torres.

"Radar?" Albury pressed.

"I think. I think so." Teal was straining now, brow furrowed, eyes framed by deep crow's-feet. "I didn't chase it or anything."

"Probably one of Tom's boys," Albury muttered.

"The reason I tell you is that they are probably still out there. The wind hasn't blown much, and if they float up against the islands you got a chance of getting 'em back. I know it's not as good as finding the whole trap, but it'll save you a few dollars, getting those buoys back."

"Sure will," Albury said. "Thanks, Teal." He patted his friend on the back, but he didn't have the heart to tell him that the markers were ancient history. Albury had no use for them anymore.

CHAPTER 7

LAURIE SAT on the bed in a thin lime-colored T-shirt. Albury stuffed random handfuls of underwear, shorts, and ratty boat pants into an old duffel bag. He crammed a wad of fifty-dollar bills into a pair of socks and tossed them in with the rest.

"So it's a big secret. Again," Laurie said sharply.

"It would be no good for you to know."

"It has to do with the bust, doesn't it?"

Albury stopped packing and sat down next to her on the bed. When he kissed her on the cheek, his eyes involuntarily dropped to her breasts and the reddish thatch of hair, dangerously visible through the shirt. Albury did his best to change the subject, but Laurie was in no mood.

"This will look bad, Breeze, you leaving like this."

"Just for a few days."

"Bobby Freed says he's going to have the grand jury call you in for questioning. He wants you to talk about Barnett. He knows your case was fixed. . . ."

"Hold on. What do you mean, he *knows?* Did you—"

Laurie tossed her head back and laughed sarcastically. "No, I didn't say anything. Jesus, Breeze, give me a little credit. I'm trying to help is all. I'm trying to give you a little fair warning that this thing will not go away. I love you, sometimes, but the dumbest thing you could do right now is run another load for those goddamn hoods."

"That's not what I'm doing. I promise."

She stared at him and her eyes softened. "Then what?"

Albury aimed a kiss for a stellate freckle on her neck, but Laurie dodged him. "Why won't you tell me?" she asked.

Albury rose, sighed out loud, and ambled to the living room where Ricky was watching television. The kid saw the duffel bag and looked up inquiringly.

"I'll be gone for a few days," Albury said softly. "Watch after Laurie."

Ricky picked himself off the floor. "Going south?" he said, grinning.

"Naw." The kid's smile made Albury's heart dive like a wounded bird. Everything he cared about was on the line this time. "I'm gonna be up the Keys for a few days is all."

"Need another hand?"

"No, thanks."

"C'mon, I'm sick of flipping burgers. I could use the fresh air."

"No way."

"God, Dad, you must think I'm still a baby."

Albury threw an arm around Ricky. "Son, you got baseball practice and your slider still needs work. Listen good, now. If anybody from the police or the grand jury comes around, you don't know where I am or when I'll be back. Same goes for that Manning lady from the Governor's hit squad or whatever the hell she called it."

" 'Kay, Dad. Just be careful this time. More careful than before."

Albury called Jimmy and was relieved to hear that his mate had decided to go along. Whether it was the money or simple loyalty, Albury couldn't be sure. Probably both.

He told Jimmy he might look for a third man, and Jimmy said fine, the more the better as far as he was concerned. Albury found Augie Quintana at a *bolita* house on Petronia Street. With Albury going light on the details and heavy on the salary, Augie took ten seconds to make up his mind.

"How long will we be gone?" was the young Cuban's first question.

"Few days at most."

"What do I tell my wife?"

"You're going to the Tortugas."

"And what do I tell my girl friend?"

"You're shopping for a new El Dorado in Miami."

Albury slipped out of the trailer at four-thirty the next morning and sweet-talked the old Pontiac to life. Jimmy beat him to the fish house by fifteen minutes and was shoveling ice into the *Diamond Cutter* when Albury drove up. Together they hoisted a fifty-gallon fuel drum into the boat; Albury knew there would be no gassing up in the Bahamas. Then he saw Jimmy's shotgun leaning in a corner on deck.

"You forget my rules?"

"No, Breeze. I ain't goin' unless we bring the Remington. Before you get all pissed, lemme tell you I've been talking to friends of mine about the Bahamas, and they said you gotta be crazy to go without the gun."

"Christ, did you tell anyone why you were going?"

Jimmy shook his head. His face was moist from the shoveling. He swatted at the night bugs and told Albury not to worry. "But the gun is a good idea, Breeze. Really."

"Get it under the deck," Albury commanded. "If we get

stopped by the Bahamians, the gun is the first thing to go over the side, understand? They got laws you wouldn't believe, Jimmy. You could piss on the prime minister and do thirty days, but if they catch you with a gun . . ."

"Bring your knitting."

"Right. Listen, Augie Quintana is coming with us."

Jimmy nodded. That would make perfect sense. Augie was insurance, good muscle and a good hand; a lean, young Cuban built like a welterweight boxer. Jimmy was feeling better about the trip already. He went back to loading the ice and stacking some crawfish traps. Five minutes later a gold Cadillac pulled up to the dock. The passenger door opened, and the dome light revealed Augie Quintana kissing a beautiful, dark-haired *latina*.

"Did you get a farewell like that this morning?" Albury teased Jimmy. "I sure as hell didn't."

Augie hopped aboard the *Diamond Cutter*, slapped Jimmy on the shoulder, and pumped Albury's hand. "You're looking good, old man," Augie said, "but not as good as this boat. Jesus, what a piece of work."

"How's your Spanish, *chico?*" Albury asked.

"My Cubish is just fine, thank you, but we'll have to see about my Colombian."

Albury had known the Quintana family for twenty-odd years. Augie's father, Cristobal, was a fine Key West lobster-man—tough, knowledgeable, honest, and, occasionally, enter-prising. His eldest son, Mike, worked the boat with him. Augie worked an uncle's boat for years, went away to the University of Miami, got a degree in business, came back to the island, and went right back to work on a crawfish boat. In his spare time, he kept the books for two of the island's more successful *bolita* houses.

Augie was bright and cocky and strong, and he owned a valuable intuition about trouble. One night he and Albury had been drinking beer at a Key West bar when Augie told him they had better leave. Albury had a quarter on the pool table, waiting his turn to beat some wiseass shrimper, so he wasn't eager to walk out. Augie looked down the bar at a small black fellow and told Albury that the guy was about to explode. The black guy had been sitting there for three hours, sipping Myer's rum, minding his own business, and largely ignoring everybody, including a topless dancer with wonderful melon-sized breasts—another reason Albury hadn't wanted to go. But no sooner had Augie whispered his warning than the little man got up from the bar, slipped a .357 out of his coat, and put a bullet in the tallow of the dancer's thigh. Then he spun around and drew down on the shrimper, who had frozen in awe while lining up the sixteen-ball for a corner.

Augie was on him swiftly. The pistol hit the floor like a hammer, followed by the snap of the man's wrist breaking. It was the loudest sound in the bar that night. Augie never said a word.

Albury had always admired instinct in a young man. The island was loaded with strong, dumb Conch kids; smart ones like Augie were a precious resource.

They cast off an hour before dawn. Albury set the *Diamond Cutter* on an east-northeasterly course up the straits. It was a healthy two hundred miles to Andros, a couple days, at least. The coordinates for the pickup had arrived in a brown envelope from Tom. The morning turned up gray, and the sky hung over them like a damp membrane. The sea was smooth and the colors dull. A stubborn pelican followed the crawfish boat, waiting vainly for the crew to start pulling traps.

Augie stretched out on the bow while Jimmy snored on deck. Albury flipped on the radio and said good morning to Crystal on the mainland.

A school of bottle-nosed dolphins came alongside after noon. Albury counted ten adults and three juveniles. They raced in front of the bow for more than five miles. Occasionally, one would peel off from the pack to perform a great, happy somersault, smacking back into the water like an eight-hundred-pound cannonball. Albury would laugh and take his hands off the wheel to clap appreciatively. Augie awakened to share Albury's delight.

"Dolphins are good luck, man. I hope they stay with us the whole trip," Augie called.

Albury smiled and shook his head knowingly. An hour later the dolphins were gone.

CHAPTER **8**

(From the deposition of Augustin Quintana, taken on the fourth day of October 1982, before Christine Manning, counsel to the office of the Governor. Also present was court reporter Mary Perdue.)

MISS MANNING: Tell me your relation to William Clifford Albury.

MR. QUINTANA: I have known him most of my life. My father, too. They fished together sometimes.

Q: Have you ever been on his boat, the *Diamond Cutter?*

A: Many times. I helped him repaint the—

Q: Did you have occasion to be on the *Diamond Cutter* in August during a trip to the Bahamas?

A: You know the answer to that, lady. Breeze needed somebody to speak the Spanish. Jimmy, that's his mate, speaks a little, but a little ain't good enough when you got a couple dozen *loco* Colombians talkin' eighty miles an hour. Which is exactly what we had.

Q: What happened aboard the boat, Augie?

A: A whole lot more than should have.

Q: Tell me what kind of weapons Captain Albury brought with him.

A: Some terrific weapons. Besides Jimmy's Remington, we had a couple fishing knives, a spear gun, and the bang stick.

Q: The bang stick is essentially a firearm, correct?

A: It's got a shotgun shell rigged to blow out on the end of a spear. You pop the shark real good and it explodes. Technically, yes, I guess it's a firearm. But it's definitely designed for sharks, not people.

Q: What was Captain Albury's destination when he left Key West on the twenty fourth of August?

A: An island off Andros.

Q: And what was the purpose of the trip?

A: To work off a debt. They spring him from jail, and, in return, he smuggles their Colombians.

Q: They? Who's they?

A: Them.

Q: Augie, that isn't good enough.

A: I'll tell you what happened on the trip. Nothing more.

Q: All right, what happened?

A: It's simple. One of the crazy Colombians, his name was Oscar, *really* went crazy. Breeze had to do something; it was his boat.

Q: This Oscar, what was his last name?

A: Which one, lady? They tell me he had three different passports in his pockets. Guys like Oscar pick a new name every morning while they're brushing the scum off their teeth. From the time he boarded the *Diamond Cutter* to the end, he had one thing and one thing only on his mind.

Q: Augie, what did Breeze—Captain Albury—what exactly did he do to stop Oscar?

A: You know the answer to these questions.

Q: Please, Augie, this is legal testimony now, for the record. Tell me what happened at the dock in Key Largo.

A: I'm supposed to meet my cousin at the dog track. I didn't realize it was so late.

Q: Augie!

A: The thing to remember is that Oscar lied about everything. The guns, the money, everything. We didn't know the rules, me and Jimmy and Breeze. And when we found out, the nature of the thing changed. The fifty grand was the least of our worries. And when the rules changed, and when Breeze knew it, there was nothing left to happen but what did happen. It was dark and the water was low and mosquitoes were so thick you swallowed them every time you took a deep breath. And, lady, I took some mighty fucking deep breaths that night at Dynamite Docks.

Q: Just a few more questions—

A: What I can't figure out is why you're so interested in all this. It's over and done.

Q: It's very important for the investigation.

A: *Cristo*, look at the time. I've really got to run.

CHAPTER 9

A U G I E   B U R S T into the wheelhouse with an infectious grin and a cold can of beer. Water pooled at his feet.

"Three nice crawfish and a couple of beautiful little yellow-tails."

Albury grunted and eased back from the counter where he had unfolded the chart. He massaged his eyes with twin knuckles and worked his back.

"Cook 'em up, I'm starved."

Augie surrendered the beer and scanned the chart. "You been at it for hours, Breeze. You trying to memorize the damn thing?"

"Something like that."

"Lotta shallow water. The tide will be important."

Albury nodded grimly. He noticed Jimmy dog-paddling abreast of the anchor rope, nudging their supper before him in a white net bag. "We'll talk after dinner," he said to Augie and turned to the chart for one last hard look.

Williams Island, a flyspeck cay off the northwest coast of Andros Island, had been a private rendezvous for quiet men of the sea since the days of Blackbeard; then, as now, a rogue's haven, no place for the uninvited. Because Williams was one of those places that suited smugglers, it meant two things: either the Bahamians would watch it closely, or they would ignore it.

Albury marked a sandbar that would block his exit from the westernmost beach; the only way out was south, and around, and that route was guarded by a nasty curving reef shrouded by a treacherous seven feet of water at high tide. Augie was right. The tide was everything.

It was one of those tropical twilights that poets proclaim and rich men squander. The *Diamond Cutter* lay at peace in a cove of crystal water on the west coast of Andros. Albury coaxed a last white piece of crawfish from its shell and reflected, not for the first time, that if people ever found out how good fresh-caught seafood really was they would never set foot in restaurants.

Sprawled on a hatch cover, he made no effort to stifle an appreciative belch. When Augie brought three steaming mugs of coffee, Albury arranged the crawfish remnants into a makeshift map on the hatch cover.

"All right, we are here, right off the coast. The pickup is Williams Island. There's a small beach here on the western side. We're probably an hour, ninety minutes, at the most, away. One of these assholes will have a big flashlight, so we should see a signal when it's clear to come in." Albury pointed with a brittle length of lobster antenna.

"There's no moon. I want to go in an hour after high tide, just as it's starting to fall. That means we load fast. The bottom is soft marl, so the prop shouldn't take a beating. I'll motor in to maybe thirty yards of the beach, turn us around and keep her in neutral, just in case."

"You want me to go ashore?" Augie asked.

"It depends. These people might have a small boat. Then we wait, let them do the work. If not, Augie, you swim in with a tow rope, tied to our stern. They get wet, so what? And, remember, I don't want them hauling a lot of shit aboard. Just them and the clothes on their back, that's the deal. No suitcases, no boxes. And, most of all"—Albury hammered the hatch cover for emphasis—"no guns. You tell them that right off, Augie, before anybody leaves the beach."

Jimmy asked, "You expecting trouble?"

"I'm trying to avoid it."

"What about the Bahamian gunboats?" It was Augie this time.

"Crystal is too far away to give us a good ear, unfortunately. But the odds are in our favor—they got half a dozen boats to patrol seven hundred islands."

"How far back to Florida?" Jimmy wondered.

"Once we pick 'em up, I figure six, maybe eight hours to Key Largo. A straight run."

"At least the weather's decent," Augie observed.

"Breeze, you forgot the most important thing of all. When do we get paid?"

"It's COD, Jimmy. We get the cash when they get their Colombians."

Augie shifted uneasily. "At Dynamite Docks?"

Albury nodded. "Hey, it should be nice and easy," he said. "Maybe we can even get a little fishing in on the way back to Key West."

The night was magic. The absence of moon had left more phosphorescence in the shallow tropical waters than Albury had ever seen. He watched mesmerized as schools of fish, their tails ablaze, darted away from the *Diamond Cutter*'s cleaving bow. A sweet breeze carried the aroma of land and, seemingly, the taste of a better tomorrow.

This was Albury's element, and he knew it. The sea was all a man would ever need. It was the land that tied you in knots and made you squirm. There was no end of the month at sea. All you had to do was to love it, and to fear it a little, and the sea paid you back.

The *Diamond Cutter* drove straight and true, like a yearling ready to run, as though it, too, could sense the majesty of soft night under an eternal canvas. Gentling the wheel, Albury watched tentative strips of cirrus play tag with the stars.

This was his last run. Albury tried not to think of that; of how he would miss the flow of the deck and the sigh of the sea; of how it would hurt to sell the *Diamond Cutter*.

He thought instead of the cheering crowds and the poised young righthander with common sense and a raffish grin, pouring it in, mixing his pitches, keeping it low, making it look easy.

Ricky wouldn't mind leaving Key West too much, Albury reasoned. It was simply the setting for his baseball. There were a million places like it around the country, the same diamond, the same subtle touches of excellence. Maybe out West was the best idea. There were some good baseball towns there, and Albury had heard men talk about the mountains the way he felt about the sea.

Would Laurie want to come, too? Probably not. She had drifted into Key West and improbably stuck to the Rock the way barnacles cling to driftwood. She loved the place now, as much as he wanted to be rid of it. So be it. If he could live without the sea, he could live without Laurie, he supposed.

Albury wanted a cigarette, but lighting it would rob him of his night vision. Instead, he fished a cough drop from a box by the wheel, eyes never leaving the quiet sea. Squinting, he could just make out a blacker piece of darkness fine on the starboard bow. Williams Island, right on schedule.

Jimmy saw it first.

"There, Breeze." His voice seemed unnaturally loud in the blackness. *Diamond Cutter* lay about a half-mile offshore, engine idling, running lights aglow. Until now, they had been safe. Interception would have meant a chewing out, maybe a fine for violating territorial waters. Now was for keeps.

"Where, Jimmy? Tell me, I can't see where you're pointing."

"One o'clock, Breeze," Augie called. "Flashing white light."

Albury saw it then, a pinprick in the vastness. He could imagine the scene on the beach; a dozen mangy Colombians, excited, probably frightened, peering out to sea, wondering if the boat that lay there was a passport to America or a ticket to Fox Hill Prison in Nassau.

Albury closed his eyes for an instant and transposed the dark half-moon of beach before him onto the chart he had studied that afternoon. It tasted right.

Behind him, water was beginning to empty out with the tide, flattening the long sinister reef. Albury pointed the *Diamond Cutter* toward the beach and nudged the throttle.

There was no dock, as Albury had known; and his passengers had no boat of their own, as he had feared. Even so, the transfer went smoothly until one of the Colombians drowned.

Augie had swum in easily, a three-quarter-inch nylon tow rope in his teeth. Albury could see him naked at the center of a knot of figures on the beach. Augie swam back alone, and Albury levered him into the boat. Gasping, the young Cuban needed no coaxing.

"There must be twenty of them, Breeze, including a few women. They all stink; Jesus, they stink. And they are in a big hurry."

"Shit," Albury sighed. A dozen, that was the agreement. Twenty was absurd; they would slow down the boat. Christ, where would he put them all? Albury furiously assessed the possibilities: he would have to take none, or take them all and try to settle with the Machine later. To leave any of them on this beach would surely spell trouble later, at Key Largo, when the welcoming committee started counting heads.

"The leader is a big guy with a mouth full of gold. Name

of Oscar," Augie reported. "I told him no luggage and no guns, and he said OK."

Albury saw his plan for a swift, easy transfer slipping out with the tide. "How's the water?" he asked Augie.

"Eight feet off the stern, no more, but the current is tricky."

"Go back to the beach, Augie. Feed them out on the line, one at a time. Tell them to hang on tight and pull themselves hand over hand, OK? Warn them about the current. Tell 'em they're going to have to move fast. You come last."

"They've got some shopping bags and other shit."

"Leave it on the beach. This ain't the S.S. *Norway*." Albury turned to Jimmy. "As they come in, you help 'em up the dive ladder and then shove 'em down below as fast as you can. No rough stuff unless you have to."

"You want me to get the shotgun?"

"Jesus, no! Leave it where they can't see it."

Dark shapes, featureless from where Albury watched at the wheel, the Colombians came up off the line like fresh-caught grouper, heaving, grunting, cascading water onto the deck, then shuttling below at Jimmy's urging. For the most part they came mutely, although twice Albury heard a whispered *gracias*, and once he smiled when Jimmy whistled appreciatively through his teeth. Even from where Albury stood, the wet silhouette, dimly seen, was spectacular. *"Hola, lindo,"* the girl called to Jimmy and was gone, like a fish to the ice.

The sea was black, calm, and empty. The Colombians were young, and they worked themselves along the rope with little trouble at first. Gradually, though, the rope began to bow as the current stiffened with the falling tide.

After the first dozen, the interval between arrivals began to lengthen. Number fourteen stopped twice for breath, and when he finally reached the *Diamond Cutter,* he could hardly climb the ladder. Jimmy had to bodily haul number fifteen, another girl, from the water.

Hurry, Albury wanted to shout. Hurry. Soon it will be impossible to come at all; soon the current will be too strong.

Augie would see the water moving. He would tell them. Albury said nothing, not even when a faint draft of wind delivered the sound, distant but unmistakeable. He scoured the northern horizon, cursing under his breath.

The seventeenth Colombian didn't make it.

Albury heard a muffled shout. He saw bubbles, then a half-submerged balloon of white—it must have been the man's shirt—separate from the tow line and float away to port.

"Jimmy!" Albury yelled. "Watch the boat and keep them coming."

He slipped out of his boots, took a quick bearing on the receding speck of white, and dove into the dark water. It felt like a warm bath. Albury swam underwater in virtual blindness toward the drowning man. When he surfaced, there was nothing.

"Jimmy," he called, treading water, "where is he?"

"Ten yards to your right. He just went under," came the call from the *Diamond Cutter*. Albury could see the Colombians clustered on deck; the transfer was going to hell in a hurry.

Albury swam ten measured strokes to his right and dove. A cave. He let the current carry him, arms extended. The water was not deep, but it might as well have been a hundred fathoms. He could see nothing.

He broke the surface.

"Nothing, Breeze," Jimmy yelled. "He sank like a rock. Come back now."

"I hear something," Augie shouted from the beach.

Albury dove again and struck out for the *Diamond Cutter*. He nearly lost his air in the involuntary grunt of surprise when a coral claw raked his left arm.

That will bleed, he thought anxiously. Shallow water or not, sharks made their own rules. Albury swam faster. He winced when the salty night air fingered the wounded arm. He knew he was dripping like a stuck pig.

Then he touched it with his foot. Not coral, or turtle grass. It was fabric.

"Here!" he shouted and dove again.

This time his fingers traced the figure of a small man. Albury found a cold arm and tugged with all his might. The figure swayed but did not yield. He pulled again.

The man was moving gently with the current, suspended like a sponge from the ocean floor. Dots of phosphorescence spangled the curly hair. Albury sensed instantly what had happened. Somehow, in his panic, the Colombian had become entangled in the stiff branches of coral. And there he would stay until the sharks came for him.

Albury kicked toward his boat. Winded, his arm aching and sticky, he swam doggedly against the roiling tide. He felt weak and tired.

Suddenly he realized that he was no longer alone in the water. If it was a shark, Breeze Albury knew, he was as dead as the luckless Colombian. He spun in the water to face it, thrashing with both fists, aiming for the blunt snout of a killer he could not see.

It took a long, shivery moment for Albury to recognize Augie, bringing him the rope so that he, too, could hoist himself aboard and complete the *Diamond Cutter*'s alien complement.

"Not too tight."

"It's got to be tight enough to stop the blood. It needs stitches, man."

Jimmy stretched the tape across the gauze. Augie held out four Tylenols and a bottle of Wild Turkey.

The deck was warm and wet, and Albury sat there puffing, like an old man. He gradually became aware of the circle of dusky feet around him, and a muttering. He looked up into gaunt, frightened faces: Colombians.

His ears rang, but it was not in his head. It was out there, much louder than before. "That's a big boat coming," Albury croaked. "Let's get the hell out of here."

Jimmy helped him to his feet. Albury breathed deeply and waited for the world to right itself.

"What are *they* doing up here?" he demanded.

"They came up when their guy lost the rope. I couldn't stop 'em, Breeze."

Augie said, "We've got to move."

"Jimmy, get the anchor." Stiffly, Albury walked to the wheelhouse and punched the ignition buttons. "Augie, get those people down below."

"I tried, but they won't go. They say they won't leave without the guy in the water."

"Tell them he's dead, Augie. And tell 'em we're all going to a very nasty jail if they don't get below. Now!"

The patter of half-understood Spanish washed over Albury; the Colombians were insistent.

"It's not the guy they care about," Augie explained. "It's what he was carrying. They say it is their luck."

"Oh, shit."

"Before they left Colombia, they got a local priest to bless a small religious statue to take along. A Virgin or something. For luck. The guy who was carrying it—they called him *El Cura*—he's the one who drowned."

"Some luck."

"It must have been made of stone, way he went down," Jimmy said.

"These people are fucking crazy," said Albury. Now he could see it, a speck where the sky met the ocean. Then twin pinpricks of light, one red, one green. Bow and stern.

"Tell them that anybody who wants to stay can be my guest. Tell them there's a boat coming and that I'm not waiting," Albury said. "Tell them to go below and say their crazy prayers."

He slipped the diesel into gear. Jimmy was at the bow, coiling another rope. Augie spoke Spanish, urgently, persuasively. Glowering, the Colombians shambled into the hold.

Twice Albury reached for a cigarette, and to hell with night vision. Twice he stopped short of the inviting pack. He felt the three ounces of Wild Turkey rampage into his gut and begin to resew the frayed nerves. A night of imaginary sharks, a stone virgin, and a dead man's hair waving in the water like seaweed. Jesus.

From the beach, *Diamond Cutter* fled into the night at twenty-five knots. Ahead, the reef waited. In a few minutes it would be bared by the tide, but now the water curled over it and broke in mocking whispers. Behind, the boat had closed to within a mile of the *Diamond Cutter*'s starboard flank. Its speed and single-mindedness left Albury no illusion: it was a gunboat.

Albury quickly backed off the throttle. The froth at the *Diamond Cutter*'s bow died, and then they were gliding like a barge in sudden silence.

"Breeze!" Jimmy cried. "Don't stop. Hit it!"

Albury shook his head. "Not yet," he said evenly. Augie stood next to him in the wheelhouse. The young Cuban eyed the reef, only fifty yards off the bow. The roar of the advancing cutter suddenly dropped two octaves as the Bahamian captain eased up.

"Augie, tell me when he hits the blue light," Albury said.

It was a patrol boat, and close enough that Augie could make out one or two numbers on the side. It was a sixty-footer. Two sailors with long guns stood forward. Another held a megaphone. In the wheelhouse, the Bahamian captain flicked a switch and the blue police light pierced the night, hitting the *Diamond Cutter* exactly once every second.

"OK," Augie said. "Blue light."

Albury threw his weight against the throttle, and the rebuilt 892 groaned. The bow rose and kept rising; below his feet Albury could feel the Colombians scrabble for balance. The

Diamond Cutter heaved itself forward and, rebelling against the weight of its cargo, planed off.

"Beautiful," Albury murmured. "Just beautiful." He turned to steer a course parallel to the coral reef, expertly following its scimitar curve, clinging to the deeper water.

The gunboat gave chase. As Albury had expected, its captain chose an intersecting course. It covered the distance in great thirsty leaps, approaching at full speed, now from the port side. To starboard was the reef; a fractional error of navigation and the *Diamond Cutter*'s hull would be lanced by a coral head. The contest would be over.

For the second time, the patrol boat, gray and menacing, drew alongside the big crawfish boat. Albury could see the black faces behind the windshield and the gunners in position on the bow. The officer with the megaphone shouted something that was swallowed by the howl of boat engines.

"Get down on the deck," Albury yelled to his mates. A quick look over his shoulder told him what he needed: that the combined wake of the two boats had obliterated the telltale curl over the reef. The jagged coral was masked in the backwash. To the naked eye, the way was clear.

Then Albury played the only card he had. Without warning, he swung hard to port, threatening collision. Instinctively, the Bahamian captain turned to starboard, crossing a few feet behind the *Diamond Cutter*. He should have paid less attention to the frantic Yankee fishing boat and more to the deadly nuances of the sea. The gunboat struck the veiled reef at thirty-three knots. It was the sound of a thousand fingernails on a blackboard.

As the *Diamond Cutter* cut a triumphant arc away from the reef toward open sea, Albury saw the gunboat scrape across the reef and settle in agony. He knew it would sink.

Some of the Colombians who had crawled up to watch from the stern began to cheer. They were still cheering when a deaththrash volley of machine-gun fire raked the *Diamond Cutter*.

CHAPTER **10**

THE CRUCIAL THING was to get away, to flee into the arms of friendly night. Albury did not expect another gunboat from the Bahamian Royal Defence Force, but he sped south for two hours off the easterly heading he needed, just in case. Aboard the *Diamond Cutter*, chaos was igniting.

Jimmy burst into the wheelhouse, his voice strained, almost falsetto. His features seemed unnaturally pale in the binnacle light.

"Breeze, these people are animals!"

"What happened?"

"I was bein' a nice guy, right? I figured they were hungry, so I go down below to make some sandwiches and stuff. Shit, as soon as those assholes smell food they mob me, like I was giving out money or something. I bet there's not a cracker or a can of beer left on the boat. They grabbed everything they saw and ran off like fuckin' rats, lookin' for a hole. And that's not the worst of it."

"What else?"

"It took 'em all of five minutes to break the head, but what do they care? Probably no fuckin' toilets where they come from, anyway. So what difference is a boat? They just squat down and go wherever they happen to be. Breeze, I swear to Christ I never seen nuthin' like it."

Albury grunted. He had expected smugglers; smugglers he understood. What he had gotten instead was a boatload of scum—coarse, ignorant gutter criminals of the most vicious sort. Albury knew the type. He had once lived in a cellblock full of them.

"Can you keep 'em below?"

"Shit, Breeze, they're everywhere. And the stink down there would choke a buzzard."

"Where's Augie?"

"He's been working on the wounded ones. Their pals don't seem to give a shit. They're too busy trying to dick it to the women."

"Jesus," Albury hissed. "How bad off are the ones who were shot?" The Bahamian machine gun had holed the *Diamond Cutter* in five or six places, all above the waterline. Two Colombians standing in the stern had gone down without a cry.

"One of them is just grazed on the head. The other is bleeding bad. Augie says he can't stop it."

"Neither can we."

By dawn, Albury knew, many vessels would be out hunting for a renegade lobsterboat. Not only the impulsive Bahamians, but also the more methodical Americans, with their spotter planes, their cutters, and their computers. But by dawn, with any luck, the Colombians would be ashore and the *Diamond Cutter* would be anonymously licking its wounds in some clump of mangroves. Maybe six more hours at twenty-four knots, Albury reckoned hopefully. They should make it, even allowing for the buffeting they would take from the heavy squall line that the radio predicted off the coast of the Upper Keys.

"Tell Augie to come up here," Albury said to Jimmy. "Have him bring the *jefe*. What's his name? Oscar?"

"His name is asshole. Like the rest of them," Jimmy snorted.

When Augie appeared a few minutes later, a young Colombian frog-marched before him, arm twisted cruelly behind his back. Augie was panting, and he said nothing. He branded the passenger with a bitter glare.

"This Oscar?" Albury said.

Augie shook his head. "Oscar is busy, Breeze, getting a hum job from one of his lady friends. This one here"—Augie gave the Colombian a rough shove—"he's had his turn. Haven't you, Lover Boy? And a few feet away, one of his buddies is bleeding to death from bullet holes. A real touching scene, Breeze."

"Easy, Augie."

"And afterwards this one here sneaks down to your cabin for a little scavenger hunt and helps himself to this." Augie tossed Albury the pair of socks in which he had hidden his money. "Only took you about two minutes to find the loot, eh, *amigo*?"

The Colombian stared at his own feet. Albury felt his control going. In a moment of self-pity, he saw himself at the helm, middle-aged, potbellied, once the master of a proud fishing boat, now only the whoremaster of a garbage scow. He reminded himself that the money that awaited was purely a one-way ticket off the Rock. Albury allowed himself a calming breath; his hands loosened their vise grip on the hickory wheel.

"Let him go, Augie."

"Shit, Breeze."

"Let him go now. Ask him if he speaks any English."

The Colombian flexed his throbbing arm. He ran his hands through oily black hair and, with an almost feminine gesture, curled two fingers along his droopy mustache.

"He doesn't speak English."

"Then talk to him for me," Albury said. "Tell him that he

is *escorio* and that he annoys me. Tell him that if he annoys me again, I will personally cut him up and feed him to the sharks one piece at a time, starting with his prick. Talk to him, Augie."

Augie talked. When he finished, the Colombian sneered.

"Tu madre," he said.

It was a mistake. Albury's hand flashed off the wheel and caught the Colombian on the left side of the face, savagely lifting him off his feet. The man capsized backwards into the wheelhouse bulkhead, his head hitting with a grating clunk. Then the Colombian slid to the deck and lay still.

"Que pasa aqui?"

The man named Oscar stepped through the wheelhouse door into a frozen tableau: Albury, right arm outstretched, a man who had just squashed a spider; Augie, rigid with fury, face contorted; Jimmy, wide-eyed, his voice raw.

"Here's the head spic, Breeze," he said.

He was a big man, balding, Indian-brown, with long and elegant sideburns that crawled toward his mouth. Albury guessed that Oscar was in his mid-thirties. A fashionably tight shirt, blood-red and open to the waist, revealed a powerful chest studded with a thick gold cross. In the eyes lay a feral street intelligence. Albury counted four rings on the right hand and a gold watch on each wrist. The man stank of sweat and sea and cheap rum. Albury could tell that he was a bit quicker, a bit smarter, and more than a bit tougher than the rest—the prototype of a coarse Latin ranch foreman or factory boss.

"Are you supposed to be in charge of them?" Albury demanded, his eyes motioning toward the man prone on the deck. "This is a fishing boat, not a zoo. You keep these people under control, or I will do it. You understand? If I have to do it, you won't like it. *Comprende?*"

The Colombian watched impassively from behind hooded eyes. Whether he understood the words or not, the tone was unmistakable.

"Many people are hunting for us," Albury went on. "The weather is getting bad, and there will be a storm soon. Go below and tell your people."

The Colombian did not allow for translation.

"I am hungry," he said in a rumbling baritone. "Where is food?"

"You assholes ate all the food," Jimmy spluttered.

"There is no more food," Albury said. *"Mañana* food."

"Then whiskey?"

"There's no whiskey for you. Jesus, Augie, talk to him."

"Captains always have whiskey, no?" Oscar insisted.

"No. No whiskey. *Mañana* whiskey. America whiskey."

Then Augie intervened, speaking harshly. Oscar cut him off in mid-sentence.

"The boat is bad. Is very small, and no *rápido.*"

"If you don't like it, swim, shithead," Jimmy snarled.

The *Diamond Cutter* began to pitch as it closed with the summer squall. Ahead, the clouds gathered in great purple bruises over the dull sea. Oscar rocked uncertainly in the crowded wheelhouse, blinking mechanically. He looked at Albury, at Augie, at Jimmy, a long measuring stare for each. The thin Colombian on the deck began to roll and moan.

"Mañana," Oscar said finally. It was a promise. He stalked from the wheelhouse, dragging the injured man with him.

A shiver danced along Albury's spine. "Jimmy," he said softly, "what have we got besides your shotgun?"

"Not much. A couple of fish knives, the spear gun, the flare pistol. And the bang stick."

"The knives are down below," Augie said absently.

"Go get them, Augie. We're all going to stay up here in the pilothouse until we reach Key Largo. Augie?"

Albury turned to look at the young Cuban. Augie's face wore a far-off gaze; his jaw was working.

"Did you see what Oscar was wearing?" he asked. "That big gold watch with the green stones on the band, like emeralds?"

Albury nodded. "I saw it when he walked in. A watch on both wrists, for Christ's sake."

"Breeze, when I left the wounded guy down there—the one who's gut-shot—*he* was wearing that emerald watch."

Later, Albury and his mates would learn that the Colombians had thrown their badly injured *compadre* into the ocean. They could never know if he was still alive when he hit.

The squall was worse than Albury had expected. The wind gusted to thirty knots and pushed the waves to nine feet. Water cascaded across the bow and lashed the windshield with opaque sheets. The *Diamond Cutter* rolled wickedly, battling the sea that snapped with white fangs at her hull. In the wheelhouse, the features of the three men were illuminated only by the green glow of the dials.

Jimmy and Augie clung nervously to whatever they could, but Albury was placid. He found the squall—it was not big enough to think of as a storm—calming. Not for a moment did he question the *Diamond Cutter*'s strength, or his own skill. He would not have taken her out on a night like this, but together they had ridden out far worse, Albury and the *Diamond Cutter*.

The weather brought three blessings. It quieted the Colombians: retching, pathetic bundles, clutching with peasant strength to anything solid. It also ruled out pursuit from the sea. And it allowed Albury to smoke. There was nothing he needed to see except the compass dial, and the jagged streaks of lightning served as eerie purple strobes.

The sole intruder in the wheelhouse then was the radio. If it had been left to Jimmy, the VHF would be off and rock music would be blaring from a tinny portable cassette deck. Augie, Albury suspected, would have steered in silence, as his forebears had.

By habit, Albury left the radio tuned to channel 16, the

hailing frequency monitored by the Coast Guard. There had been the normal nighttime banter as the *Diamond Cutter* approached the Florida coastline, and one boat captain laconically reporting engine trouble, but not much else. Reception was capricious amidst the thunderheads; the radio mostly crackled and spat.

Listening to it with half an ear while he conned the *Diamond Cutter* to an uncertain homecoming was the worst mistake Breeze Albury made that night. He should have listened to Jimmy's rock music. Or to silence. For the radio destroyed his pride.

All three men heard the call for help. It was weak, the transmission scored by static, but they heard it.

"Mayday! Mayday! This is the *Darlin' Betty*, Whiskey Kilo Alfa Three Six Six. I lost my bilge pump and I'm taking water about two miles east of French Reef. I've got three men and a boy aboard . . . can you read, Coast Guard?"

"That's a lobster boat," Jimmy said. "What the hell is he doing out here?"

By law, crawfish boats were not permitted to pull traps after dusk or before dawn. "Maybe he's just on his way to Miami for engine work," Augie said, "or maybe he's out here doin' what we're doing."

Jimmy said, "Breeze, he's only about ten miles south of us."

"Mayday, Mayday!" the radio cried.

"I *know* where he is," Albury said. Sweat sprouted. His guts churned. The rain fell softer.

"Let's go," Augie said.

"Hot damn, a rescue," said Jimmy. "It'll be another *Vixen*, Breeze."

Albury could have wept for their innocence.

The *Vixen*. He hadn't been able to buy a drink on Duval Street for nearly a year after that. What had it been, eight, nine years now? The boat had been still new, still the *Peggy*, and one morning just to shake her down he had run over to the

Dry Tortugas; to fish, to snorkel, and to wander the ruins of old Fort Jefferson.

On the way back the weather had gone to hell in a hurry. Albury had just about decided to run for cover in the Marquesas when the *Vixen* came on channel 16. A motor ketch, fifty-two feet, a lovely boat she must have been, but when Albury got to her she was dismasted and listing badly, the captain fighting feverishly to free the dinghy and keep the lines around three crying kids and a sick wife. Albury had been lucky to get them all off, and even luckier to get back to Key West. It was not until then that he had discovered the captain he had saved was a United States senator. The clippings were someplace in the trailer, together with the letter of commendation from the Coast Guard. Unless Peg had taken them.

But this was not the *Vixen*, not a famous stranger but a member of Albury's own tribe: a Conch fisherman. Albury knew the *Darlin' Betty;* it worked out of Marathon. And he knew the captain, a gangling retired Navy CPO named Hawk Trumbull. The boy on board would be his grandson.

And Albury knew there was nothing that he could do to help. He averted his face so the two young mates would not see the tears of rage and shame.

The distress call echoed again over the VHF.

"Breeze," Jimmy urged, "we got to change course." He reached for the microphone. "I'll tell them we're comin'."

Albury brushed the hand away. *"Think,* goddamnit. Think."

Jimmy withdrew his hand as though it had been scalded. He looked like a baffled puppy: Albury never yelled at him.

"What's wrong?"

"What the fuck do you think is wrong? Have you forgotten about our cargo? Hawk Trumbull might understand why I'm carrying twenty dirtbags named José, but the boys at the Coast Guard station won't—"

"But their boat is sinking. . . ."

"I know, Augie. I'm praying that somebody else is nearby. I can't get caught with these assholes on board, son. They'll lock the three of us up and seize the *Diamond Cutter*. I can't afford that. Now, turn up the radio and let's listen."

The next ten minutes were the longest Albury would endure. Hands wrapped protectively around the wheel, he stared straight ahead through the rain-streaked windshield. The silence was wracking; Albury could taste the resentment and bewilderment that flowed from Jimmy and Augie. Jimmy did not really understand. Augie did, and, understanding, he would have run hell-for-leather to the sinking boat anyway. From the corner of his eye, Albury watched Augie. If he were five years older, he would cold-cock me and take the helm, Albury thought. That is what I would have done. Once.

The squall was losing its fury, and the *Diamond Cutter* rode easier. Albury willed the radio to life. The Coast Guard, a tanker, a long-liner, surely somebody had heard the *Darlin' Betty*'s distress call. They were near the shipping lanes now, but tonight, perversely, there were no ships at sea. Or they were all deaf. No one had heard the dying call a Conch fisherman had launched into the thunderheads. There was no one but Breeze Albury to lift the microphone and say he was on his way.

He had to go, but he could not. Twice his hands began to spin the wheel for a more precise course toward the stricken craft, but twice he drew back. To go would be to lose everything: his boat, his freedom, his ticket off the Keys, even his son. Not to go was to lose his manhood. Feverish with self-disgust, Albury could devise no alternative. He looked straight ahead.

Then the radio whined to life a final time.

"Mayday, Mayday, somebody . . ." It was the excited voice of a boy. "Grandpa is hurt and we are leaving the boat. Good-bye."

"Dear God in heaven!" This time Albury made no attempt to hide the tears. Jimmy bit his lip and turned away.

"Mayday, please," came the last faint transmission.

Albury flicked the wheel a few points to port and opened

the throttle to its last stop. He snatched the microphone, but he did not say what he wanted to say. The squall was abating to a mist. There was one chance for Hawk Trumbull now, one that would save Albury as well.

"Mayday! Mayday!" Albury barked through a dry throat. "This is the fishing vessel *Darlin' Betty*, Whiskey Kilo Alpha Three Six Six. We are sinking two miles east of French Reef, six miles southwest of the Elbow. Abandoning ship. Can you copy, Mayday!"

The response was instantaneous.

"*Darlin' Betty*, this is Coast Guard Islamorada. Could you repeat your position?"

Thank God, Albury thought. Thank God the *Diamond Cutter* had a decent radio. He repeated Trumbull's position, nine miles southwest of his own, then broke off in mid-sentence to make it sound as though he had lost power.

"Stand by," the Coast Guard operator said. "Stand by."

Albury could imagine figures hunched tensely around a plotting table, a duty officer rubbing sleep from his eyes, a klaxon sounding to awaken a crew. It was too dark for a helicopter. It would have to be a patrol boat.

Even flat out from the Coast Guard station at Plantation Key, an able patrol boat would need thirty minutes. The *Diamond Cutter* would be there first.

"What are the Colombians doing, Jimmy?" Albury asked, as though it mattered. They could do anything they wanted now; their presence alone was enough to destroy Albury and his boat.

"They're mostly liyin' around on the deck, Breeze. I think the storm made 'em wish they were dead."

The radio swamped Albury's response.

"*Darlin' Betty*, this is Coast Guard Islamorada. The cutter *Dauntless* is thirteen miles north northeast of your position and will assist."

Dauntless. A good ship. Probably looking for me, Albury thought ruefully. And now she'll find me.

Then, with mournful precision, the Coast Guard operator began that universal sailors' litany of hope and despair.

"Calling all ships. The fishing vessel *Darlin' Betty* reports she is sinking off French Reef in two hundred feet of water. Coast Guard has lost radio contact. All ships in the area please respond to a sector two miles east of French Reef, over."

Albury cursed himself for forgetting to say how many people were aboard Trumbull's boat. He listened without expression while better men accepted the challenge of the sea.

Out in the Florida Straits, the Norwegian captain of a giant bulk carrier, Maracaibo to Boston, rang for more speed and to hell with the company computers that would later demand an accounting for unprogrammed fuel expenditure. Bending over his ship-to-shore, the Chinese deck officer of a rusty freighter bound for Charleston from Shanghai decided to risk criticism and altered course. Marine radios were suddenly alive with promising voices intent on a single purpose. In their midst, the *Diamond Cutter* sailed alone, in shame and silence.

As the ship captains exchanged positions, Augie listened somberly, his jaw set. "Too far away, all of them, Breeze," he said.

"Yeah. Looks like we're up."

"It'll work out," Jimmy offered. "It's a rescue, Breeze, what are they gonna do? Give us a medal, then throw us in jail for smuggling?"

"The law is the law," Albury replied.

"This is the Keys, man," Jimmy said.

"We'd better get on the radio and tell 'em we're in the area," Augie urged. "We're so close now they might mistake us for the *Darlin' Betty.*"

"Yeah."

They were good boys, both of them, Albury reflected. Maybe he could tell Customs that they hadn't known about the illegals, or that he had forced them to come along, threatened them. Maybe that would get them off the hook. And thank God he had not let Ricky talk him into coming, too.

Albury's palms were moist, but his hands were steady when he lifted the VHF microphone from its holder.

"Let's go out in style," he murmured, then cleared his throat.

"Coast Guard Islamorada, this is the fishing vessel *Diamond Cutter*, Captain William Albury. I'm in the area of French Reef and I will assist the Mayday, over. My posi—"

". . . in the storm."

The foggy voice leaped from the *Diamond Cutter's* tinny radio speaker. It was a Latin voice, speaking slow and deliberate English.

"Por Dios, he must be right on top of us. Who is he?" Augie grabbed a pair of binoculars and bounded from the wheelhouse.

"Your transmission is broken up," the Coast Guard operator said patiently. "Vessel calling, please repeat."

Albury took a deep breath, the microphone dangling loosely from his right hand. Talk! he wanted to scream. Talk back and save me.

"This is the motor vessel *Rio Limay*," the Latin voice answered at last. "Buenos Aires to New York, general cargo. My antenna was damaged in a storm, but I have heard the Mayday. I believe I am now in the location of the vessel in distress. Coast Guard, do you read?"

"This is the Coast Guard Islamorada calling the motor vessel *Rio Limay*. You're breaking up on the VHF; can you call on ship-to-shore, over?"

"Breeze!" Augie shouted from the deck. "Dead ahead, about half a mile."

Albury saw the squat form of the freighter, black in the predawn grayness, almost dead in the water. It lay straight off the *Diamond Cutter's* bow.

A white flare suddenly burst farther inshore, spitting pink

sparks into the mist. Albury eased the helm, dropped the throttle a couple notches, and killed his running lights. In a dense stillness, the crawfish boat wallowed parallel to the freighter.

"Coast Guard calling all vessels. The motor vessel *Rio Lamay* reports contact with the crew of the vessel in distress. Cutter *Dauntless* is en route with ETA of fifteen minutes."

"Breeze, I see a raft," Augie called. "About thirty yards off the freighter's stern."

Albury opened a hatch and withdrew another pair of binoculars, a heavy Zeiss. Quickly he sighted the raft; inside were three men and a young boy, who stood rubber-legged, waving. The crew of the Argentine freighter was waving back; a skiff was dropping from its portside davits. It was obvious that the *Darlin' Betty* had gone down.

Albury watched from afar as the shivering survivors clambered into the Argentine skiff. The boy, wearing an orange slicker, went first; Hawk Trumbull, his head swathed in a makeshift bandage, was last.

"Que hacemos?" It was the Colombian named Oscar.

"He wants to know what we're doing," Augie said.

Albury lowered the binoculars. "Tell him to shut the hell up and get down."

He fed power to the big diesel, and the *Diamond Cutter* stole away like a thief.

When he was certain that his boat was safely anonymous, northward bound in a lazy predawn procession of marine traffic, Albury gave the wheel to Jimmy. Then he made his way toward the stern until he could no longer be seen from the pilothouse and vomited into the sea.

The ride in went smoothly after that in a gray smuggler's void, an oily swell, a fine drizzle that became fog near the coast.

Albury felt empty. His arm ached. Sandpaper scoured his

eyelids. Otherwise, he was numb. Even when Augie returned from the quick foray aft to report that the Colombians were quiet except for the gut-shot one, who was missing, Albury felt nothing.

His chore was precise and mechanical now. There could be no threat of pursuit, or any danger from the sea. All he had to do was to find Dynamite Docks, discharge his cargo, and escape. He would hide the *Diamond Cutter* someplace quiet. He would sleep and try to forget. He anticipated no problems from the Colombians. Not after the beating they had taken in the squall. They would limp ashore like whimpering kittens. Jimmy and his Remington would oversee their departure. Good riddance.

The channel leading to Dynamite Docks is tricky, even in daylight. Shoals to north and south are deviously marked by ugly metal rods that look as though they have been borrowed from a construction site. Coming in off the open sea in the hour before dawn, *Diamond Cutter* made a landfall that would have made any sailor proud. Twin red flashes appeared fine cn the starboard bow; lights atop a Bell microwave dish that were a warning to fliers, and to sailors, a welcome. Albury, who had no pride left, nodded silently when he saw them. They were just where they should have been.

"Nice goin', Breeze," Augie remarked.

"Now look for the channel markers. They begin about a half-mile out. Don't use the searchlight unless you have to."

They found the markers, and Albury nudged *Diamond Cutter* between them at dead slow. There were no lights from shore: the docks weren't used much, except by smugglers and the occasional fisherman, and at this hour, Albury expected them to be deserted.

When the Colombian named Oscar appeared in the wheelhouse, his swaggering machismo had vanished. He seemed shrunken and haggard, his fancy red shirt soggy with sweat and salt rime.

"He wants to know if we are there," Augie relayed.

"Tell him we will arrive in a few minutes. Ask him what to expect on the docks."

"He says there will be two or three big cars waiting. I think he means Winnebagos."

"How about the money?"

"One of the drivers will have it, he says. I guess he'll bring it out onto the dock."

"Tell him that I hold him responsible. He will be the last to leave. If there is trouble for me, I'll make big trouble for him."

"He says there will be no trouble."

"His people are to leave in an orderly way. A few at a time. No mobs. No running. He goes with the last group. Him and Lover Boy and one or two others. Make sure he understands that he doesn't leave until the money is on board."

"He says he will do as you say."

As the limestone jetty slid into view through the fog, Albury could hear Oscar talking to the Colombians. Beside him at the wheel, Jimmy fidgeted. The first magenta blush of dawn teased the horizon.

"You believe him, Breeze? That it's all gonna go smooth?"

It was Augie who answered.

"When a shark smiles, man, don't look at the grin, look at the teeth."

"You watch them with the Remington, Jimmy. I checked it; it's all ready to go." Albury was judging the glide of the boat toward the shrouded docksite. "Augie, you reckon any of them is good enough to take a knife away from you?"

"Sh-it."

As the *Diamond Cutter* eased against the rocks, a muffled figure appeared. He wore a dark windbreaker and slacks, sneakers, and a New York Yankee baseball cap. He carried an attaché case, which he slipped under his arm to deftly catch the bowline and make the *Diamond Cutter* fast.

An excited chorus rose from the cargo. Oscar quelled it

savagely. Then the Colombians were gone in untidy groups that scrambled onto the dock and reeled away into the fog. At the end of the jetty Albury could see the sidelights of four vans, customized with smoked-glass windows.

"Four left, Breeze. Oscar, Lover Boy, and two others," Augie called softly.

"Get the money."

The figure on the dock had not moved. Now Oscar called to him, and, in a smooth underhand motion, the man tossed the briefcase.

"Have him bring it up here," Albury ordered.

Oscar stiffly climbed the short ladder to the wheelhouse, followed by the twin barrels of the Remington. He placed the attaché case on the chart table and undid the twin catches.

"You will see, captain. It is all here," the Colombian said.

"Your English has certainly improved," Albury noted.

The Colombian smiled.

"There are times, you see, captain, when it is convenient not to speak English. And other times when one must speak it. *Comprende?*"

Intuitively, Albury reached for the attaché case, but he was too late.

The stubby black revolver slid into the Colombian's hand, and with a downward slash, barrel first, it caught Albury on the side of his head. He staggered back, blood gouting from his scalp. The Colombian kicked him hard in the stomach, and Albury went down. The Colombian struck the way a shark strikes, silent and overpowering.

Albury writhed on the wheelhouse deck. The Colombian kicked him again.

"Hijo de puta," the Colombian cursed, and then, in English, he called down to the deck: "Throw down your gun, or I will shoot your captain."

"Breeze!" Through a haze of pain Albury heard Jimmy's shocked cry.

"Do what he says, Jimmy," he heard Augie say.

The Remington clattered to the deck, and the Colombian they called Lover Boy hopped forward to retrieve it. The other two vaulted ashore and ran with the man in the Yankee cap toward the last of the four vans.

Albury groped to his feet. One eye was closed. Blood coursed down his cheek and ran onto the deck. His belly churned. His arm was bleeding again.

" 'Tell him if there is trouble, I will make trouble,' " the Colombian mocked. "Come on and kill me. Make your big trouble. *Gringo de mierda.* It was you who was the dead man. From the very first, this was a one-way trip for you, *puto.* I am only sorry that I do not have time to do it with a knife."

Albury concentrated with every fiber to make the wheelhouse stop swimming. He raised both arms, as if in exhaustion or surrender, until the hands rested on a tubular aluminum object latched with hooks to one of the roof beams. It was smooth and cool to his touch.

"Look, please . . ."

"Beg, *gringo,* beg."

"Not for me. But for my mates. They are only kids, like sons to me. They can't hurt you." Albury lurched back half a step. The object was free now in his hands.

"They are shit, *mierda,* like you. And they will die first because it will hurt you to see them die. And then you, not with one shot, but with many, *como en la Guajira.*" Foam flecked the Colombian's lips. His eyes burned like a madman's fire. "Luis," the Colombian yelled. *"Dales. Ahora!"*

He grimaced, like a man about to ejaculate, waiting for the twin booms from the Remington.

But from the deck came only two muted clicks, and only Albury was ready for them. In a blurred half-second, he saw the Colombian turn aft in perplexity. He heard Jimmy sob and Augie roar like an angry panther.

Then Albury's arms were moving, coming down from the rafters with the bang stick, and he was thrusting like a demented swordsman against the Colombian's chest. In a single frenzied motion, Albury pulled back the rubber sling and let go. The long tube shot forward.

The bang stick is meant for sharks, not men. The twelve-gauge deer slug exploded on impact and blew a hole the size of a softball in the Colombian's belly and out his back. The dead man flew one way. Deafened, only half-conscious, Albury collapsed against the opposite bulkhead.

He lay there for what seemed like eternity but could only have been a few seconds. He jerked upright at the sound of pounding feet and the sight of Augie bursting into the pilot-house, a bloody fish knife in his fist.

"Shells, man. Where are the fucking shells?" he demanded.

"My right pocket," Albury mumbled. His last thought before he passed out was that he had been right not to trust Jimmy with the shotgun.

Later, it was Jimmy who told him how Augie had fired both barrels at the last of the Colombian's vans, and how one of the shots must have hit the gas tank because the van had exploded in a ball of fire and screams. That was Jimmy's story. Augie wouldn't talk about it.

CHAPTER 11

BOBBY FREED cosseted his patient with iced mountain chablis and a tingling back-and-front rub smoothed by liberal applications of coconut oil.

"The doctor says another ten days and you'll be as good as new." Freed rubbed gently. "Does this feel nice?"

Beeker lay impassively, hands folded behind his head, staring at the fan. After a time his back arched and a grunt forced its way through his teeth.

"Well, at least my favorite part of you has survived nicely," Freed whispered.

"Sure. That will make everything right?"

"You're all better now; the doctor says so. It's over."

"No, it is not over."

"I know how you feel. But we'll get even with Fatso Barnett. I promise."

"I don't care!" Beeker buried his head in a down pillow. "I'm leaving. This place sucks. I'm going, Bobby, I am."

"Don't be foolish. This is our home now. It could have

happened anyplace . . . anyplace where people are still *backward*."

"No, there is a special evil about this place. I want to go home to New York."

"Absolutely. You get your strength back, and we'll go back for a visit. Laurie could run the restaurant for us, no problem."

"Do we have any pot?" Beeker asked, his voice muffled by the pillow.

"What?"

Beeker rolled onto his back.

"Pot. I want a joint."

"You know I disapprove of pot, Neal; that's part of the trouble with this town. It is run by pot."

"You knew I was coming out of the hospital. The least you could have done was to buy a lid."

"I will not buy it for you. You know that."

Beeker hurled the pillow. It snagged on the rattan peacock chair and a cloud of feathers settled on the rough-weave peasant carpet they had bought in Mexico.

"You are so innocent," Beeker spat.

"Really, Neal, I . . ."

"*Innocent*. You strut around like a big man at the council meetings and talk and talk, but you don't really know what is happening in this anus place. You don't know at all."

"What do you mean?"

"Fatso Barnett, Fatso Barnett. That's all you can think of. He's only part of the problem. A fat little leech, a nobody. The real problem is bigger scum, like that lawyer Boone. *They* really run this town. Barnett is only their puppet. They laugh at us."

"Drake Boone?"

"Scumbag."

Freed was surprised. He had always thought of Beeker as the

ethereal sort. Neal always signed the petitions and dressed well for the rallies, of course, but you could tell his heart wasn't in it.

"What do you know about Drake Boone, Neal?"

"Lots."

"Tell me."

"No, I just want to go away."

"Please tell me. It could be important."

"What's the use?"

"It all fits together. Believe me, I know more than you think." Freed stroked Beeker's hand. "Please tell me."

Beeker sighed.

"Bring some ice for the wine, and I'll tell you," he surrendered.

Later that morning, with Beeker asleep, Bobby Freed walked alone to Singleton Docks to watch the shrimp boats come in. His mind was in turmoil, sickened. He would have to control his fury before the council meeting that night. Beeker had told him a story of a fifteen-year-old girl named Julie Clayton; it was the kind of thing you read about in the tabloids. But it had happened in Key West. And no one knew. Let me find some proof of what I have heard, Freed prayed silently. And the whole world will know.

Julie Clayton lay in Room 177 of Duval Hospital. She had been there for weeks, with a snake's nest of tubes to feed her and drain her, and machines to preserve the pretense that she was still alive. Julie Clayton was a vegetable.

Once, the way Beeker told it, she had been a student at Key West High, a fun-loving girl who took her kicks wherever she could find them.

She had found one too many, and his name was Drake Boone.

She must have been a cinch, huh, *counselor?* What a change from slap-and-tickle with panting adolescents in seedy drive-ins: a blow-dried, big-shot lawyer with three-piece suits, a fancy car, and an office with its very own private entrance.

What a wonderful secret for a fifteen-year-old girl, right, Drake? No band practice for Julie. No empty afternoons before soap operas in dingy trailers. For Julie, rather, after-school excitement, adventure, sex, perhaps even the illusion of love. Did you pretend it was love, Drake? Did you lovingly roll her joints? Was it you who introduced her to the wonderful high that comes from a couple of tiny pills? Was she *wild*, Drake, at those wonderful impromptu office parties? How many more like her were there? And where were you, Drake, you *hideous bastard*, the afternoon that Julie Clayton popped so many pills that they shut down her nervous system and left her a cabbage? Were you there, Drake, or could any fifteen-year-old wander in and help herself to joy juice at the private entrance of Drake Boone, Jr., *attorney-at-law?*

Neal Beeker had told the story in the strained tones of a sinner at confession. His hospital room had been across the hall from where Julie Clayton lay. And late one night, restless and unable to sleep, he had padded to a first-floor lounge for a cigarette and there encountered the girl's mother: a haggard, work-worn woman, Key West blue collar.

"I think she must have had a few drinks, Bobby, because she was real uptight at first, but then she opened up. She must have talked for half an hour, a monologue, almost like she was in a trance, talking to herself. Then suddenly she looks up and sees me and goes all white. That was the worst of all, Bobby, what she said then."

"What did she say, Neal?"

"She said, 'Mister, please forget what I told you. Mr. Boone, he made me promise not to tell anybody. He says he'll pay the hospital bills as long as I keep my mouth shut. But if anybody finds out what Julie done, Mr. Boone says he'll have them turn off the machines, and my baby will die.' "

In the summer, Manolo always rose with the dawn. The skylight in his studio had an eastern exposure, and in the mornings the light was perfect. He would paint in total absorption for several hours, until it became too hot. Manolo disliked the heat, and to have air-conditioned a studio with a high vaulted ceiling would have been wasteful. Besides, even air conditioning could not have helped with the glare. And to have fought the glare would have meant sacrificing the light. It was a closed circle: Manolo only painted by morning. It was his conceit that he could have made it as an artist if he had not become a doper, although he knew his subtle abstracts with occasional flashes of a dark vision were not truly of international standard. Still, he sold one every now and then, and he even had a show once, in Miami. For Manolo, art was at once a smuggler's cover and a private passion.

While he painted, Manolo tolerated no interruptions. At first, he had had the Cuban maid answer the phone while he worked. But she always got the messages wrong, and even the ringing, dimly perceived though it might be from another part of the house, was sometimes enough to break his concentration.

That morning, after wrestling with an improbable seascape, Manolo walked to the shower wondering for the thousandth time whether he had turned to pastels from natural predilection, or in rebellion against his environment because the Rock was a universe of gaudy, primary colors.

Among the calls Manolo extracted from the recordings over a sting *cafecito* that morning were two he expected: one tedious, one dangerous.

"Hey, big chief, give me a call chop-chop, *urgente,* like bang-bang, man."

Winnebago Tom. Asshole. And if I called you, fool, what would you say? Probably you would tell me exactly what I heard myself this morning: big shoot-out in Key Largo, two dead men in the water and a bunch more in a burned-out van, a missing boat, a search. Well, Tom, for now only you and I know it was an alien run gone wrong. But we had nothing to do with it, did we? All we provided was the transportation and the captain to run it. The rest was somebody else's problem. That is all I want to know. If you know more about it than that, loudmouth Tom, then keep it to yourself. Manolo did not call Winnebago Tom.

The second call had been short and to the point, a girl's voice in rough Caribbean Spanish that was not Cuban.

"Matilde a las dos," she said and hung up.

Manolo winced. The trouble with Jorge, sitting there in his sumptuous ranch in the emerald hills of Colombia, was that he had too little to do. Jorge loved spy stories. He devoured them.

"Tradecraft, Manolo," he insisted, "that is important to learn. It distinguishes us from the amateurs. It is a sign of maturity and dedication."

And of pretension, Manolo had added silently. Still, he had played Jorge's game, as usual. Part of it was to memorize a list of telephone booths, each assigned the name of a girl. When Jorge had something important to say, a terse call would arrive—from Miami, Manolo supposed—naming the booth and the time. *Dos* meant two. This was an even month, so subtract two. Jorge would call a telephone booth on Little Torch Key, twenty miles north, precisely at noon. Which meant that Manolo would have to get there early to be sure of getting the booth. When a secret agent needed a booth, it was always empty in Jorge's novels. A busy signal from Matilda would discomfit him thoroughly. Manolo tossed the Cadillac keys to the dumpy *cubana.*

She knew the drill. She would start the car and let the air conditioning run full blast. Manolo could not bear to touch hot metal, and he hated the feel of stuffy cars. That was what he told the *cubana.* He didn't tell her that, in his business, sometimes cars blew up.

Manolo liked to watch the landscape as he drove. He saw with an artist's eye, and sometimes he was later able to transmute swatches onto canvas—a pelican in awkward flight, a bridge stretching whitely away across blue waters. In truth, though, there was less of natural beauty to contemplate each time he drove north, from the Rock to Stock Island, to Boca Chica with its naval air station, across a procession of bridges that followed an old railroad line, into the Lower Keys.

Manolo's grandfather, that turn-of-the-century refugee from some forgotten political battle in Cuba, would not have recognized anything beyond the aching glare and the inviting clear water. When Jorge made the ride on his infrequent visits to the Rock, what he saw in satisfaction was a string of satisfied customers, puffing away, snorting, popping, in a chain of baked cinder-block settlements clinging tenuously to the mangroves.

What Manolo saw was destruction. The Keys had become all the rage of late: a tropical asylum from crime, cold, and high taxes. That was how they were advertised. The developers loved that line. They loved to plow up the mangroves and bulldoze the gnarled, disorderly native vegetation and replace them with block houses closed to the breeze and decorative shrubs that belonged somewhere else.

It was, to Manolo's eyes, a disaster; fragile beauty gone forever. Still, he supposed, one could not have it both ways. The venal officials charged with protecting what little of beauty remained in the Keys were the same ones who were supposed to suppress the commerce in which he himself traded. If they were effective at one, they might also be good at the other.

Manolo directed his full attention to rehearsing the lines he would say to Jorge. The conversation with Colombia that awaited him would be an ordeal. The time and location made that plain. Matilde was a punishment.

The booth sat in the middle of a desert, the survivor of a get-rich-quick scheme gone bust. "Trade Winds, a Community for Tomorrow," read the slick aqua-and-tan billboard along US 1. For perhaps ten acres the land was totally flat and absolutely barren, limestone broiling in the sun. Nothing grew and nothing moved. The fifty-foot lots, each with its carefully carved finger canal, were a study in desolation. The square stucco sales office, single-story with a cypress fronting, was marked by broken windows and the smell of urine. A few come-on flags still hung limply from the roof, colors faded to gray by the merciless sun.

It must have been 120 inside the blue-and-white phone booth. But at least the phone worked: in Jorge's books the phones always worked. Manolo jammed the door open with a chunk of coral in the forlorn hope some fresh air might seep in. Then he sat in his Cadillac with the engine running, waiting.

The phone rang precisely at noon.

"Con Carlos Ibañez, por favor," the voice said.

"El no está," Manolo gave the prescribed response.

"Cuando vuelve?"

"Para la pascua."

"Momentito," the girl's voice said, and Manolo heard some clicks. Electronic games, probably.

"Manolo. What the fuck is going on up there?"

Manolo sighed. For Jorge, no pleasantries.

"Business is fine. Is there a problem?"

"Not the business. The transportation. What happened? What went wrong?"

"You asked for a boat and I provided it. You asked for a first-class captain and I found one, although I told you it wasn't easy. That nobody here would touch that kind of job. What else should I know?"

"What I know is that I have had about a half-dozen hysterical phone calls from Miami already this morning. Fewer than half the people I sent have arrived. And they were screaming about shooting and explosions. One van apparently got caught by the highway patrol in the fallout. I need twenty people in Miami, and right now I got nine. How come?"

"I can't answer that. But if there were big problems, I would have heard it already. The pickup was by your people from Miami, remember? I don't know what went wrong. I only did what you told me."

"Don't feed me that Pontius Pilate bullshit, my friend. You are paid to take care of things for me up there. If things got screwed up, it was because something went wrong with the boat, or the captain got smart. I had a good man on that boat to run things for me, and he's one of those missing."

"Was it a clean pickup, Jorge? Like I suggested? Cash and no hassle?"

From Colombia came only static and silence. Instantly, Manolo understood.

"Because if it wasn't," he continued, "maybe the Conchs didn't like the way you wrote the ending. Maybe that's what happened, huh?" The booth was an oven. His soggy shirt stuck to his ribs like a rag; his tongue seemed bloated.

"I believe that is what happened," said the voice from Colombia. "And now you must repair the damage for me— permanently. My prestige has suffered. I will not tolerate it."

"Look, for God's sake, Jorge, like I told you, people don't like that kind of thing around here. This is not Colombia."

"That is no concern of mine. Without a reputation I have no business. My reputation has been damaged by someone you provided. I don't have to spell out what must come next."

"This is a lousy connection. Let me get some facts and I'll call you in a couple of days, OK? After the next shipment."

"The shipment will arrive on schedule. Your other instructions are not subject to change," the Colombian said, and the line went dead.

Manolo sprawled across the front seat and gratefully let the air conditioning wash over him. Unbelievable. The Colombians were not simply from another country but also from another century. Why couldn't they just hire a man and pay for his labor? No, that would be too civilized. Now, because some hapless fishermen had apparently had the temerity to balk at his own execution, Jorge's machismo was all out of joint.

Which left brother Manolo between a rock and a hard place, didn't it? If he didn't have Breeze Albury killed, then he himself might become a victim. If he did have Albury killed— Winnebago Tom and his gay band of Marielitos would relish that job, no doubt—that would scare off half the decent boat captains left on the Rock and leave the rest of the Conchs thirsting for blood. Manolo's blood.

Manolo killed the engine and tumbled into the heat, keys in hand. It was a moment's work to uncover the concealed compartment he had had built into the trunk. His escape kit. It was all there: a virgin Canadian passport that had cost him ten thousand dollars and two bank passbooks, one for the Bahamas, one for Luxembourg.

He studied the comforting columns of figures. The next shipment hence would swell them nicely. Then he would decide. If there was no graceful way out of his dilemma, then Paris would simply have to find room for one more aspiring artist.

". . . two days of surveillance by detectives resulted in apprehension of two pushers and the seizure of two hundred and seventy grams—that is, nearly eight ounces—of high-grade marijuana." Huge Barnett looked up. "Those college kids from up north think they can come down here and flout the law."

He resumed reading.

"As a consequence of 'Crusade '82' your police department has broken the back of the underworld drug business. I am proud to report that the situation in Key West is now under control. Sincerely yours . . ." Barnett constructed a tired man's sigh to follow a carefully timed pause. "That's it, gentlemen. As you can see, we have been busy." Too busy, he thought. He wished to hell he knew what had happened up at Dynamite Docks that morning.

"Thank you, chief, a nice report," said the mayor.

"Move-we-accept-the-report-and-thank-the-chief," intoned Councilman Biggs.

"Second," muttered Councilman Dawson.

"All in favor . . ."

"Wait a minute!" Bobby Freed objected. "I want to ask some questions. This is just nickel-and-dime stuff. He hasn't told us about the real drug business at all."

"Possession of ounces or pounds of marijuana is real business to me, Councilman," Barnett said levelly. "Anybody with that much drugs is in real bad trouble with the law here."

"Let's talk about the law down here. The federal drug-enforcement agencies pinpoint Key West as a major entry port for marijuana—not ounces or pounds, but *tons* of it."

"Look, the feds don't live here. I do. I know what's going on here, and as I have just told you, everything is under control," Barnett replied.

"Is that so? I am not talking just about the DEA, but also Customs and the Coast Guard. They both say that drug smuggling is a major industry here. Let me quote one Customs report: 'Its tentacles reach in all directions.' Is that news to you, Chief Barnett?"

"News? It's not news. It's wrong. Those guys see a grunt and think it's a shark. I know. I talk to them all the time."

"Do you also talk to the Governor's task force? Don't you find it interesting that it should be here at all? Or that law enforcement—or the lack of it—is one of its concerns?"

"The Governor's folks have been here for almost a year, councilman. They have made no accusations."

"Let us hope some will be forthcoming."

"Bobby, Bobby . . ." the mayor implored, not unkindly. Huge Barnett liked Mayor Gibbs. His wife was a skilled and determined shoplifter, but she would never have a record while the mayor was mayor and Barnett was chief.

"You gentlemen asked for a report on what we are doing to combat the evil of narcotics in this city, and I have given it," Barnett said softly. "If there is nothing else, I would like to get back to work."

"At least make him answer for the Ramrod Key fiasco. There were tons there, all right. And then what do we get?

Headlines one day, and the next day everybody goes home and it's all forgotten. Isn't that *real bad trouble,* Barnett?"

Barnett reined his temper.

"You're out of order, Bobby," the mayor shouted. He pounded his gavel with one hand and with the other wrenched Freed back into his chair.

"With your permission, mayor, I *would* like to talk about the Ramrod Key incident," Barnett said. "I didn't put it in the report because I did not consider it one of our successes. But it's important, and it's the sick kind of thing that is happening all over the country today. It's the kind of thing that happens when the police are handcuffed and criminals coddled."

Barnett spoke slowly: Margie, the middle-aged divorcée who covered council meetings for the local paper, God bless her patient soul, took lousy notes.

"Now, I had that scu . . . criminal dead to rights. I had 'em with probably the biggest load of dope anybody has ever tried to smuggle into the Keys. So it was a few miles outside the city limits, so what? Does that make it right? I knew that dope was comin', and I knew it was intended to be sold on the streets of this city to our children, yours and mine. So I went out and got it. And I didn't tell the feds and I didn't tell the state; I didn't tell anybody. It's not anybody else's kids, it's ours. I did it and I'm glad. No loophole justice is going to stop me from doing my job of protecting this city, no sir."

Loophole justice. It had taken Barnett hours to think it up. He bestowed an avuncular smile on openmouthed Bobby Freed.

Barnett hitched his belt and adjusted his cowboy hat in that special way so it would not mess up his hair.

Bobby Freed's voice cut like a knife.

"That is the most hypocritical bullshit I have ever heard in all my life."

Barnett boiled to his feet. His overworked chair collapsed behind him. He snarled.

"Now look, princess . . ."

"Order, order," the mayor yelled and watched in perplexity as the head of the gavel parted from its stem and shot across the room to bounce harmlessly off Huge Barnett's belly.

Freed was like a virus that would not die.

"And what about the campaign of violence against businessmen in this city? Whose kids are behind that? And why does *our* police department stand by and watch it? Tell me about that, Fatso!"

"Faggot! Freak!" Barnett bulldozed across the floor toward the defiant Freed.

It was the precise and normally timid clerk of the council who averted bloodshed. He could not abide disorder and there he sat, the council in uproar, his minutes in shreds.

"Motion on the floor!" the clerk hollered with all his might. "There is a motion on the floor. The council must vote on the motion before proceeding to the next order of business."

Somehow that was enough to restore sanity. Freed was led back to his seat. The council voted 4–1 to accept their chief's report.

Outside, Barnett savagely slammed the custom Chrysler into gear. He ignited the flashing blue lights and switched on the siren. He was late for an important appointment.

In the trunk of the police car lay a neat, brown-wrapped parcel. Drake Boone had dropped it off at headquarters. Inside the parcel was fifteen thousand dollars.

Barnett reckoned it would take only about a third of that to convince the accommodating bureaucrat he was meeting to arrange the quick, quiet transfer of a hospital patient named Julie Clayton to a public hospital upstate.

Bobby Freed walked home alone down Simonton Street in deeper depression than he had ever known.

CHAPTER 12

THE SOUND of a lone mosquito buzz-bombing a blood-ied ear rattled Breeze Albury from a four-hour sleep. He rolled off his bunk and clutched his head with both hands to suppress the vertigo. His arm stung and his stomach roiled. His skull burned where Oscar had clubbed him with the pistol.

Albury dragged himself to the deck where Jimmy and Augie lay like gaping, snoring corpses. He let them sleep. Dusk was settling in on the Florida Keys; a faint, a cool gust from the west chased away the choking heat. Albury climbed to the pilothouse and studied his chart through blistered eyelids.

The *Diamond Cutter* lay tranquilly at anchor off Lignum Vitae Key, a pear-shaped mangrove islet west of Islamorada. Here Florida Bay offered deep water, and concealment. After the killings at Dynamite Docks, the crawfish boat's flight had been breakneck, confused, haphazard. Instinct had warned Albury to run south, home toward Key West, as swiftly as the big Crusader would take him. But prudence told him to lay low, hide for a few days, ask quiet questions.

Augie had grabbed the helm for the first leg while Albury's head had cleared. The kid had steered safely southward in the heart of Hawk Channel, past Rodriguez Key, with the idea of slipping through the islands to the Gulf side at Tavernier. It was a good plan, but Augie didn't know the Upper Keys like he did Key West; numb from the shootout, Jimmy had been no help, either.

As the *Diamond Cutter* had cleared Tavernier Key, Augie had wheeled her starboard and promptly deposited all forty-three feet of Albury's pride and joy on a shallow mud flat. There the three of them had sat for two hours, watching the traffic crawl by on U.S. 1, squinting into the sky for some sign of the Coast Guard helicopter that was surely on its way to arrest them for murder.

Finally the tide had come up and gentled the big fishing boat back into the channel, where Albury had taken the wheel. Hunger and dwindling fuel had persuaded him to call at the first oceanfront marina. But a Monroe County sheriff's car innocently idling in the parking lot had run the *Diamond Cutter* off.

From then on it had been damn-the-fuel, forget-the-hunger, and run for cover—and for the *Diamond Cutter* no cover was good enough on the Atlantic side of the Keys. Albury had taken the boat through to the Gulf side under the Indian Key Bridge and anchored behind Lignum Vitae, one of the largest islands in Florida Bay. Sheltered from the badgering southeasterly winds of summer, the *Diamond Cutter* could at least expect a calm last leg back to Key West.

That would be more than Breeze Albury could expect—if he dared go back to Key West at all. Albury swigged at a can of warm beer that had somehow escaped the aliens' marauding and tried to think it through.

By now everybody and his brother should be looking for the *Diamond Cutter,* from the Bahamian Coast Guard to the

Florida National Guard. Sunk patrol boats and exploding vans have a way of attracting attention. But it might not be too bad. Suppose they caught him? There was no evidence on the boat to link him to anything, no scars he couldn't explain away. Augie had spent the whole trip down on his hands and knees scrubbing the blood off the wheelhouse floor. So they caught him, so what? He and his mates had innocently motored north to look for new fishing grounds; a lot of people knew Breeze Albury was fed up with Key West and wanted out. What aliens? An explosion? A Conch jury might believe him, certainly if the only testimony to vouchsafe the charge came from Colombian wetbacks. And who else was there to tell? Not Jimmy, certainly not Augie.

Albury tuned the VHF to channel 4 and tried to raise Crystal. Silence. He flipped to 16. Right after they had fled Dynamite Docks the air had been full of excited voices. Now there was only the routine chatter of pleasure boaters.

"How hot are we?" It was Augie, stretching.

"Not very."

"I'm not surprised. You think those asshole Colombians would tell the cops anything? No way."

"They knew the name of the boat."

Augie laughed.

"Maybe some of them. But they have forgotten it by now. They don't get paid to remember names and faces. Those that got out of Key Largo aren't saying shit to anybody, except maybe to their boss. If any got caught, all they're saying is *'No comprendo, señor policeman. No hablo English.'* Don't worry about them, Breeze. Worry about their *patrón.*"

Jimmy shambled into the pilothouse, rubbing his eyes.

"It's like a bad dream, Breeze."

"It's all over now."

Except that it was not. While part of Breeze Albury calmly plotted a defense, the rest of him howled bitter outrage. Now what, sucker? Anybody else want to come by and punch me out? No, it was not over.

"Is there anything to eat?" Jimmy asked. "I'm starved."

"Nothin'," said Augie.

"We need to let things cool off some more, Jimmy," Albury said. "In the morning we'll go up to Bud N' Mary's for food and fuel. No sense risking it now."

"Guess you're right, but I gotta eat." Jimmy vanished into the hold and emerged with a rusty spinning outfit with a frayed bucktail jig tied to the monofilament line. He began casting from the bow.

Albury noticed that Augie's T-shirt was crusted with dried blood and that a bandana had been tied as a makeshift bandage on his left forearm. Augie's eyes were bright and intent, but his voice was tired.

"What the hell happened, Breeze?"

Albury said, "I don't know for sure. We were double-crossed."

"That much I figured out by myself. Tell me the rest, man. We almost died up there at Key Largo. Killed some people ourselves," Augie said. "Least you can do is tell me why."

"I don't know why," Albury repeated. He swatted at a cluster of gnats, whining around the open wound on his scalp. "I don't know who in Key West would want me killed. Maybe it was Oscar's brainstorm."

"Or Oscar's boss."

"Christ."

Augie asked, "Why did you do it at all, Breeze? The *Diamond Cutter*'s an honest boat. That's your reputation. You wouldn't work for a snake like Tomas Cruz."

"Blackmail," Albury said in a dead voice and explained the whole story. "Boone promised that the dope charges would be thrown out if I made the run," he finished. "Tom said it was worth fifty grand. Fifty thousand dollars, Augie."

"That I understand. But Tom and his people work for the Machine. They run weed, 'ludes, cocaine when they can get it. Not illegals."

« 128

Albury shook his head tiredly. "My guess is that this was a favor for somebody, Augie. That's not important. I told them 'yes,' that's what's important. I said 'yes,' and I wish to God I hadn't. I thought it would solve everything for me and Ricky. The money would do it. But I thought the same thing a few years ago when Veronica was so damn sick. They always give you the same line, the same bullshit: 'We need a good captain and a fast boat. One run is all, captain. One run and all your troubles are over.' This time they *helped* me make up my mind. That's the only difference."

The words came out raw and tremulous. Augie felt embarrassed. "Shit, any fisherman would have done the same. And for a lot less," he added. "Don't sweat it. Nobody's gonna catch us. We're almost off the hook now."

"That's not enough."

"I knew it wouldn't be."

"I'll drop you and Jimmy at the gas docks tomorrow."

"Forget it," Augie said. "A captain's got to pay his mates. Fifty grand, you said, right? For my share I'd swim through a school of bull sharks. Nude!"

Albury laughed hard and in his exhaustion kept laughing. He needed to wind down, to back away from the cliff. The boat, the boys—solid, Lord, in damn good shape. If only he was as sure of himself.

"Hey, bubba!" came a triumphant cry from the bow of the *Diamond Cutter*. Albury and Augie turned in time to see Jimmy hoist a silvery five-pound barracuda into the boat.

"Goddamn," Augie exclaimed. "The white boy's caught us some supper."

Crystal was hunched over the workbench when he heard the light tapping on the door. His wife came in quietly, kissed him once on the cheek, and whispered something.

"OK," Crystal said. He yanked the plug on the soldering

iron and placed it, still smoking, on a slab of plywood. "Go ahead and send him in."

Crystal's wife led Shorty Whitting into the repair shop. The policeman's uniform was starchy clean; he carried his hat in his hands. His eyes surveyed the electronic jungle with a certain awe.

"Hey, Crystal."

"Hello, captain. What's up?"

Whitting shifted uneasily from one foot to the other. "Chief Barnett asked me to stop by."

"And what does that fat fucker want that he can't ask me himself?"

Whitting's face turned the color of fish flesh.

"I'm sorry, Shorty. I can't help it if the guy makes me puke. What does he want?"

"Were you on the radio yesterday morning?"

"When?"

"Early. Around dawn."

Crystal shook his head no and gave a roar of a laugh. "No, sir. Yesterday morning about that time I believe me and the old lady were rolling around in the sack. I didn't put my ears on till about ten or so."

Whitting asked, "You're sure?"

"Positive, captain. Why?"

"There was some shooting up in Key Largo. Supposed to be a crawfish boat involved. Chief Barnett heard about it from Tom Cruz—"

Crystal wheeled himself over to a small refrigerator. "Wonder how Tom knew so fast. Want a beer, Shorty?"

"No thanks," Whitting said. "Apparently several people were killed. The sheriff's office hasn't identified the bodies yet. A truck blew up and some of them got fried."

"Where did this happen?" Crystal asked, popping a Miller Lite.

"A place called Dynamite Docks. It's a little jetty on a piece of private property up there off Card Sound Road."

"Sounds like dopers," Crystal said.

"That's what the chief thinks. He also thinks the boat might be the *Diamond Cutter*."

"He's crazy. You guys just busted Breeze Albury last week. He's not dumb enough to try again so soon. Tell your lardass boss he's crazy. No way was it the *Diamond Cutter*."

Crystal could tell that Shorty was damn uncomfortable with this errand.

"Just the same," Whitting pressed, "the chief wondered if you could ask around on the radio today. See if anybody heard anything or saw anything up there. Albury's boat isn't docked at the fish house, and most of the guys haven't seen it for a couple days. If you hear anything, maybe you could call me over at the office."

"Sure," Crystal said. What a poor sap this guy was. "But I really don't see what the big deal is. It happened a hundred miles away, Shorty. It's not a Key West case, is it?"

"The chief is interested," Whitting replied curtly. As he moved toward the door, a suitcase-sized radio mounted over the workbench crackled to life.

"Smilin' Jack, this is Lucky Seven, do you copy, over?" The signal was weak, but the voice was distinct. Crystal swiftly rolled himself across the workshop.

"Smilin' Jack? Can you copy, please? This—"

Crystal twisted the volume control to zero. The voice died in the speaker box.

"Who's that?" Shorty asked curiously.

"Some fuckin' crank. He's been jamming up the radio all morning. The Coast Guard ought to throw his sorry ass in jail."

Whitting studied the sophisticated VHF radio. "How far can you listen with this thing?"

"Depends," Crystal said. "Depends on the atmosphere."

Crystal waited until he heard Whitting's patrol car roll out of the gravel drive. He turned back to the radio, playing the dials like a maestro.

"Lucky Seven, this is Smilin' Jack, over. Can you copy?" he asked urgently.

"It's about time, you lazy sonofabitch," came the voice of Breeze Albury.

A few minutes later Albury came down from the pilothouse. Jimmy and Augie were scrubbing the mess from Key Largo off the fishing deck.

"Anchors up," Albury said. "We got trouble." He told them of his conversation with Crystal. Word was out about the fiasco with the Colombians. Tom knew about it; Barnett already was asking questions.

Albury took the *Diamond Cutter* to Bud N' Mary's to gas up. Jimmy and Augie went for groceries, Albury for a telephone.

"Good morning," said Mark Haller on the other end.

"I was afraid you'd be out rousting trap robbers," Albury said.

"Naw. I used up my gas allotment for August, so I can't take the boat out. How d' you like that shit—a Marine patrolman who can't go out on the water?"

"The State of Florida strikes again," Albury said. "Mark, I need a favor. I was around Key Largo yesterday . . ."

"You weren't involved with those damn Colombians?"

"What Colombians?"

"Christ, Breeze, I remember back when you were a decent fisherman."

Albury grimaced. Jimmy stood outside the phone booth and pointed to the palm of his hand. Albury opened the glass door and handed him a damp fifty-dollar bill.

"I talked with a friend of mine," Albury said. "He said there's a load coming in at Bahia Honda tonight."

"So what do you want from me? I told you I ain't got a boat with any gas in it."

"Just tell me, is it Tom's load?"

"That's what I heard," Haller said. "Five tons. If I knew

exactly where they were bringing it in, I'd go sit there in my truck and cut loose a few rounds when the boats came."

"Well, I know exactly where," Albury said. He told Haller his plan, and he told him what he needed.

"You've got magnesium balls," the Marine patrolman sighed. "John Cotter is on air-patrol duty this week. His truck is parked at the Exxon station in Marathon. What you need is in there, under the front seat. Don't get caught."

Albury asked Haller to pass the word to Ricky and Laurie that he was alive.

"Where are you?" Haller asked.

"Moving," Albury said. "Fast."

"I got some news about your crawfish traps, if you're still interested. I know it's pretty dull stuff for a big-time smuggler. Just fishermen's gossip."

"I'm interested," Albury said impatiently.

"There's a boat called *El Gallo*. Captain's a Cuban named Willie Bascaro. Forty-six feet. Radar. A dope boat. Willie works for Winnebago Tom."

"That's the boat that cut my traps?"

"Willie got drunk the other night at the Casa Marina and started bragging in Spanish about it. Some of the Key West Cubans heard. Tom was there. Had one of his goons slap the shit out of the guy. I checked the story with a couple of captains I know, and they heard the same thing. It's not much consolation, Breeze, but at least you know. There's not enough to file charges yet."

"You did good just to find out," Albury said. "Thanks, Mark, thanks for everything."

Haller was right: learning the truth was no consolation, but it certainly enhanced the clarity of Breeze Albury's situation.

He untied the *Diamond Cutter* from the diesel docks at Bud N' Mary's and motored quietly, almost serenely, seaward past Teatable Key. Jimmy opened three cans of cold beer, and Augie constructed huge sandwiches from fresh cold cuts.

It was an overcast morning, the sky gray and shrouded with the distant purple promise of an afternoon squall. A three-foot chop followed the fishing boat south-southwest, toward Vaca Key and the town of Marathon.

Four hours later, Augie Quintana was using an eight-inch screwdriver to pop the locks on a gray-over-black Chevrolet Blazer, property of the Florida Marine Patrol, that was parked at a Marathon gas station.

Back in Key West, Crystal's wife was escorting another visitor into the muggy workshop.

Tomas Cruz gave Crystal's massive hand a perfunctory squeeze, then pressed an envelope into the palm. "Three thousand even," Winnebago Tom said. "Just like I told you: one boat only, coming in through the Bahia Honda channel about midnight."

"Fine," Crystal said neutrally. "Your people will be listening on channel eleven, as usual."

"That's correct." Tom wore a silk shirt, open to the breastbone. Crystal counted four gold chains on his brown neck.

"Since when are you guys running aliens?" Crystal asked. "Shorty Whitting told me about the mess up the Keys."

"It's a long story," Tom said.

"It was stupid. You guys don't know when to quit."

"We pay you for your ears, not your lip." Tom pretended he was kidding. He flashed his teeth and cuffed Crystal on the shoulder. "You gonna count your money?"

"Nope."

"Well, OK. You don't think there's gonna be any problems with the law tonight, huh?"

"No problems," Crystal said. "I'll take care of it. If I hear anything, your boys will be the first to know. I'll use the police scanner, the single sideband, the VHF, the works."

"As long as you got the cops covered."

"Don't worry, Tom," said Crystal. No cops, he thought, but you're going to wish there were.

CHAPTER 13

THERE WAS a light knocking on the office door. Christine Manning folded that morning's edition of the *Key West Citizen* and placed it on a corner of the desk. As usual, she wasn't expecting anybody.

"Yes?"

"Can I come in?" It was a woman, tall, with dark red hair and eyes both shy and alert. She wore blue jeans and a tissue-thin pullover that clung to her breasts. Christine Manning knew who she was: Breeze Albury's girl friend.

Laurie Ravenel introduced herself and sat down stiffly.

"Am I interrupting anything?"

"Oh my, no." Christine smiled. "I don't get many visitors. Not many of the locals would be caught dead talking to me."

"They don't like interference, especially from Tallahassee," Laurie said. "You shouldn't take it personally. The Governor himself would get the cold shoulder down here."

The special task force had been formed a year earlier in the Pavlovian politics that logically followed the embarrassing arrest of a number of Key West's finest, who had been caught taking big bribes. The Governor declared that the new squad was going to root out the island's most egregious scoundrels, but, in reality, most of its paltry budget had been squandered on publicity junkets before Christine Manning had even been handed her plane tickets.

Newly divorced, bored to numbness with sleepy Tallahassee, and admittedly hungry to make a crusading name for herself, Christine had accepted the Governor's offer. The Key West locals had promptly given her the smallest office in the courthouse, a peeling desk that did not lock, and a telephone upon which half the civil servants in Monroe County could eavesdrop, if they wished.

For nearly eleven months, Christine had tried to make friends and cultivate dependable sources, quietly building up her files but accumulating almost nothing of prosecutorial value. In the meantime, she had watched enough sunsets at Mallory Square to last her a good long lifetime. She was ready to get off the Rock.

"Laurie, you're obviously not here to give me the cold shoulder," Christine said.

"No."

"You want to talk about Breeze?"

"No!" Laurie blushed. That was the last thing she wanted to talk about. "It's Drake Boone," she added quickly. "What have you heard about Boone?"

"I supposed I've heard everything," Christine said. "That he's a bagman for a big smuggling operation, a fixer here at the courthouse, an errand boy for Chief Barnett. I've heard about his home on St. Thomas and his apartment in Manhattan. He's a snake."

"What about his personal life?" Laurie asked.

Christine shrugged. "He snorts coke, like everybody else

in this town who can scrape up a dollar bill." She decided not to mention how, after only one week in town and knowing full well who she was, Drake Boone had greeted her with a hug and a small amber vial of Peruvian flake. Terrific sense of humor.

Laurie fidgeted nervously. "There's a young girl over at Duval Hospital that you ought to see. She can't tell you why she's there or what happened, but her mother might. What I heard was that it happened at a party at Drake Boone's office."

"What happened?"

"This kid ate about a dozen Quaaludes."

"And she's still alive?"

"That's a matter of opinion. Go look for yourself. My boss heard about it from a friend who was a patient at the hospital. Says the girl's a veggie. He says Boone fed her all those 'ludes from a mason jar." Laurie sighed and stood up. "I don't know what else went on, but I think it's just as well that the girl can't talk about it."

Christine asked, "How old is she?"

"Fifteen."

"What's her name?"

"Julie. Julie something. Bobby knows. My boss."

Christine Manning began to write in a legal pad. "That would be Bobby Freed, the councilman."

"Yes. He's very upset."

"Were there any other witnesses?"

"Probably," Laurie said. "It's awful. After I heard Bobby talking about it, I figured somebody ought to do something. Somebody ought to know, even though nothing will come of it."

"You might be surprised," Christine said.

"It's awful," Laurie said.

"It certainly is a nasty little yarn. I'll pursue it, I promise," Christine said. "While you're here, tell me how Breeze is doing."

Laurie smoothed the crease from the front of her jeans, picked her purse off the floor, and moved toward the door. "Oh, he's fine," she said earnestly. "He's out on a fishing trip." Then she was gone.

Christine Manning turned back to the newspaper on her desk. In red ink she underlined a short and sketchy front-page article under a headline: "Six Die in Shooting/Van Wreck at Largo/Smugglers Sought."

Another nasty little yarn.

Eddie Fontaine followed the convoy through Big Pine Key, past the federal prison, past the bleached waterfront cottages, past the Old Wooden Bridge Fishing Camp, and over a ten-million-dollar concrete bridge that would have been a scandal anywhere but the Keys. It was a bridge to nowhere, to an island called No-Name Key. No one lived on No-Name. There was no water, no electricity. The bridge and the highway existed only because some clever politician had a stake in such things. Bugs thwacked the windshield of Fontaine's pickup and hung by the glue of their blood. A tiny Key deer, the size of a golden retriever, dashed between the speeding cars and disappeared into the red mangroves. There was only one reason on God's earth that Eddie Fontaine would have pulled himself out of that pretty second-grade teacher, kissed her good-bye on the left breast, climbed into his old Army greens, and driven off into the ravenous night.

Eddie Fontaine smelled money. When Winnebago Tom called, Eddie came. He wasn't proud. Ten thousand bucks was a new trailer, or a new truck, or maybe one of those Checkmate speedboats that Boog Powell was selling. Fontaine chuckled to himself and took another draft from a flask of Jack Daniels. There were a dozen ways to look at it, ten thousand dollars. Enough cocaine to keep that little teacher bucking for weeks.

Fontaine fixed his eyes on the taillights of the car in front of him. The road would be ending soon, not at a fishing village or subdivision, but at water's edge. Ahead, the other cars slowed and brake lights winked red in the night. One by one, the drivers turned off a dirt road that cut a washboard trail to the loading site. Fontaine put the flask between his knees and used both hands to steer. A family of raccoons, hunkered down at a trash pile, gave a green-eyed stare to the caravan but never budged from its supper. Night swallows swooped through the glare of the headlights to snatch june bugs and mosquitoes.

A car's horn sounded. The off-loaders cut their headlights and parked. The water of the Big Spanish Channel was visible through the mangroves; Eddie Fontaine and the others wordlessly picked their way through the roots and rocks to the shore. There, parked at the end of a man-made jetty, sat two Winnebago campers and a beer truck.

Eight men comprised the off-loading crew, including Tom's lieutenant. From past experience, Fontaine knew that Tom's man wouldn't be doing much of the heavy lifting. Well, that was fine. As long as he brought the cash.

The men gathered at the tip of the jetty, murmuring, smoking, slapping at their arms and legs to kill the bugs. Fontaine knew four or five of them as neighbors, high school buddies; the rest he knew by sight. It was a small fraternity of regular faces. Tom said it was best that way.

Fontaine looked at his wristwatch. It was ten minutes past midnight.

"What kind of boat this time?" he asked Tom's man.

"Just a boat," the man said, frowning. Eddie had been drinking again. How many times had Tom warned him?

"What do we load first, the beer truck or the campers?" said Eddie Fontaine.

"I'll let you know," said Tom's man, walking away.

Fontaine climbed into one of the Winnebagos to look for a

place to lie down, but the insides of the camper had been stripped to the bare aluminum. Fontaine hopped out and sat on the corner of a bumper. Across the water, in the distance, was the Seven Mile Bridge. The only lights along the blackened ribbon were trucks and cars; the only sounds in the night were their engines.

Eddie Fontaine took another sip of whiskey. The real question was whether to tell his wife about the money. He couldn't just go out and buy a speedboat and not expect her to ask questions. She was no damn fool. The kid needs braces; that would be noted, too. The other times he had managed to stash a little and lie about the rest. Shit, she never cared where it came from. Throw in a gold necklace or a new color TV, and she all of a sudden forgot what she wanted to ask about.

A shoe box, Fontaine decided with a sour belch. That's where tonight's wad was going. Fuck Junior's rotten teeth.

He got up and weaved a few yards to the edge of a mangrove clump, where he unzipped his jeans and began to urinate. He yelped when a voracious horsefly scored a direct hit on his pecker.

"Eddie!" shouted another off-loader. "The boat's comin'."

The men swarmed to the end of the jetty. One of them began to light Coleman lanterns. The belabored sound of a diesel rode the breeze up the channel. Huffing, Eddie Fontaine joined the others, watching from shore.

"For Christ's sake," grumbled Tom's man. "Tuck yourself in, willya, Eddie?"

A crawfish boat with three men aboard hung fifty yards off No-Name Key. Tom's man could see the bales stacked to the gunwale. With an obliging wind you could have smelled the stuff all the way to the mainland. He lifted a lantern and swung it like a pendulum for several seconds. A spotlight winked back at him from the fishing boat; the captain aimed its bow toward the jetty.

"OK, let's keep it short and sweet," said Tom's man, addressing the group. "We load up as fast as we can, the

Winnebagos last. Then give the drivers thirty minutes to get out of here."

"When do we get paid?" someone asked.

"After the load is gone," answered Tom's man. "And if I catch one of you bastards ripping off even a handful of weed, you'll be swimming."

The boat nestled up to the jetty. A porky man on the bow tossed a rope to one of the off-loaders; the others formed a makeshift fire brigade from the boat to the beer truck. The first fifty-pound bale was on its way when the shotgun punctured the summer night.

"Fuck me," whispered Eddie Fontaine, dropping the bale.

Tom's man raised hands, imploring silence, like the marshal at a big golf tournament. The other men turned their eyes north, to Little Pine Key and a new sound. Another boat.

"Let's get out of here," one of the off-loaders murmured.

"No!" barked Tom's man. "No, not yet. Maybe it's just trap robbers or something. Sit tight for a second." He snuffed the lantern he was holding.

The boat came anyway, rounding the point of Little Pine, faster and faster, the rasping of its engine followed by the sound of pushing water.

"That fucker's crazy," Fontaine said.

Tom's man strained to see the new boat. "Where are his goddamned lights?"

Then there was one; blue, whirling ominously in the wheelhouse, firing cool beams every second into the sweaty faces on the shore of No-Name Key. The shotgun roared again, and this time the off-loaders scrambled for their cars. The smugglers cannon-balled off the grass boat and hit the water swimming.

Eddie Fontaine lurched through the mangroves to the spot where he thought he had parked the pickup. He was off the mark by forty yards; half-running, half-stumbling, he made it to the truck breathless and nearly sick. The mangrove roots had shredded his jeans and left bloody tracks along both shins.

Fontaine turned the key and gunned the truck in the general direction of escape. As it barreled down the dirt road, another fugitive exploded from the mangroves. Fontaine spun the steering wheel and swerved off the road. The pickup came to a stop at a dump site, crashing into an old Frigidaire.

"Hey!" the runner called. "Gimme a lift."

Fontaine waved and opened the passenger-side door. It was Tom's man. His face was damp. The scarlet remnants of an Izod shirt hung from his neck. Fontaine told him to get in.

"Thanks, Eddie. My car's up the road about half a mile. It's the El Dorado."

"Shit." Fontaine backed his truck out of the trash heap and punched the accelerator. "What happened, man? Who the hell called the Marine Patrol?"

"I don't know."

"Was it Haller? Could you see?"

"Couldn't tell."

"Fuck me," Fontaine said, scowling. "Tom said the cops were taken care of."

"That's what he promised," said Tom's man, glumly.

The intruders waited twenty minutes. By then, the frightened crew of the grass boat had scrabbled ashore and escaped with the other smugglers. All that remained at the jetty was the boat; its cargo; the Winnebago campers, deserted forever; and two Coleman lanterns aglow against the tangled mangroves.

Breeze Albury guided the *Diamond Cutter* toward the island. Augie knelt on the bow, cradling the shotgun. Jimmy stood shirtless at his side, holding a coiled rope.

Effortlessly, Albury sidled the *Diamond Cutter* up to the grass boat, Tom's boat. The pirates worked swiftly.

CHAPTER 14

(From the deposition of James E. Cantrell, Jr., taken on the sixth day of October 1982, before Christine Manning, counsel to the office of the Governor. Also present was court reporter Mary Perdue.)

MISS MANNING: Jimmy, can you tell me how you knew that load of marijuana would be coming into the Big Spanish Channel that night?

MR. CANTRELL: Breeze found out, somehow. On our way back from Key Largo, we gassed up the boat in Islamorada. Breeze got off and made a couple phone calls. When he came back, he told us that Tom had a load coming in.

Q: That would be Tomas Cruz?

A: Right. After that, we brought the *Diamond Cutter* down to Marathon. Augie got out near the Vaca Key Bridge. I guess he was gone an hour or so before he came back with this police bubble. You know, the light they flash at you when you're supposed to stop. Like the troopers have on top of their cars. I don't know where Augie got it, and I don't want to know.

Q: What did Captain Albury say?

A: Nothing. He just hooked it up to the twelve-volt we had in the pilothouse. This was after we already anchored behind Little Pine Key.

Q: While you were waiting to ambush the other boat?

A: Ma'am, I wouldn't call it an ambush. All we had was the blue light.

Q: And the shotgun.

A: Yes, ma'am. That was my idea, firing the Remington into the air. I figured it would speed things along.

Q: Did Captain Albury ever explain why he wanted to hijack the other lobster boat?

A: He didn't have to. Part of it was the money, the fifty grand Winnebago Tom owed us. Breeze needed something to bargain with. And let me tell you, five tons of weed is good for openers.

Q: Jimmy, what took place after the hijacking at No-Name Key?

A: Breeze took the dope boat around to the Mud Keys. Me and Augie followed in the *Diamond Cutter*. Made good time, too. Then Breeze got on the radio to somebody and passed the word. He told them to let Tom Cruz know that we had his five tons.

Q: Isn't that blackmail?

A: Is it? It seemed pretty damn polite, compared to what those fuckers put us through. Tom should have given us the money. The right thing to do was pay us, like he promised. Breeze didn't want his fucking grass.

Q: So Mr. Cruz learned what had happened to his boat?

A: Oh, yeah.

Q: And he knew what Breeze Albury wanted?

A: I'm sure he did.

Q: Did he give Captain Albury an answer

A: Yes, ma'am. It was quite an answer, too. Just about the worst thing I ever heard of. Nothing surprised me after Winnebago Tom did what he did. Not a goddamned thing that happened after that really surprised me. Not the least.

CHAPTER 15

THE GIRL sat cross-legged on the bed, the lute's fretted neck leaning gently against her left breast:

> Come by sea, come by flight;
> Bring it to me by the crate.
> Fly by day, sail by night,
> But honey please don't be late
> 'Cause I gotta have my Florida freight.
> Bring me speed,
> Bring me weed.
> Bring me snow,
> I love it so.
> Florida freight, oh Florida freight,
> I jes' gotta have my Florida freight.

Propped on an elbow, Manolo raised his glass in silent toast.

"An improvisation," she smiled. "I call it 'Smuggler's Lullaby.'"

"Amusing."

"Actually, there is another very good line." She sang: "Float a Donzi, drive a Porsche . . . but the trouble is I can't think of anything to rhyme with 'Porsche.'"

"The next time, perhaps."

"Shall I go?"

"I am afraid so; I am expecting guests."

"At this hour?"

"Irritating, but unavoidable."

When he arrived a half-hour later, Tomas Cruz headed straight for the bar. He drained off three ounces of scotch and then splashed some onto his hands and across his face.

"Christ, the mosquitoes almost ate me alive up there. What a mess . . . an all-time blue-ribbon fucking mess."

Manolo, in a knotted dressing gown, sipped Cointreau from leaded crystal.

"Help yourself to a drink, Tom; no sense being shy."

"Yeah, thanks, I'll have another one. Jesus, we're really screwed this time."

"Short and to the point, if you don't mind. It's late."

Tom trailed mud across the white carpet and hunkered onto a suede sofa, scratching his ankles.

"OK, look, it's a routine run, right? Five tons, one boat, a drop-off we've used before. Three vans, eight off-loaders, and by dawn the stuff is already in Miami, right? Sweet and simple. Then it all went to shit."

"Do you know who did it?"

"At first, I thought it was the cops—the Marine Patrol, blue light 'n all. It wasn't."

"Let me guess. It was Breeze Albury."

"Jesus, Manolo, you're really sharp. How'd you know that?"

"A desperate captain in a rogue boat. Who else would try something like that?"

"Who woulda figured it? Breeze Albury, and him like all

the rest: lean on them a little bit and they keel over like it was a hurricane. You shoulda seen him when we cut his trap line, like a little kid who'd lost his puppy."

"The next time we need a patsy, Tom, I think you should look harder." Manolo sipped at his drink. "If there is a next time."

"What the fuck is that supposed to mean?"

"If Albury was a patsy like you say, he never would have left Dynamite Docks alive, would he? Your patsy comes snapping back and rips us off for ten thousand pounds. Some patsy."

"Yeah, that's what he is, a potbellied patsy Conch. I ain't afraid of Breeze fucking Albury."

"That's good, Tom, because I expect you to deal with him. The business at Dynamite Docks has upset our Colombian friends. They are mad at Breeze Albury. That is enough. I want the load back, and I don't want any more trouble from him. We need to make an example before he gives other people ideas. I want you to deal with it."

"I'll take care of him, all right. Just tell me where to find the motherfucker."

"He will tell you himself, Tom."

"Huh?"

Manolo stifled a sigh.

"Think, Tom. Think every now and then, and you might learn to like it. What do you suppose Albury is going to do with five tons of grass?"

"I dunno. Sell it, I guess."

"That's right. He will sell it—to us. What else can he do with it? He will offer to swap it for the money due from the Key Largo run, plus a little more, maybe. And he will do it quickly because that much grass is going to be spotted, sooner or later."

"Well, I'll be goddamned if I'm gonna pay to get our own grass back."

"Of course not. But you must encourage Albury to negotiate. Make him see that it is not merely a question of money."

Tom Cruz tossed down the scotch with a smile. "Damn, that's good. I like it. I'll make him want to negotiate." He rolled the syllables around in his mouth.

"You had better leave now, but remember one more thing, if you can. Our business is built on *control,* Tom. We have lost control because of your patsy. We must reestablish it. If we do not, think of how it will appear. I shall be forced to tell our Colombian associates that you are the one who was responsible."

With satisfaction, Manolo watched Tom Cruz scramble anxiously for the door.

He was Winnebago Tom, but there were times when a lumbering camper, his symbol of status, would not do. Tomas Cruz dropped the Corvette into third and whipped past a tractor-trailer. Ahead, the Overseas Highway gleamed starkly in the afternoon sun. He fed it to the Corvette.

"Shithead legless bastard," Tom muttered into the slipstream. Manolo must be right. He must be losing control. Or else he would have checked into the post office first thing. And the crippled radio jockey wouldn't have been such a wiseass.

"Message for you, Tom, from Breeze Albury." Crystal had delicately laid the glowing tip of a soldering iron to a tangle of transistors.

"Where is he?"

"He didn't say."

"You could tell from the radio, couldn't you—the direction finder?"

"No."

"Don't give me that shit. I know about radios, shortknees. You try and cover up for Albury and you're in deep shit with me, hear?"

"I'm trembling, Tom, I really am. Do you want the message, or what?"

"Tell me, Stumpy. Give me the message from Mr. Breeze fucking Albury."

"Breeze says you can have your grass back for fifty-three thousand . . ."

"Shi-it."

". . . that's fifty you owe him for something—he didn't say what—and another three for his traps. He says to let him know if you want to deal, and he'll tell you when and how."

"He'll tell me, huh? Big-shot Breeze Albury will tell me. You tell him I'll get back to him."

Crystal had nodded and for the first time looked up from the radio he was fixing.

"One more thing, Tom."

"What?"

"Breeze didn't say it right out, but I think that after this deal goes down you'd better haul ass out of Key West."

"Ain't that too bad? You tell him he'll hear from me. A message he can understand . . ."

Tomas Cruz wheeled the Corvette off the highway onto a gravel track that led to a dilapidated marina a few miles north of Key West.

El Gallo lay at its berth. It seldom left, for Willie Bascaro never fished. At first glance, *El Gallo* seemed a spanking-new Key West crawfisherman, ready for sea. Tom knew better. The engine wheezed before its time. The brightwork was pitted, a deck seam needed caulking, the bottom was fouled, and the radar had quit working two weeks after it was installed. Easy come, easy go. Willie had earned enough for the boat in one night's work. He was a Marielito, one of the tens of thousands of misfits Castro had flushed from Cuba to South Florida in a fit of pique. He was unskilled, barely literate, a slob. But he had lived long enough around the Havana docks to learn to run a boat, more or less, and sometimes he was useful. Tom picked his way across the littered deck and went into the cabin to awaken the captain of *El Gallo* from a rum-fueled siesta.

"At least tell me what kind of trouble my dad is in. I'm not a kid."

"Ricky, take it easy, OK?" Tomas Cruz eased the Corvette through the afternoon traffic toward Stock Island. "He told me to pick you up after work and bring you to see him. That's all he said, OK? He didn't say anything about trouble."

"He must be in trouble."

"What makes you think that?"

"Or else he would have come himself. Or maybe sent Jimmy. He wouldn't have sent you."

"You think your dad doesn't like me, don't you? Well, you'd be surprised. Him and me, we've done a lot of business together. And I know all about you: best right-handed prospect in the state of Florida, that's what he says about you. A real prospect."

"Yeah, sure."

"Wait and see."

Cruz maneuvered slowly along a pier littered with fishermen's debris: traps, buoys, lines, a discarded anchor, a stove-in dinghy. He stopped alongside a lobster boat, its engine idling.

"This is not the *Diamond Cutter*," Ricky protested.

"No shit. Your dad's waiting offshore. We're going out to see him."

Instinctively, Ricky shied.

"That's OK, Tom. I've got someplace to go. I'll wait till my dad comes in."

The Beretta appeared in Tom's fist. A silencer glared from the end of the barrel.

"Get in the boat, kid."

They rode in silence for about twenty minutes until they were alone on the sea. Ricky could see only the angular back of the man who was running the boat. Winnebago Tom lounged on the engine cowling. His gun never wavered.

"Basta?" called the man in the wheelhouse.

"Basta," Tom replied.

Ricky felt the engine go into neutral. The helmsman walked back to join Tom. He was a short, wiry man with sharp features and three missing teeth on the right side of his jaw. Ricky thought of him as Rat Face.

"This is my friend Willie, kid. He doesn't speak much English, but he's a mean sonofabitch, believe me. He likes to hurt people. You answer some questions for me or I'll let Willie hurt you. Understand, Ricky?"

Rat Face saluted with a tire iron. Ricky licked his lips.

"Fuck you, Tom, and fuck your Rat Face friend, too."

Tom fired once. Ricky flinched. The bullet twanged past his head like an angry bee.

"This is no game, Ricky. Where is your father?"

"What do you want him for?"

"He stole something belonging to me. Where is he?"

"I thought you said you were going to take me to him."

"Don't play games with me, shithead. Where is he?"

"Tampa . . . he said he was going to Tampa to check out a bigger boat he wants to buy. Or was it Galveston? He took a Greyhound bus."

"Dale." Tom's voice cracked in fury.

The Cuban named Willie came at Ricky with the tire iron held like a baseball bat. Ricky leaned back against the transom, as though huddling in fear. His kick caught the Cuban full in the stomach and drove him back toward the wheelhouse. Ricky sprang after him. He was reaching for the tire iron when Winnebago Tom clipped him along the side of his head with the butt of the pistol.

Pain awakened Ricky. Greater pain than he had ever known. His arm was on fire. He hung suspended by his pitching arm from the lobsterboat's winch. He tried with all his might but could get no purchase. His toes grazed the deck. He bit back a scream.

Winnebago Tom held the tire iron now. He stood in front of Ricky, shouting.

". . . like your father, a patsy, a stupid Conch patsy."

Ricky could smell the rum on his breath. He tried to make his left hand come up to hit Tom. It would not move. He groaned and was ashamed.

". . . a *real* prospect, huh? Well, Mr. Smartass Prospect, you tell your fucking patsy father that nobody fucks with Winnebago Tom. Nobody, hear me?"

Like a demented batter, Winnebago Tom slashed the tire iron across Ricky's upper arm. Ricky screamed, and then he fainted. He never felt the second blow.

CHAPTER 16

"I'M SORRY, sir, we're closed tonight. Private party."

"Oh." The tourist shuffled uncertainly on the sidewalk.

"If it's seafood you want, I'd recommend El Pulpo on Duval Street. And if you come back here tomorrow night, we'll make up for the inconvenience with a free cocktail. Just ask for me. My name is Laurie."

She closed the door and looked toward the back of the restaurant, where the owner of the Cowrie sat at the edge of a table, legs swinging. Facing him sat about thirty men. Laurie was the only woman. She sighed to herself: many of the men, like Bobby Freed himself, were very good-looking. What a waste. They had come from all over the Lower Keys at Freed's urging. A marshaling of forces, he had called it.

"Somebody asked me why we are here," Freed said suddenly in a voice that silenced the room. "We are here because we've had enough. It's time we started dishing it out."

There were a few cheers, a whistle.

"Some of you were asking over dinner about my friend Neal. Let me tell you about Neal. He was beaten and robbed in full sight of a so-called policeman just a few blocks from here.

"I complained to the police and to the mayor and to the council, but nobody cared. He went to the hospital and came out scared of his own shadow. Neal couldn't make it. He was too weak. Yesterday I put him on the plane. Neal is gone for good." An excited murmur coursed through the room. Neal and Bobby had been together a long time. "Neal is gone . . ." Freed milked a dramatic pause ". . . and I say 'good riddance.' "

There was rapt silence. From her post at the door, Laurie's eyes shone in admiration.

"I say 'good riddance' because Neal was afraid and he couldn't cope with his fear. Well, a lot of us are afraid. Some of us have been beat up, like Neal. I don't mind confessing that I've been afraid, too. But I am not leaving. I am staying here and I am going to fight."

Several men started talking at once then, and the loudest among them, a motel operator from Lower Matecumbe, asked the question for them all.

"Shit, Bobby, what *can* we do? Buy guns? Get bodyguards? Hire a hit man?"

"I think Neal had the right idea," said an architect from Caroline Street. "These Conchs suck."

"No, you're wrong," Freed insisted. "The Conchs would live and let live, I know they would. It's the system that's bad here, not the people. If we show the Conchs we are worth their respect—stop being punching bags—then they will respect us."

Laurie could control herself no longer.

"Bobby is right. Listen to him," she begged. "Use your brains."

"There is strength in numbers," Freed said. "There are thousands around here who feel the same way we do about life. Thousands who resent living like second-class citizens because of what they believe. Collectively, we know a lot, and there are many things we can do. We need to pool our talents, band together."

"That's an interesting proposition, Bobby," said a Miami lawyer who had just moved his practice to Key West. "Exactly what do you have in mind?"

Freed told them.

"We aren't vigilantes," the lawyer objected.

"No, that's the beauty of it. We don't have to be. We can make the circumstance speak for itself."

"It has possibilities," the lawyer observed.

"I like it," said a teacher.

"So do I," said a bridge tender from Marathon.

"Do it, do it!" Laurie clapped her hands in excitement. "Make a list of all the assholes. Get them one at a time. It's great!"

"A list," someone cried in a room suddenly alive with righteous enthusiasm. "A hit list."

"Can we agree on who is to head the list?" Freed asked.

"Fatso Barnett," came the unanimous shouted reply.

When the last of the men filed out of the Cowrie near midnight, Laurie leaned against the door with a contented sigh. Bobby Freed sat alone, staring vacantly at a yellow pad.

"Bobby, you're wonderful. I'm so proud." Impetuously, Laurie leaned over the table and planted a kiss on Freed's lips.

"Why, uh, thanks, Laurie. I hope . . . I hope it works."

"Work? Sure it will work. Let's celebrate. I'm going to open a bottle of champagne, OK?

"Sure."

Their glasses clinked.

"To justice," said Laurie.

"Amen," said Freed.

They drank in companionable silence for a time, until Freed spoke at last.

"Laurie, I don't think I could have done it without your help and . . ."

"Of course you could."

Freed seemed suddenly unsure of himself, perplexed. He drank deeply.

"Look, Laurie, I meant what I said about Neal. He's not coming back. I bought him out. And I wondered, you know, I thought you might be interested in becoming my partner. You know, a business like this is easier with two people. . . ."

"Oh, Bobby, you are sweet. I'd love it. But you know I'm broke."

"Oh, the money wouldn't matter," Freed said quickly. "It's just that . . . well, I like having you around. I mean, you already make a lot of the decisions. Besides, I . . ."

"Besides what?"

"Well, Laurie, I've never related to women well, but, what I mean is . . . I find you tremendously attractive."

"Bobby, you're blushing."

"I'm sorry, I didn't mean anything." He looked away.

"Bobby, I think you are one of the sweetest and most gentle and strongest men I have ever met."

He looked back. "It's more than that, Laurie. It's not that I find you attractive as a person—I mean, I do, of course— but you're attractive to me as . . ." He took a breath. "Jesus, this is funny to say. As a *woman*."

He leaned over then and hesitantly, awkwardly, kissed her on the lips.

Laurie sat back, startled.

"Oh, Bob."

"Did you like that?"

"Well, yes. You surprised me, that's all."

"I'm surprising myself, too, Laurie."

She smiled.

"Then do it again."

They kissed then, in earnest, and embraced with a heat that eventually carried them off the table onto the floor, where Laurie led Bobby Freed through quick pathfinder's love.

CHAPTER 17

THE MUTED THUMPS of bare feet on the deck aroused Breeze Albury from sleep. Jimmy stood in the doorway to the cabin, a lean silhouette in the twilight.

"Breeze," he whispered. "Breeze, you awake?"

Albury propped himself up on the bunk and massaged the fatigue from his forehead. "Yeah, I'm up. What's going on? Everything OK with the other boat?"

Jimmy nodded. "Augie flicked the lights about an hour ago. He's fine. Someone just came on the radio for you."

"By name?"

"No. Lucky Seven. Same as before."

Crystal, Albury thought. Winnebago Tom is ready to talk. He's sending his answer through Crystal.

"I'll go call him back," Albury said, rising.

"He doesn't want you to, Breeze. The message was real short. He said to wait. Someone is coming out to meet us. We're just s'posed to wait."

"Who for? Did he say?"

"Nope."

Albury was puzzled. He had told Crystal that the *Diamond Cutter* was holed up in the Mud Keys, but he had not told him exactly where. A search party could look for days and still not find the narrow channel, snaking through the mangroves, where Albury had hidden the two fishing boats, his and the Machine's. Yet Crystal, who knew the confusing vagaries of the Keys, was sending a messenger; the mud flats had grounded many a Coast Guard search boat at night. An amateur stood no chance at all.

Something was wrong. Maybe Crystal was in trouble. It had, after all, been his task to make sure the coast was clear for the off-loading at No-Name Key; Tom Cruz would have been counting on it. And, of course, when Tom's crew had seen the *Diamond Cutter*'s bogus blue light, they had been sure it was cops. The load of grass had been lost. No doubt Crystal would have had some serious explaining to do.

"Jimmy, can you swim over and help Augie move the other boat farther up the creek?" Albury stretched his arms on deck. The grass boat was anchored thirty yards away, its white prow tucked into the tangled red roots. Augie waved amiably at Albury from the stern.

Jimmy peeled down to his underwear and dove in. Phosphorescent plankton scattered in bright green shreds as he stroked up the creek toward the hijacked crawfish boat.

Albury rubbed hard at his chin and cheeks to get the blood moving. He longed for a jarring cup of Cuban coffee.

He and Crystal had worked out the scenario over the radio. After the pot was stolen, Winnebago Tom would arrive in Crystal's trailer in a fury; he would demand to know what had gone wrong. How could the cops have found out about the operation? Good money had been spent to make sure that wouldn't happen.

Crystal was to tell him the truth, that the boat with the blue light did not belong to the Marine Patrol or Coast Guard;

that it was not a bust but a ripoff in the Big Spanish Channel. Who? Tom would shout. Crystal would tell him.

Then Tom Cruz would understand. His next question would be a simple one: how much?

But now, instead of an offer, a visitor. It was a twist that worried Breeze Albury. He climbed to the pilothouse and played the dials on the radio. Again and again he called for Smilin' Jack, but only static answered. Albury believed that Crystal was listening. This time of night, Crystal always listened.

Up current, the grass boat's diesel hacked and came to life as Jimmy and Augie guided the boat deeper into the green arms of the tiny island. Albury flipped the VHF to channel 12 and called his mates.

"Hey there." It was Jimmy's voice; he loved to talk on the radio. "This boat's a cow, captain. A pregnant old cow."

Albury said, "Take her up around the first bend. Tie her off in the trees and swim back. Augie, too." To leave the boys on the boat with all that dope would be a mistake, especially with company on the way.

Two hours later, the three of them were stretched out on the deck of the *Diamond Cutter*, dozing under a sliver of yellow moon. The Remington lay at Albury's side. The fishermen were far enough from the mainland that the howling truck noises on the Overseas Highway were smothered by the sounds of the Keys—insects, herons, gulls, the trill of raccoons, the gentle percussion of wavelets on the wooden hull. Albury was dreaming of an old man, steering a slow old boat from a bleached whiskey crate, following a rich trap line west.

A faint noise at his feet made him open one eye. A stranger's shadow blocked the moon. Albury sat up, stiffened by a volt of fear. His right hand groped for the shotgun.

"Breeze," said a voice from the stranger. "It's me. Teal."

"Jesus!"

Augie stirred and rolled to his side. Jimmy snored placidly.

"You scared the shit out of me," Albury said.

"Crystal wanted me to find you," said the tawny flats guide. "Breeze, I'm taking you back to Key West. We'd better go right now." Teal motioned to his bonefish skiff, tied to a cleat on the *Diamond Cutter*'s stern. "The tide's up. I can take you straight in."

Teal's mahogany tan made him look like a Cuban in the night. "Wake the boys," he said. "Tell them you're leaving."

Teal climbed into his skiff and started the outboard engine. Jimmy and Augie wobbled to their feet. Albury told them he was going to Key West.

"Stay with the *Diamond Cutter*," he instructed. "Give me a couple days. If I'm not back, you get out of here."

"What about the grass?" Jimmy asked.

"Fuck it. Leave it on the other boat. If I'm not back in two days, you guys take the *Diamond Cutter* up the Keys and lay low for a while. There's a couple hundred bucks left in the cabin."

"What's the story?" Augie asked. "Is something wrong?"

"I don't know."

"Teal, what's going on?" Augie called. "How come Breeze has got to go back?"

Teal shrugged and said something that was swallowed by the growl of the engine. Jimmy and Augie watched Albury lower himself into the skiff; he waved at them once as Teal punched the throttle. The lightweight bonefish boat planed off quickly and cut a creamy stitch in the sleepy Gulf. Teal found an invisible channel and followed it along the edge of the flats toward the mainland. An unlit cigarette poked from one corner of the old guide's mouth. Though tearing from the wind, his eyes never left the dark water.

Albury smiled. Crystal must have known. Only Teal could have found the *Diamond Cutter*, could have navigated by instinct through the serpentine flats. Teal hunted the Mud Keys for bonefish every spring; if anyone, he would know where to look for an old Conch captain and two hot lobster boats. Crystal had picked the perfect scout.

Ahead of them, the mainland took form. Albury recognized the brontosaurus profiles of construction cranes along Highway One on Stock Island. Then Key West itself, where one of the ball parks was lit up. Probably the men's softball league.

After a few more minutes, Teal found the channel into Garrison Bight and throttled back to accommodate the no-wake signs posted along the shore. As the skiff approached the bridge by Trumbo Point, Teal turned off the engine and let the boat drift. He lit a fresh cigarette and held out the pack. Albury shook his head.

"I've known you your whole life," Teal said awkwardly.

"We caught some fish together, didn't we?" Albury said. "I'll never forget that one trip to the Tortugas. The twenty-eight-pound permit on six-pound mono. Remember?"

"Yeah. On a goddamned dead shrimp." Teal hacked ferociously. "You made a good cast on that fish."

"I should have got him stuffed."

"Damn right. I could have used the commission." The skiff hung in the channel, caught between the wind and the current, as if tied to the big bridge. Teal stared hard at the water, looking all the way to the bottom, or seeming to.

"Breeze," he said, "the reason I came to get you, it's your boy. Ricky."

Albury's ears filled with the sound of his own heart drumming.

"He got hurt," Teal stammered. "Somebody hurt 'im."

"How bad?"

"I'm gonna leave you at the charter docks," Teal said, turning the ignition. "You go to the hospital right away. He's on the third floor. He's not critical or nuthin' that bad." Teal was talking faster, in a cracking voice. He took the skiff under the bridge. "He's not critical, Breeze, so don't get all panicked."

Albury grabbed Teal's elbow. "How bad?" he groaned.

"Some broken bones. He'll be all right. We're here now. Grab onto that piling and pull yourself up."

163 »

Albury bounded from the bow of the skiff to the docks, where a row of gleaming deep-sea boats rocked together.

"Breeze, I'm sorry," Teal said, standing at the steering console, looking up at his old friend. "It's all gone to hell, this place. We talked about it all the time. We talked about it but never imagined it would come to this. Goddamn, going after your boy."

Albury's shoulders sagged. His arms hung at his side, swinging slightly with his breathing. He dropped to one knee and bent forward over the edge of the dock.

"Teal," he whispered plaintively, "who did it?"

"Go see your boy, Breeze," said the fishing guide. "Before it gets too late."

Half-hour until shift change. Lina Spurling gulped down her Tab and fumbled for a cigarette. Five-minute breaks—when was this hospital going to join the twentieth century? You can't run your fanny off for nine hours with a five-minute break here and there. Then they wonder about the turnover. Jesus. Kathy called in sick tonight, as usual. Leaves me with pediatrics *and* orthopedics. Terrific. Thanks, pal. Shit, Lina thought, I'd have called in, too. If I'd had a date. Just try to find a straight guy in Key West who doesn't smell like fish guts. Just try.

Lina unlocked the pharmacy and loaded up the syringe. She lay it on her tray, next to the doctor's prescription, and padded quietly to Room 307. On the way, she doused her cigarette in a bedpan in the hallway. Some wise guy put it there. Very subtle, Lina thought. Wait your turn, pal. Sick people can be so pushy.

Lina whisked into Room 307 and braked, her rubber soles squeaking on the floor.

"Sir?"

The man said nothing. He sat in a darkened corner, hunched

in a chair. His skin was chestnut; a mottled rag was knotted around one arm. His salt-and-pepper hair was moist and matted; a purplish gash glared up from his scalp. He wore the white boots of a commercial fisherman. Lina Spurling could not see his face: it was buried in his arms. Nor could she see precisely how large a man he really was, for he was folded so compactly that his arms were on his knees. He appeared to be sleeping.

"Sir?" the young nurse repeated.

Breeze Albury raised his head. He looked lost.

"It's past visiting hours," Lina said.

"He's my boy."

"He's going to be fine. You're welcome to come back tomorrow when—"

"What's that?" Albury was out of the chair, standing at the foot of Ricky's bed. "Is that for him?"

Lina spun and headed for the door. Albury seized her elbows and lifted her off the floor. He put her down in the far corner, then closed the door quietly.

"I asked you a question."

"It's Demerol. To help him sleep."

"He *is* sleeping."

"He won't be for long, not if you don't lower your voice. Look, I know you're upset. Why don't you let me call the doctor? He'll explain everything."

Albury examined the syringe. "Seventy-five milligrams," he read out loud. "This is for pain."

The nurse looked at Ricky. The boy stirred slightly. His right arm, encased in plaster, hung from a pulley. His fingers, orange from the iodine, poked like carrot tips from the end of the cast.

"Sit down," Breeze Albury said tiredly. "I'm not going to hurt you."

Lina Spurling did not sit down. She held her ground, eyeing the intruder. He was a wreck. Looks like he went ten rounds with Joe Frazier. Contusions, lacerations, the look of the dead in his eyes. He could use a doctor himself, Lina thought. Suppose I could dress that cut on his head.

"Tell me what happened," Albury said.

"I've got to give him the shot." Lina moved to Ricky's side and pulled back the blanket. Albury watchfully stood behind her as she inserted the needle into a pale hip.

"His arm is broken," Lina said, "in two places."

"The same bone?"

"Two different bones. The ulna and the humerus. Right about here." The nurse touched Albury's forearm lightly, then his upper arm, midway between the elbow and the shoulder. Jesus, she thought, he's certainly got the arms of a boxer. Be nice if he'd change his shirt every couple weeks.

"Were the police called?"

"What for?" Lina replied. "It was an accident. That's what your son told the ambulance driver. Fell off his bike or something. Didn't anyone call you when it happened?"

"I was out of town," Albury muttered. "Just got back."

"Sir, I have to go now. I've got thirty-one other patients on this floor, and I'm supposed to look in on all of 'em before I get off. . . ."

Albury nodded toward the door. "Sure. Sorry if I scared you."

Lina Spurling scampered out.

"Is it all right if I sit with him?" asked Albury to no one. He moved a chair to the left side of Ricky's hospital bed. He reached under the blanket and took his son's hand in his own. The boy's rhythmic breathing filled the yellow room.

They were alone for fifteen minutes before Ricky shifted and moaned. Albury stiffened.

"Ricky?"

The boy's eyes opened and he saw his father through a Demerol gauze. "Hey," he said with a weak smile. "You're back."

Albury squeezed the kid's hand.

"So how was fishing?" Ricky asked.

"Shitty."

"My throat's so dry."

Albury filled a styrofoam cup with ice water and held it to Ricky's mouth. Half of the water dribbled down his hospital gown.

"You too tired to talk?"

"Naw," Ricky said. "Just feel a little weird. They gave me all kinds of drugs. What time is it, dad?"

"I don't know. What the hell happened? Some nurse gave me a horseshit story about you falling off your bike."

"Oh. Yeah."

"What's left of your bike has been rusting under the trailer for two goddamn years," Albury said. "Tell me what happened."

"Coupla guys grabbed me after work. Didn't say much except that you cheated 'em out of something. I figured it was money, but they didn't say."

Albury asked, "Who?"

"Tom Cruz and some other guy. They took me over to some crawfish boat on Stock Island. *El Gallo,* it was called."

Ricky told Albury exactly how they had mangled his arm.

"My God."

"It hurt, sure, but it wasn't as bad as it sounds. Think I passed out before it was over." The words came like syrup. Ricky took a deep breath and closed his eyes. "Dad, can I take a rest?"

Albury raised the blanket to his son's neck. "I'll be back in the morning," he whispered. Before leaving the hospital room, he refilled the cup with ice water and left it on the nightstand where Ricky could reach it with his good arm.

Lina Spurling punched her timecard into the wall clock. Great, she thought, only ten minutes late tonight. Could have got off on time, for once, if it weren't for Captain Ahab back in 307. She thought about what to do next and decided on the Casa Marina; there was a rock band down from Fort Lauderdale. All oldies. Supposed to be pretty good.

"Excuse me, are you Miss Spurling?" The question came from a tall, attractive woman. She wore a forest-green dress that buttoned at her neck under a small bow. Here was another one who didn't belong in a hospital in the middle of the night.

"My name is Christine Manning," said the woman, holding out some kind of glossy identification card. "I'm with the Governor's office."

"Are you a cop or something?"

"No. An investigator is more like it," Christine said. "I have some questions about one of the patients on the floor."

"Lemme guess. The boy in three-oh-seven?"

Christine shook her head. "No. I don't know anything about him. It was another patient. A young girl."

Lina pointedly glanced at her Timex. "I'd like to help you, lady, but I'm already late getting off. I got a date, believe it or not—"

"Her name is Julie Clayton," Christine said.

"Lord." Lina walked to the nurses' lounge. Christine followed her inside.

"I don't know what I'm allowed to say," Lina began. "The hospital has got rules. Privacy rules."

"And the state of Florida has laws," Christine interjected. "Obstruction of justice is one of my favorites. . . ."

Lina raised a hand. "Save the speech. I don't know that much. The ambulance from Miami showed up this afternoon. Said they were supposed to move the girl to a hospital up there. Thing is, Mrs. Clayton, the mother, didn't know anything about it. She started crying that she wouldn't be able to visit the girl if they moved her from Key West. There was a big stink. The administrator, Jenks, he finally came up to the floor and took Mrs. Clayton to his office. A few minutes later, Mrs. Clayton comes out and says it's OK. Jenks hands me the discharge papers, but I tell him the girl's doctor hasn't signed her out yet. Jenks says he'll handle it. The ambulance is waiting downstairs, he says."

"Is it so unusual to transfer a patient up to Miami?"

"Of course not," Lina said. "But the Clayton girl was an overdose case, a bad one. She was vegged out in a coma. I heard one of the neurologists say she didn't have a prayer. That's why I was a little surprised that they'd bother to move her to a new hospital. The girl's family had no money for that. But Jenks, he told me to drop what I was doing and get the girl downstairs."

"So she's gone now."

"Right," said Lina.

"Do you remember," Christine asked, "which hospital?"

"Flagler Memorial. But don't waste your time up there." Lina fished in her purse and came out with two quarters. She got a Tab from the vending machine. "The girl died, Miss Manning. While we were wheeling her downstairs to the ambulance, she died." Lina took a sip from the can. "Her heart just went to sleep. It was the last thing left that was working right."

"Sounds like a blessing," Christine murmured.

"She must have been pretty important," Lina added. "Chief Barnett hurried over this afternoon right after it happened. And that lawyer, Boone, he called about an hour after that. Wanted to know if it was true. Tell me, Miss Manning, was that Clayton girl related to some big shot, or what?"

CHAPTER 18

PITCHING isn't all in the arm. Fifty percent is smarts. Look at Spahn or Robin Roberts. They didn't have to dish it up at ninety-five miles an hour every time; hungry hitters go for the bad pitch. If you've got smarts, you make 'em hungry. Look at Tug McGraw. God, think of Reggie, corkscrewed at the plate after whiffing a third strike. A hungry hitter, always waiting on that fastball.

Breeze Albury slid lower into the bathtub so the steaming water puddled on his chest. He kept his eyes closed.

The fastball is an overhand pitch, of course. Ricky throws it straight over, so straight that his arm seems to brush his right ear on the way down. A lot will depend on how the bones mend. He'll lose some speed, that's only natural. May take a year or so to get the muscle tone back in the forearm. There's a chance he'll lose the slider altogether, unless the bones mend just right. Good slider depends on a healthy arm, depends on an arm that can come right back at you with the big fastball.

Albury reached for the bar of soap, fragrant and oval. He lathered his chest and shoulders.

You can't keep this sort of thing from the pro scouts. Word gets around fast. There's no sense pretending it won't hurt Ricky's chances. Who wants to gamble a bonus on a lame arm? There's a Nautilus machine at the high school. Still, it would be better to have one at home, so Ricky wouldn't ever have to wait. Could probably buy a secondhand one from a gym in Miami.

Albury dried off with a pink towel. He struggled into a pair of too-tight French jeans, pulled on a strange blue T-shirt, and walked out of the bathroom.

"Now, that's much better," pronounced Christine Manning, sitting on the edge of her bed. "I hardly recognized you in the hospital."

"It's been a bad week," Albury said. She handed him a cup of hot tea with lemon. "Hope I don't split these trousers."

"Don't worry. They belonged to my ex. I don't know why I haven't tossed them out." Christine shrugged. "Come on, I've got dinner cooking."

Albury followed her out of the bedroom, glancing sideways at himself in a full-length mirror. He felt like a fag in the silly jeans, but his appearance was an improvement over the haggard figure Christine had led from the elevator at Duval Memorial. Moist-eyed, shaking like a sick hound. God, what must she have thought? His state of embarrassment was not relieved by the fact that he had completely forgotten her name. The face and figure stood out with clarity from that afternoon at the jail, but her name had eluded him. Albury had remembered it just as they were climbing the rain-warped stairs to her second-floor flat in an old Conch house on Margaret Street.

"All I've got is leftovers," Christine said. "Part of a tuna casserole."

"It sounds wonderful."

She still wore the forest-green dress but had untied the bow at her neck and kicked off her high heels.

"I've got some stuff in the medicine chest. Disinfectants or antibiotics. You ought to put something on that cut. Exactly what, I don't know. First aid is not my specialty. However"— she spooned some casserole on Albury's plate—"if you ever want to sue the bastard who did this to you . . ."

"Miss Manning, I need a place to stay."

"Please, it's Christine. No man who's used my bathtub has ever called me Miss Manning."

"Christine, I can't go back to the trailer. I'm sure they're watching the trailer," Albury said.

"The men who hurt your son?"

"Yes. They're waiting for me to come back. They'll be watching the trailer. The fish house, too. I only need a day or two."

"It's probably not a good idea," Christine said. "How about some more tea?"

"Two days is all I need," Albury said. "I'll behave, counselor."

Christine took her place across the table. Albury ate ravenously, rarely looking up, saying nothing. She watched his energy return and noticed something hard at work behind the deep green eyes.

"Consider my position down here," she said. "It would hardly help the cause—mine or yours—if it became known that one of Key West's celebrated dope smugglers was shacking up with the Governor's special prosecutor."

"No one will know," Albury replied through a cheekful of tuna, "unless you've got a . . . friend. Someone who stays with you."

"No," Christine said. "That's not it."

"It's all right, I don't blame you," he said. "I ought to be thanking you for letting me clean up. And the food, by the way, is very good."

He certainly knew how to back off. "I couldn't let you wander around the hospital looking like some kind of refugee," she said.

Christine rose and began clearing the dinner dishes. She thought to herself: this man definitely is not an animal. A criminal? Probably so. But not a killer or a rapist. She remembered Veronica; Laurie and Peg Albury both had mentioned Veronica. Albury had been in prison when the girl had died. He had gotten out, gone back to the sea, and now stood an excellent chance of going to prison again. Another Conch success story.

Yet he was different from most of the Keys fishermen Christine had talked with. The gentleness was one thing, but it was the intellect behind the eyes that intrigued the lawyer. The first time they met she had longed to ask him: Captain Albury, why are you still here? Why haven't you gone north, with the rest of the smart ones? You don't sell seashells, peddle postcards with palm trees, or own one of the big beachfront hotels. Your heart obviously isn't in the fishing anymore, and what you pay on that firetrap trailer each month could get you a sixty-foot lot in Ocala. With trees, no less, and shade. Why stay here? she had wanted to ask but had not. That first day, Breeze Albury had worn the ambivalent look of a big mutt that was either going to wag its tail or lunge for her throat.

"Let's make an arrangement," Christine said.

"Everyone wants to make a deal," Albury grumbled.

"You can stay the night *if* you agree to talk to me about a few things."

"You mean answer questions."

"No, just talk. Tell me what you can about what's happened. I know it's bad. Chief Barnett is asking around about your boat, and I saw one of his men in the Cowrie talking to your girl friend this afternoon. If you can tell me something about it, I might be able to help, captain."

"Please quit calling me captain. I'm not a Pan Am pilot,

I'm a goddamn fisherman. Can I have a beer? Do you *have* a beer?"

"Sure . . . Breeze."

Later, sitting at opposite ends of a lumpy sofa, they talked. Two beers extracted Peg's story. For Albury, that was the easiest: everybody sympathizes with a rotten marriage. Three more beers revived Veronica; he saw her with a can of orange spray paint, assailing the lobster buoys strung up behind the trailer in winter; and during the season, waiting in the dusk at Ming's fish house for his boat, squealing when the rust-colored lobsters scrabbled and twitched on their way to the ice.

Albury was into a second six-pack by the time he began to recount Key Largo. The details of the killings were, he thought, unnecessary. He resolved also not to mention the Mayday, or the *Diamond Cutter*'s pathetic reply. What he did not mind discussing was the betrayal.

"Who ordered Oscar to kill you?" Christine asked.

"I don't know, but his mind was made up. It all fell apart when he pulled the gun."

"I saved the clipping from the paper. Somehow I had a feeling it was your boat."

"It was, but I'll deny it. If it comes to that, I'll lie. In fact, I'm afraid there's not much of what I've told you that could be put in a file. It's true, all of it, but it's no good to you, Christine."

"You could give me some names."

"No way."

"I know a few."

Albury laughed derisively.

"Tomas Cruz?"

"Brilliant work," Albury said. "And what will you do with the names? Put them in a file. What will you do with the file? Add it to the other files. And then what?"

Albury could see the sarcasm sting, but Christine pressed on. "What did you do," she asked, "after the shootout on Key Largo?"

Albury crumpled an empty beer can. "Simple. I stole something that belonged to somebody else. Somebody who owed me a lot of money, and more. I told him he could have his property back when I got paid. His answer is there." Albury jerked a thumb in the air. "In the hospital. My boy."

"What are you going to do now?"

"Do you ever stop with the questions?"

"I'm worried about you," Christine said.

Albury slid closer on the couch. "What I'm going to do now," he said, "is stop answering your questions. I've told you what happened. The good parts, anyway. If you want to know what's going to happen tomorrow or the day after, try Madame Zuzu over on White Street. Five bucks for a thirty-minute reading, and you don't even have to get her drunk."

"Are you drunk, captain?"

"I suppose so, Miss Manning. I'm drunk and I'm tired and I hurt all over. The thing I care about most is lying in the fucking hospital with his arm pretzeled by some asshole Cuban. The thing I care about second is anchored out on some mangrove island with nothing but an antique bilge pump and two hare-brained boys between her and the bottom of the Gulf. The thing I care about third is probably doing crosswords or writing couplets about spoonbills to keep from worrying about me anymore. And, before you have a chance to ask, the reason I moved closer is that you smell so good and look so wonderful in your dress and your nylons—"

"Jesus."

"You're the one who wanted to talk." Albury leaned over and kissed her on the lips. Christine pulled away until she felt his hands on her shoulders.

"What are you doing?" she said crossly.

Albury took her hands and stood up. "We're going upstairs," he announced.

Tentatively, Christine followed him out of the apartment, up two peeling flights to the roof. They stepped outside to a

175 »

small wooden platform, framed on four sides by a hand-carved railing.

"It's called a widow's walk," Albury said. "In the old days, Conch wreckers would come up here to search for ships on the rocks. You can see the reef from here." He pointed east, out to sea, where a long slick curl of water shouldered the coral shelf. "The storms would throw the ships up on the rocks, and Key West would empty like a whorehouse on a Sunday morning. Boats out of every harbor, racing for gold or guns or rum. Whatever they could salvage."

"Your relatives, too?" Christine said.

"Oh, I'm sure."

"Did they find any treasure?"

"You bet," Albury said. "Found it and lost it a dozen times over. It must have been a hell of a time. A regular tropical Klondike."

Christine found his hands and moved them to her waist. "Are you sorry things have changed down here?"

"But they haven't. Not really," he said with a dark laugh. "Come up to the widow's walk some night when a shrimp boat runs aground with a load of grass. The crew will start heaving those bales overboard to lighten her up, and pretty soon you'll see the boats. From here you can see 'em racing out to scoop up anything that's floating out there. Just like the old days. The spirit is the same."

Christine pressed closer and Albury felt her hair against his cheek. "I can't blame you for being so bitter," she said.

"I would rather watch the moon," he said, turning her around by the shoulders. His fingers found the top button of the forest-green dress. "You'll never see a moon quite that color in Detroit or Huntsville, Alabama."

Christine laughed softly. Albury's fingers moved to the second button, then the third. "These islands have their own sky and their own moon," he said.

A soft gust rustled the royal palm trees and brought goose bumps to Christine's shoulders. She glanced down and noticed that her dress was below her waist, and that somehow a pair of coarse fisherman's hands had managed to solve the riddle of her bra clasp.

"Breeze?"

He had dropped to one knee, cursing the skintight jeans. "Was your ex-husband in the ballet?"

"No, he was just . . . what are you up to?"

Albury found her nipples and moved his tongue from one to the other. Then he kissed her belly and played along the tan line. "These nylons have got to go."

"Come up here," Christine said, pulling at his shoulders until he rose to his feet. She stood on her toes and kissed him tenderly, her hands around his neck. "Let's go back to the apartment."

"I like it out here."

"But I'm chilly."

"I'll cover you with something warm." His hands dropped to her buttocks and she drew against him tightly.

"Jesus, Breeze." She kissed at him feverishly, lips, neck, cheeks. "Where can we lie down?"

"We don't have to lie down," Albury said. "Can't see the water if you're lying down. Take off the stockings before you drive me crazy."

Later, with their clothes in a pale heap on the roof, he lifted her easily, kissing her the whole time, lowering her onto himself until her legs tightened on his hips. Under a milky half-moon they made love standing, harder and harder, until they were both drenched in sweat. He stopped moving only when Christine cried out twice. He held her around him until her breathing softened.

"I thought we were going to fall off this thing," she whispered.

Albury moved a hand absently along her bare back, the skin like cool velvet under his calloused fingers. It struck her that he had been silent as they had made love, not in the shy or preoccupied way of some men, but in a manner totally dispossessed—all muscle and mouth and movement, without the smallest sigh or groan. And she was quite sure that his eyes had been open, fastened hard on the deep blue light of the sea's horizon. Still, there had been a tenderness to it, a melancholy need every bit as urgent as the frantic passions of other lovers.

Christine nuzzled at his ear and smiled when she felt his light kiss. She rocked back, holding him by the shoulders, as he supported her full weight with a single hand under her buttocks.

"Let me down now," she said. "I've got one more question. Now, don't shake your head like that; just one more and then I'll quit for the night."

"OK, counselor."

"Why do they call this a widow's walk?"

"That's easy," Albury replied. "Because the sea is a widow-maker." His eyes were fixed beyond the reef, and in the moon's light, Christine was startled to see that they were not weary or cold, but almost exultant.

"It's not the sea itself," he went on, "but the chances that it makes a man take. Full of promise one moment, fury the next. It won't often surprise a keen and reasonable man, but even after years it will make him take extraordinary risks. Not all the widows who watched from these roofs lost stupid fools out on that reef. Some of their men were fine, courageous. They just took a chance and lost. The sea itself behaved as it always has, and it didn't really kill those men as much as it made them believe . . . made them believe they could do something that they could not."

Christine spoke in a small voice that seemed to drop off the edge of the old house. "Is that what happened to you?"

"More than once," Breeze Albury said, "but never again."

CHAPTER 19

QUARRELING BLUE JAYS woke Albury. He felt stiff, and stale. Scrabbling for a cigarette, he encountered the note: "You sure beat hell out of a sleeping pill, but you'll have to make your own breakfast, anyway." Signed with a bold "C."

Breakfast would have to wait. Albury reached for the bedside phone.

"Hey, champ, how they hanging'?"

"Hey, dad." Ricky's voice sounded faraway, as though through a gauze. Probably was still doped up.

"Hurts, huh? But I took a look last night, and it didn't seem too bad to me," Albury lied. "Pain'll go away quick."

"Where are you, dad? I called the trailer and you weren't there. . . ."

"You must have scared the shit out of Laurie, telling her about the arm."

"She wasn't there, either." Nor had she been long past midnight when Albury had called from the kitchen phone of a sleeping Christine Manning. "Dad, it's my pitching arm. I asked the doctors this morning if I could pitch as good as ever once the cast is off, and they just shrugged."

Ricky was fighting back tears. Albury watched his knuckles whiten against the plastic receiver.

"That's no sweat, man. I talked to the chief doctor, and he said you'd be good as new. Then just to be sure, I called this guy in Boston—I was in the Navy with him—and his brother is the doctor who takes care of the Red Sox, a specialist. He wants to look at you as soon as they let you out of there. We'll fly up."

"The Red Sox?"

"I know they ain't the Orioles, but they ain't bad, either. You just got to be careful in Fenway that the right-handed batters don't pull you over the wall—the Monster, they call it."

"Yeah. Dad, they want to know if we've got insurance." Ricky's voice was fading.

"Sure, we do. The best. I'll stop by and straighten that out when I come see you, maybe later today. Tomorrow for sure."

There was a long pause, and Albury thought Ricky might have dozed off.

"Dad?"

"I'm here."

"I will be able to throw again, won't I?"

Tears stung the fresh cut on Albury's cheek. He tried to keep his voice firm.

"If you stay off bicycles you don't know how to ride, for Chrissakes."

Albury scoured himself in a melancholic shower. He made coffee and called Crystal.

"Hey, sunshine, any mail for Smilin' Jack?"

"Hi, bubba, how's Ricky?"

"Doin' fine. What do you hear?"

"There's a picture postcard from our favorite asshole. He says he hopes you got his message. He means Ricky, I'd say."

"What else does our friend say?"

"He says he'll pay twenty thou F.O.B. for the merchandise, and—get this—no hard feelings."

"Friendly soul, isn't he?"

"Asshole."

"Tell him I accept. I'll make contact with him."

"You crazy? You know how much that stuff is worth," Crystal spluttered. "And what makes you think he'll really pay?"

"He sure doesn't want any more trouble, and neither do I."

"I'll tell him, if you're sure. . . ."

"I'm sure. One more thing: Can you find out for me where a lobster boat called *El Gallo* docks?"

"I already know. Up at Big Coppitt. The captain is some scumbag Marielito friend of the man you're doing business with."

"Right, thanks. I'll see you around."

"Hey, wait a minute, mister businessman."

"What?"

"You're liable to get killed, you know."

"I'm not looking for any more trouble. I told you."

"All this sweetness and light is very noble, Breeze, but I've known you since I was a kid."

"So?"

"So remember ole Crystal. He can't run much anymore, but he can drive a car and he can outshoot any asshole doper in town and talk on the radio at the same time. Teal and Spider and a couple of the others already called this morning to say more or less the same thing. And ole catch-'em-quick Haller was around here at dawn in his Marine Patrol uniform, sayin' how much he'd admire to drink a beer with Breeze Albury. I guess they all heard about Ricky."

"I read you, bubba, loud and clear. Tell 'em I said thanks."

On a rickety and old manual typewriter that was all the town fathers had said they could offer the Governor's repre-

sentative—"Sorry, ma'am, things are tight around here"—
Christine Manning pecked out her case against Drake Boone.
Of his guilt she was certain. He had seduced a minor, fed her
pills that had blown her circuits, and then tried to cover up.
That was the working hypothesis. It would be enough to see
that Drake Boone never practiced law again. It should be
enough to cost him his freedom. And it could be the key she
needed to unravel the whole mess. Squeezed, Drake Boone
would talk.

Christine Manning felt feverish. One moment the words
before her were sharp, incisive, and her mind hopscotched
through a dozen prosecutorial tricks she could use against
Drake Boone. The next instant she seemed floating in space.
She allowed herself a luxurious shiver and pressed her legs
tight together. Christine had not had a man for almost six
months, and she had never had a man like Breeze Albury.
Three times her hand, unbidden, reached for the phone. Three
times she intercepted it. Was he still asleep? Perhaps he had
already gone. Would he come back? Did she want him to?
What could she say? Thanks for making me feel like a woman
again, Breeze; too bad I have to put you in jail. That's not a
very nice morning-after hello, is it?

Christine lay her head against the cool black metal of the
typewriter. It was resting there when the visitor walked in.

"Good morning, remember me?"

Christine jerked up, guiltily.

"Oh, oh, Miss Ravenel, uh, Laurie, yes, hello." Christine
felt the blood rush to her face.

"Am I interrupting anything?"

"No, no, please sit down."

They exchanged pleasantries, Christine battling for com-
posure. How could Laurie know? Only if Breeze had told her.
Maybe he had called her from Christine's own phone, her
own bed. Maybe they had joked about how easy it had been
for the big fisherman to make her. Christine felt mortified.
For one paranoid instant she loathed Breeze Albury.

"We have something important to talk about," Laurie said.

"Yes," Christine said grimly.

"Last night . . ."

"Look, Laurie, what I . . ."

"Last night there was a big meeting, maybe an historic meeting for Key West. I think you should know about it. Unofficially, of course."

"Oh. Well." Christine toyed with a pencil.

"Bob Freed and his friends have decided to fight back. They are fed up with the harassment and the corruption around here, and they're going to do something about it."

"Oh."

"You OK? You're sweating."

"No. Yes, thank you. Please go on."

"They have a list of targets, and they are going to investigate them systematically. They are going to trace the course of corruption—up to the top—and then they are going to root it out. . . . Can I get you a glass of water? I can come back another time. . . ."

"No, no, I'm fine, really. What exactly would they do with the information they acquire?"

"That's where you come in."

"Tell me."

Laurie spoke for ten minutes with great animation, a righteous Valkryie. Christine took great care not to look her in the eye, but the lawyer in her was intrigued by what she heard.

"I think that is fascinating, Laurie," she said at last, "but one thing I must caution you against is trying to take the law into your own hands."

"That's a joke. You know the law around here as well as I do."

"I know, but the second you start behaving like the people you're after, I can't help you anymore."

"I am sure we can find some common ground." Laurie smiled, and it occurred to Christine what a handsome woman she was.

"At least let's talk again. I appreciate your coming."

Laurie rose to go.

"Oh, I'm sorry, I forgot to ask before. How's Ricky?"

"Oh, he's fine, thanks, eats and breathes baseball."

Laurie's hand was on the doorknob.

"No, I mean his arm. How is his arm?"

"His arm? What's wrong with his arm?"

"It's broken, didn't you *know?* He's still in the hospital, isn't he?"

Laurie paled, staggered a step.

"Hospital? God, I didn't . . . the meeting lasted so late I stayed with . . . Oh, Ricky."

"I'm sorry." Christine reached across the desk to comfort Laurie.

"Oh, God, I'll go there right now. . . . Thanks for telling me."

"I'm sorry," Christine said again, uselessly. Even then she didn't realize her mistake.

Laurie turned again for the door. Then she stopped.

"How do you know about Ricky's arm?"

"Breeze told me," Christine Manning said in the voice of a little girl.

"Breeze told you!"

"I . . ."

"You've seen Breeze." It was an accusation. "How? Why? I've been worried sick about him. Where is he?"

"I don't know. I talked to him, that's all. He's been helping me. . . ."

"Breeze? Helping you?"

They stood there for a long, strained moment, two strong, confused women, each realizing that the other had no secrets, each loving and hating a battered fisherman. Crying, Laurie fled. Alone, Christine dialed her apartment. There was no answer.

* * *

The small boat came with the twilight, a bonefisherman with its engine throttled back. It made no wake and disturbed no one. An egret fishing on a mud flat paused momentarily to stare. A school of mullet ran perfunctorily toward some mangroves to escape its path and then, sensing no threat, darted back to play in the mottled shadows around the dock. The bonefisherman nudged gently against the dock and tied up around a piling draped with a fading orange-and-blue bumper sticker. "Florida Fishermen Have Bigger Rods," it said.

Willie Bascaro never noticed. He lay on a chaise longe in the lee of his wheelhouse, snapping his fingers to *salsa* piped through headphones from a cassette deck on his belt. He felt a thump on his deck and looked up incuriously. Then he sat straight up and yanked off the headphones. Before him, silhouetted by the sun, was the figure of a man, arms crossed, waiting. Bascaro shaded his eyes but could see only a black bulk. It reminded him of a ghost. Reflexively, he crossed himself.

"Willie Bascaro?"

"*Si.*"

"My name is Albury. I have come to burn your boat."

Bascaro only half-understood the words. That was enough. He jackknifed from the lounger and sprang to the rail. He had learned many things in the streets of Havana, and the most important was knowing when to run. In another second he would have jumped. Albury grabbed him from behind and lifted him off the rail as though he were a baby.

"No, Willie. No running this time. Now is the time to pay the bill, Willie. *Pagar la cuenta, comprende?*"

Albury rifled through the Marielito's pockets for the engine keys. He shoved Bascaro into the fetid litter of his cabin and locked the door. In the new darkness, a few minutes later, *El Gallo* headed out to sea, skiff towing merrily behind.

Albury drove without thinking, pointing east toward the vastness of the Gulf Stream. From the cabin came the piteous babble of Spanish. Breeze Albury ignored it. He spoke only to himself.

"This is a shit boat, Willie, a real dog. Engine needs an overhaul, the compass is off, and it steers like a scow. I wouldn't give you a nickel for your chances in a real sea. You probably don't know how it is in the Keys, Willie. Maybe you can steal a Conch's woman, but if you cut his traps, you're a dead man. You should have figured that sooner or later I'd come for you.

"But not you, Willie. *Muy macho,* huh? You bragged in a bar about cutting the traps, and you even stole the buoys. Saw a whole pile of them up there on your dock, orange-and-white buoys. Been in the Albury family a long time. Those are the last ones, though. I'm leaving the Rock, Willie. Me and Rick."

Albury broke his monologue to listen. The babbling from the cabin had stopped a few minutes before. Albury lit a cigarette and waited, relaxed at the wheel.

Willie Bascaro erupted from the cabin just as Albury was pitching the butt into the sea.

Albury turned to meet him with a savage smile.

"I knew you'd be coming, Willie. It's better that way. What is it you've got, *macho,* a gun? No, a tire iron. Is that what you used to cripple my boy, Willie? Come and cripple me, motherfucker."

With a ferret's scream, Willie Bascaro lunged, the iron pointed like a sword. He was younger and too quick for Albury. The metal rod caught him in the gut. He felt something tear.

Albury staggered back against the wheel, winded.

"Cobarde de mierda," he gasped.

Bascaro attacked again in a frenzy. Albury ducked under a roundhouse, the tire iron grazing his ear. He caught the Cuban with a left hand to the face and a right above the heart. Bascaro sagged against the curved coping where the open wheelhouse ran toward the deck. Albury got inside his next weak swing. He seized Bascaro's arm with all his strength and pushed it back against the coping. Back, back, until finally, with a sickening snap, it broke. The iron fell into the sea. The Cuban screamed. Albury released him to slide onto the deck and poked gently at his own belly. It hurt like hell.

When his head cleared, Albury pulled in Teal's boat and tied it off close to the stern. From it he took two jerrycans of gasoline. Bascaro lay moaning on the deck.

Albury went into the cabin and came back with a life jacket. It was covered in mildew. He threw it at Bascaro's feet.

"Put it on or not, it's up to you."

Methodically, Albury drenched the engine compartment and the wheelhouse with gasoline. Bascaro watched from the deck with dead man's eyes.

Albury stepped over the rail into the skiff.

"*Adios*, Willie."

"*No, no, por favor. No quiero morir. Por favor.*"

The Cuban scrambled to his feet and staggered toward the skiff, beseeching. A trickle of urine ran down his pant legs and onto the deck.

Albury watched him coldly for a full minute.

"No, I'm not going to kill you, Willie. Not yet. Come aboard." He gestured to the bow of the skiff. Willie Bascaro stumbled into the skiff. He fell heavily onto his broken arm and screamed. Then he cowered quietly in the bow, like a beaten dog.

From twenty-five yards away, Albury fired *El Gallo* with a shell from Teal's flare pistol. It burned like a wrecker's beacon on the dark sea. Then he turned the skiff toward shore.

"*Policia*, Willie, *mucha policia*," said Albury. He put a hand around his neck and squeezed. A noose.

Six miles off the coast, the skiff came abreast of a drum-stick-shaped island. Albury reduced speed as the water shoaled to less than two fathoms. Albury saw that his prisoner had noticed the shallow water and was gauging the distance to shore. Albury left the wheel and bent in the stern, fiddling with the outboard engine.

Willie Bascaro went overboard in a clumsy dive. He found his feet and began slogging toward the beach.

Albury laughed out loud. Willie had snapped at the bait the way a crawfish tears at horse meat.

"One more monkey," Albury grinned.

The island was called Loggerhead Key. The University of Miami ran it as a research center for the study of the rhesus monkey. There were at least a thousand of the noxious, quarrelsome beasts on the mangrove island. And nothing else. They had taken over.

Every third day, Albury knew, a boat would come. Young researchers would quickly shovel a mountain of dog food onto the beach and hastily retreat. The monkeys would gulp the food and remain with nothing to do but fight and fornicate until the next boat came. Willie Bascaro would be a diversion.

With a phone call from Christine's apartment, Albury had learned that the next food boat would not come for two days. That was time enough. For two days Willie Bascaro could grovel in the sand for leftover dog chow and battle one-handed with the monkeys for his clothes.

Unsuspecting, Willie was in knee-deep water now near the beach. He looked back, as though disbelieving his good luck.

"*Adios,* Willie," Albury called. In the instant before he opened the throttle, Albury heard the monkeys shrieking their hatred for the intruder.

CHAPTER 20

LAURIE RAVENEL urged the old Pontiac down Whitehead Street, one eye on the temperature gauge. Breeze had often warned her about the radiator, which leaked itself dry every couple of days.

She parked across from a laundromat and brushed her auburn hair in the rearview mirror. The Cowrie was only two blocks away, and Laurie was early, an hour at least. But she knew that Bobby was already there, setting up for lunch. She checked her lipstick.

Suddenly the passenger door swung open and a bundled-up man slid into the car. Laurie instinctively grabbed for her purse. Then she saw who it was.

"Breeze! God, oh my." They hugged each other in silence, awkwardly bunched on the front seat. Laurie kissed him wetly, lightly, on the lips and held him back by the shoulders. "I love the hat."

Albury sheepishly snatched the blue knit cap off his head. "Borrowed it from a shrimper at the West Key Bar."

"And the jacket? Looks like it might have fit you back in junior high school."

The navy slicker belonged to Christine's ex, though Albury didn't say so. "I'm not much on disguises," he said. "But I needed something so I could walk around town without being noticed."

Laurie burrowed into his shoulder. The Conch Train clattered by, canary-colored boxcars loaded with children and tourists, lobster-skinned, bandoliered with Nikons. The driver was giving an animated monologue on the Hemingway House.

"Breeze, what happened to Ricky?" Laurie's words were muffled in the folds of his jacket.

"A couple of the Cubans busted his arm."

"Why?" she cried. "What for? He's a boy."

"He's my son. They wanted to get back at me."

"God." Laurie sat up and fished in her purse for a Kleenex. Her eyes were moist, her voice tiny. "I spent an hour with him today. He's a strong kid, thank God."

"I've got to settle this. Then I'll be leaving Key West." Albury took her hand. "I won't be able to stay."

"Breeze, I won't be able to go."

He had seen the look before, not often, but enough to know it. This time he felt nothing but tired.

"Things are starting to happen, honey. Bobby's getting a group together. Businessmen, shop owners, professionals. They're going after the core of all this. Bobby says they're going to work with the Governor's office, the federal people, anybody who needs help down here. Eventually, I think they're going to clean up the island. Think of it, Breeze."

"You and Bobby gonna clean it up, huh?"

"It all started when Beeker got beat up and that cop just stood there, watching—"

"I remember," Albury said. Laurie and Bobby, lovers. A soft touch and a fair-weather faggot. Why not? They were hopeless reformers, both of them. Maybe Laurie needed some-one like that; together they could Save the Whales.

"You wouldn't consider going with me?" Albury asked.

"Breeze, I love this place. It's gorgeous. You . . . well, you've been here too long. You walk down Duval Street and all you see are the hustlers, bikers, and bums—"

"And who do you see? Mother Teresa? A dozen budding Picassos, maybe? Poppa's ghost?"

"Breeze!"

Albury sighed. "You knew I was ready to get out."

"And now I don't blame you," Laurie said gently, "but I can't go. I think what Bobby's doing is exciting. I know you don't; you think it's fanciful and naive."

"Nothing will ever change here," Albury said. "Nothing ever has."

"You've been poisoned by the place," she said. "You'll never be able to see it, but it will change, honey. It will go on and change without you."

Albury sat quietly for a time, his hand resting on her knee. Then he laughed.

"It'll have to, Laurie, I'm through with the Rock. But maybe before I go, I can come up with a little present for you and Bobby."

"What, Breeze?"

They talked across the car for fifteen minutes; Laurie got out a notebook and scribbled seriously. Albury, the knit cap pulled down to his eyebrows, hunkered down in the car seat, explaining everything slowly and twice.

"Can he marshall the troops today?" Albury asked finally.

"For something like this? You bet."

"Good. Now, I gotta go before somebody recognizes me in this car."

"Breeze, why can't you tell me what's happened?"

"Not yet, Laurie."

"I saw Christine Manning."

"Me, too," he said quickly. "Ran into her at the hospital when I was up with Ricky."

"Oh." Laurie smiled fondly and touched his cheek. "You've been out on the boat, haven't you? I can always tell, Breeze. Your face is shining, burnished."

"It's the summer sun off the water."

"More than that," she said, tidying herself for the walk to the Cowrie and fighting back words. "It's more than just the goddamn sun, Captain Albury."

It was five minutes to two in the afternoon when Drake Boone, Jr., sauntered into his office, a tall young woman on his arm. His timing could not have been worse.

"Long lunch?" asked Christine Manning, rising from a pillowy chair in the lobby.

"Did you have an appointment?" Boone demanded.

Suzanne, his secretary, wore a vaguely helpless expression. "I thought your afternoon was clear, Mr. Boone," she said, thumbing with mock concentration through the day's mail.

"Drake, you'd better ask your friend to leave us alone," said Christine, as if it were merely a suggestion. Boone followed her anxiously into his office. This was not good, not good at all. He closed the door hurriedly.

"You're finished," Christine announced crisply. From her briefcase she produced a thick manila file.

Boone laughed sharply. "Sugar, you been tryin' to nail my ass since you first got to town. I told you then and I'll repeat it now: it can't be done. Not by you, anyway. Want a drink?"

"No." She laid three legal documents side by side on his desk. One of them was fifty-seven pages; the other two were much shorter. The oral interviews had been completed by ten-thirty. Finding somebody to transcribe them so quickly had proved an ordeal.

"I think you ought to read Irma Clayton's first," Christine said, pointing to the thickest affidavit.

Boone shook his head. "Don't need to, sugar. The woman's obviously distraught. Her little girl is dead and she's ready to blame it on somebody, so why not me? The only problem," Boone continued, "is proof. She says that on the afternoon of August whatever-it-was, I stuffed her little girl with Quaaludes, right? Well, it so happens that a young fella from Key West High by the name of John Henry Russell was with Miss Julie that very afternoon, and it also happens that he saw her gulp down a dozen pills she had bought from some longhair during lunch hour. And in there"—Boone aimed a manicured finger toward a file cabinet—"I have a sworn deposition from young Mr. Russell himself."

It was Christine's turn to smile. "I'm disappointed in you, Drake. An old Conch fixer like yourself, and the best you can do is buy off some jock from the local high school."

Boone poured himself a scotch. "You are wasting my time, Miz Manning," he said icily. "You're not gonna pin that girl's death on me. Don't get me wrong. I'm sorry it happened—I *did* know the girl; she liked me, I guess. She'd come around to the office now and then, looking for a little action. I told her to go home, play with somebody her own age. I was nice about it."

Christine waited placidly across the desk, listening with an expression of unbearable politeness. Boone sensed that he was talking too much.

"I'll wait while you read the other affidavits," Christine offered.

Boone set aside Irma Clayton's and studied one of the short ones. "Kerry McEvoy?"

"One of Julie's friends."

Boone shrugged. "Never heard of her."

"Her nickname is Daisy," Christine said. "She was also in your office on the afternoon of August fifteenth. Tall girl, nice figure."

Boone's mouth turned to powder.

"Looks a lot older than fifteen," Christine said pleasantly.

"Her statement there is only about twelve pages, but she gets right to the heart of the matter. You'll see that she even uses the proper terminology—fellatio instead of blow job. Right there on page three, Drake. And Kerry is also conversant about certain sadomasochistic practices for which you—by her account—recruited Julie Clayton."

Boone smiled again, only this time his tile-square teeth did not show. "Christine, who is going to believe this? What jury in Key West is going to believe some junior-high whore?"

"Good point, Drake, and precisely the reason that I bothered with a third affidavit."

Boone looked at the name and groped for the phone. "Suzanne, no calls." He tried to pour himself a refill but splattered the desk blotter instead.

"Where the fuck did you get *this?*"

"The Governor made a phone call," Christine replied. "Judge Snow was at your little party, was he not?"

"I will fight this the whole way," Boone snarled. "The jury will never hear a word of this. Not a motherfuckering whisper of it. Judge Snow is a known drunk."

"Is that any way to talk about your old friend?"

Boone wrung his hands under his desk. Every shred of common sense told him to clam up and get a lawyer, but he was a persistently curious man. And his adversary, for God's sake, was a *lady* prosecutor. His blow-dried ego would not permit retreat.

"It's all hearsay, Christine, but still, I am interested in knowing how you—how Judge Snow came to offer this affidavit."

"Simple. He was there; he saw everything and was understandably appalled. When Julie died, he chose to tell us what he knew."

"And I don't suppose," Boone snorted, "that the Governor threatened to yank his drunken ass off the bench if he didn't cooperate in nailing ole Drake Boone, right?"

Christine returned the file to her briefcase. "Drake, trying to put you in jail with a big trial would be a waste of time and taxpayers' money. There are easier ways to ruin you. You can scream and shake your fist and strut indignantly in your sappy little corduroy suits; you can do all that till you're blue in the face. Go ahead and fight, put on a show. But I am telling you that this package is as good as in the mail to the Florida Bar, and that the Governor is prepared to pick up the phone and cash a few political chips with some buddies on the grievance committee. Tom Cruz and the rest of the sewer rats you represent better start hunting for a new lawyer, Drake, because your name is poison from now on."

They were both standing now. Boone, the shorter of the two, was so red that his head trembled and bobbled, as if his neck itself were a spring.

Christine thought that he might punch her, but she delivered the clincher. "The money you gave Irma Clayton is now the property of the state of Florida," she said. "Twenty-five thousand dollars in two envelopes. Mrs. Clayton saved them. Don't bother to deny it, your fingerprints were all over them. Sloppy. Very sloppy. You'll be hearing soon from the IRS about your charitable contribution."

"All right!" Boone charged around the desk. He spoke in a dark whisper. "What do you want? How much? I got forty thousand in a wall safe. I can get more."

"Good-bye, Mr. Boone."

"Wait, please wait." He held her arm. "It's not money, is it? You want somebody. Who, Cruz? I'll give you Cruz. If you keep my name out of it, I will deliver Winnebago Tom."

Christine removed his hand from her elbow and eyed him. "Not enough," she said. "But maybe we can work something out."

"Tell me."

"I want everybody. Everybody you know. Starting with Cruz and working up."

Boone stepped back. "I can't. That's impossible, it's suicide," he blubbered. "They'll kill me, damnit!"

"See you in Tallahassee," Christine Manning said.

Drake Boone locked the office door behind her. Slumped at his chair, he pawed listlessly through the desk until he found a bottle of white pills. It was empty. He gulped another glass of scotch and closed his eyes.

Boone's heart pounded louder but slowly, so slowly that he found himself inserting completely formed ideas between each beat. One of the ideas was suicide. Another was murder. Yet another was to pick up the telephone.

No, Miss Manning had not yet returned to her office.

Drake Boone left his name and number.

He shambled to a wall, lifted a Monet print, and fumbled with the office safe. He piled the contents in his arms and returned to his desk.

My, my, my. He was wrong about the money. There was only thirty-four thousand here. Suzanne? "Suzanne!" No one answered.

Boone pushed the cash to one side and leafed through some photographs. They were Polaroids. He frowned at the quality. The focus was oily—or was it his vision? There was pretty Julie on the charcoal sofa, her wrists taped together over her head, her legs spread apart, held apart. From her body you could never have guessed her age. Boone could not discern from the photograph whether Julie was smiling or shouting something. He was in the picture, too, on top of her. Sort of. That Daisy took lousy fucking pictures.

Julie had been such a lovely girl. In one of the snapshots, she was stretched out on her tummy on the same sofa. Boone noticed something around her neck, and he squinted at the picture to see. It was one of his own belts, beige beneath an indigo stripe. Julie didn't mind that part, as long as he didn't make it too tight. Boone smiled narcotically. The goddamn Polaroids had given him an erection.

The phone rang. Christine Manning. Miss Bigtime Prosecutor.

"What is it, Drake?"

"I know who attacked the Albury kid. Gimme a break and I'll tell you."

"I already know," Christine said. "It was Winnebago Tom."

"Yeah, but wait, sugar. Wait a minute," Boone slurred. "You don't know who ordered it. *I* know who ordered it. I know who runs the goddamn Machine. I really do, lady lawyer. I know who."

That's my boy, Christine thought triumphantly. "Meet me later at the Pier House," she said. "About ten."

It was three-fifteen and Huge Barnett's stomach, a considerable force in his life, growled. Barnett fired the big Chrysler through a red light at Duval and Petronia, made a right on Whitehead Street, and coasted to a stop in front of the Cowrie Restaurant.

"Whose fucking El Dorado is this?"

A microwave salesman from Michigan, sitting with his plump wife at a corner table, dropped half his egg-salad sandwich at the sight of a lantern-jawed blimp with a badge on his chest, filling the doorway.

"It's my car, officer," the salesman replied. "I thought I put plenty of money in the meter."

"That's a police emergency zone you're parked in, pal. Better move it."

"Can I at least finish my lunch?"

Barnett's fist came down on the counter and the salesman's ass came out of his chair. The police chief got his parking space.

Barnett took a table for four, by the window. He would have preferred a place at the counter, where it was easier to flirt with the waitresses, but a single stool could not contain his tonnage.

"Darling!" Barnett called to Laurie Ravenel. "Could you bring me a pitcher of Budweiser, please?"

Barnett studied Laurie salaciously as she crossed the floor of the restaurant: tight jeans, a feathery tank top, her dark red hair tied back with a ribbon.

She set the beer next to a chilled glass mug on Barnett's table. "What would you like to eat, chief?"

Barnett winked.

"That's not on the menu."

The chief chuckled. "Well, then," he said in a wheezy voice, "how 'bout some black beans and rice, and chicken? Bring me a couple breasts. White meat only."

"Comin' up," Laurie said gaily.

"You sure look fine today, Miss Ravenel."

"Thank you, chief," said Laurie, offering a shy smile that lasted two seconds longer than Barnett had counted on.

Laurie placed the order with the kitchen, then popped her head into Bobby Freed's private office. "Our fat friend is here," she said. "Better keep your voices down."

Freed nodded soberly and turned back to the men gathered at his desk: a truck driver from Sugarloaf Key, a bridge tender from Marathon, a gas-station man from an Exxon up on Big Pine. They had been part of the crowd at Freed's civic rally the night before; this afternoon there would be no cheers or applause, only grave talk.

"What about Mark Haller?" continued the trucker.

"Taken care of," Freed answered.

"I can't miss the car, can I?" said the gas-station man.

"There's only one like it in the whole world," Freed said. "There'll be an elephant driving."

The men laughed together.

"Don't you ever wonder how come I eat lunch here every day?" Huge Barnett was draining a second pitcher of beer.

"Because the food's so good," Laurie said.

"No, darlin', because you've got the most delicious-looking pair of tits in Key West, that's why." Barnett chomped into a piece of hot chicken with such porcine vigor that the breast-bone cracked in his mouth.

"I wish you wouldn't talk like that around the customers."

"Then let's go somewhere by ourselves so I can talk the way I want." Barnett lowered his voice. "Ever been for a ride in a police car?"

"Oh, please." Laurie drifted to another table and started clearing plates. "You know, chief," she scolded in a whisper, "you wouldn't be half-bad if you weren't always so . . . so crude."

"Darlin', I can be a gentleman." He put down the remains of his chicken and looked up at her, panda-eyed. "You think I can't be a gentleman if I want?"

Laurie carted the dirty dishes back to the kitchen and puttered around for a minute or two. Through the window in the swinging door she watched Barnett shifting at his table, craning with great effort to look for her. Slowly, she made her way back to the table.

"How about some Key Lime pie?" he said.

"All right. The usual two slices?"

"Right," Barnett said. "How come you never go out with me?"

"Not so loud."

"Is it Albury? Is it because of him?"

"Nope."

"Why, then?"

"Shhh." Laurie took her time cutting the pie.

"Why, then?" Barnett repeated when she returned.

" 'Cause you don't ask like a gentleman. You want a slice of lime on this?"

Barnett buffed his lips with a napkin. "Miss Ravenel, ma'am, could I have the pleasure of your company for a cocktail tonight over at the Casa Marina?"

"Ohh . . . all right," she said. Then, bending over the table: "But not at the Casa, OK? I don't want any of Breeze's friends to see us. Can we go up the Keys? Marathon, maybe?"

"Abtholootely," Barnett said enthusiastically through a mouthful of meringue.

"And not tonight," Laurie added. "Tomorrow, 'kay? I get off around five."

Barnett's crotch tingled as he wolfed down the Key Lime pie. She would want to get on top, of course. Most women did, except that fat hooker who worked the topless joint on Roosevelt. Yes, this would be the high spot of the weekend. Laurie was a lush-looking woman . . . experienced, he was sure . . . patient, artful even. Not like the stringy, hair-triggered hitchhikers he was always picking up. Sluts. Clumsy, too.

Barnett pushed the table away from his belly and rose, as if in slow motion. Laurie was crossing the restaurant with the check in one hand.

"Just put it on my tab, darlin'," he called. "And this old gentleman would be grateful if you wore those jeans tomorrow night. Whaddya say?"

CHAPTER 21

TOMAS CRUZ wheeled the big Winnebago into a handicapped-only zone and exchanged a cheery wave with the flaccid foot patrolman whose job it was to see that the tourists behaved themselves in the heart of Key West's Old Town. Winnebago Tom often came to Mallory Docks to watch the tourists watch the sun slip into the sea. With the Winnebago as his traveling office, the docks at sunset were a good place to transact business, pick up snippets of information, and troll for fresh meat to be savored later on the pull-out double bed beneath the ceiling mirror. Tom gnawed at a boiled shrimp. He had two hours to kill before sunset; plenty of time to mellow out. From the cutlery drawer he extracted three pills from a shipment that had come from Colombia the month before. He washed them down with a long swig of champagne from the bottle. Then he slipped off his loafers and sprawled on the sofa in front of his Sony. . . .

". . . two weeks in Aspen or the prize behind the green door. The choice is yours. Which will it be?"

Tom knew that scam. The green door was horseshit, nine times out of ten.

"Take the vacation," he screamed.

The contestant chose the green panel and won a year's supply of dog food.

"Air-headed bitch," Tom scoffed.

When the door of the Winnebago sprang open, Tomas Cruz sat up sharply, upsetting the champagne onto the pile carpet.

"Don't you ever knock?" Tom recovered the bottle, rubbed the lip on the sleeve of his T-shirt, and proffered it to Drake Boone.

The lawyer ignored it. He dropped a green attaché case onto the floor and stripped off his matching tie.

"Where's Manolo? I need to talk to him right away."

"Booney, baby, relax. Relax. Have a drink. Have a pill."

"Christ, what are you on? Your pupils look like Frisbees."

"What do you want Manolo for?"

"It's important. I'll tell him myself."

"You're talkin' to him."

"What do you mean?"

"Manolo had to go out of town on business for a few days. He left me in charge. You got a problem, tell me."

"Where did he go? When will he be back?"

Winnebago Tom didn't notice the strain in Boone's voice or the sweat that spotted his forehead despite the camper's air conditioning.

"Where he went is Manolo's business, and when he'll be back is my business. You got somethin' to say, say it or go away. I'm tryin' to watch television."

Exasperated, Boone flicked off the Sony.

"We got bad problems."

"Keep it short and to the point," Tom said, mimicking Manolo. "That prick Breeze Albury is comin' by anytime now. He's finally going to give us back the grass he stole. I sent him a little message, and he read it loud and clear."

"I don't want to talk about Albury, Tom. It's that Julie Clayton business . . . it's all coming to pieces."

"Good ole Julie. She sure did love Demon Pill, didn't she? But she was overrated. Never could understand what you saw in her." Tom yawned.

"Listen, asshole, I'm not going down the tube for Julie Clayton or anybody else."

"Oh, c'mon. You're not going down the tube, counselor. You got a problem, I'll have Barnett fix it."

"It's not Barnett who's after me. It's that Manning woman, the Governor's bitch. She's got me cold, man."

"We'll fix it." The Machine paid Drake Boone to be precise, but sometimes he was simply tedious. Tom decided to pop another pill.

"We won't fix this one, Tom. Look, we've run this town for almost ten years. It was fun, but it's over. I'm leaving for St. Thomas—now and for good."

"Horseshit."

"It's the truth. And do you know something? I think Manolo has the same idea. Is he really away on business? Or did he split? Manning is after me. The queers are crazy for Barnett's blood. Albury ripped off a load. Maybe Manolo just read the tea leaves and walked away while he still could."

"No, no way. Manolo's coming back."

"OK, Tom, if you say so. I'm leaving town, and I want a hundred thou to go with me. I'll take cash."

"Are you out of your gourd?" Tom was becoming agitated. He wished Manolo was around to handle Boone.

"Let's call the money a parting gift. A silence gift, like all the ones we have paid to patsies over the years, OK?"

"No, it's not OK."

"Hey, baby, if I go down, I don't go alone, remember that."

"What is that supposed to mean?"

"It means what it says. Remember where Julie's pills and everybody else's pills come from. That's you, ain't it, Winnebago? And the pot, the enforcement, and all the other little things you'd rather your ole mama never read about you in the newspaper. It costs a hundred grand for me to forget all that. For good. Otherwise, I meet the lady prosecutor. Tonight."

"That's not funny."

They quarreled for another forty-five minutes, while the sun dropped ever lower, as though on a pulley, and the tourists gathered along the seawall to celebrate its departure.

At sunset, the broad concrete promenade at Mallory Docks is street theater the way Fellini would stage it. That night a juggler-comedian with a wispy mustache and a pink jump suit played the star. Around him, as he tossed flaming rods and evil-looking machetes, stood several hundred people: cruising homosexuals and shagged newlyweds; bemused straight tourists in white shoes and matching belts; an eccentric piano teacher from Akron with a broken arm cast in praying-mantis position; a creature of indeterminate sex in a knee-length white fur coat, mirror sunglasses, and a rainbow-colored wig. About the periphery, a frizzy-haired woman bicycled in a green dress and high-topped leather boots. "Guava cookies, carrot cookies, Key West sweet, Key West treat, warm and chewy," she sang to the strains of an off-key black bongo drummer. Alone on an elevated pump housing, smiling benignly, stood a barefooted gray-bearded man in white duck trousers of an Otavalo Indian and a poncho cut from an army blanket. Around the Rock, people called him Moses.

In the Winnebago on the fringes of the spectacle, Drake Boone was adamant. Tomas Cruz ricocheted between incredulity, anger, and stupor.

"One last time, Boone," Tom said, "this will all blow over. Forget it."

"I've had it. You and Manolo can get yourselves another lawyer."

They stared at one another for a long moment—Tom gummy-eyed; Boone glacial. Outside, the sun was dying. The tourists watched in rapt silence. When it vanished, they would clap; every night the tourists clapped.

"OK, have it your way," Tom said at last. "One hundred thou it is. Small bills?"

"I don't care. You got it here?"

"Yeah." He had much more than that. "But turn around while I get it. If you ain't a part of the team anymore, then I don't want you seeing where my bank is."

"Just put it in the briefcase, OK?"

Drake Boone turned. From behind a cushion, Tomas Cruz pulled the silenced Beretta and shot Drake Boone twice in the back.

On the seawall outside, the tourists applauded.

"How much is that shell there?" He nudged it with his boot. It was a queen conch, a beauty.

"Ten dollars," she said without looking up. "It may sound expensive, but it's real cheap. That's a Queen of the Sea, comes from over a hundred feet deep."

"Not as deep as all that, Peg."

"Hello, Breeze."

It hurt to look at her. Once, her eyes had flashed a sensual yellow fire. Now, as she peered up at him from under a floppy straw hat, they were lost in the swollen face and as colorless as the gin that had destroyed them.

"How're things, Peg?"

"Fine, I guess."

"You haven't been around to see Ricky lately."

"I keep meanin' to, honest. But you know how it is. Besides, he stopped by the other day. He's so big, Breeze. And Veronica, she'd be nearly fourteen. Veronica."

"Yeah." Albury had come to tell her about Ricky's arm. He decided not to.

"Where did it all go, Breeze? Us, and the island? It was so good, once. Then it went someplace, all of it, all rotten. Can you tell me where it all went?"

"I don't know."

"Fast. It all went so fast. Like my little girl. And now, what's left? This place, my office." She gestured. The sun had left. Shadows speckled the tiny shingle of sand and the fading red-and-white sign that proclaimed it "Southernmost Beach in the U.S."

"These are hard times, Peg," Albury said gently.

"No good times." Then she smiled. "It was so bright, like the sun on a summer day, so hot it makes you feel good all over. Remember? We saved and bought that house. The kids loved that backyard, and then you said one good season and you'd build a Florida room on the back with air conditioning, but you never built it. Only a tree house in that ugly old ficus, and me scared to death the kids would fall out. 'Course, you didn't know that because you were out fishin', and you were going to buy another boat and then one day a fish house so you could be home more."

She poked at the cool sand with dirty toes. Then she looked up.

"I'm sorry, Breeze."

"Me, too."

Albury took the heavy ivory-and-pink conch shell and left her a twenty-dollar bill.

He was nearly back to the car when she called, a figure lost in shadow.

"Take care of my boy, Breeze. Take care of my Ricky, hear?"

"I will, Peg," he replied softly, "Oh, I will."

Breeze Albury found Tomas Cruz sprawled on the Winnebago's burgundy leather sofa. A pistol lay on the carpet alongside an empty champagne bottle. Tom watched him through hooded eyes.

"Hey, Tom, how they hangin'?"

"What's that you're carryin'?" Tom asked warily.

"This? A queen conch. I'm going to take it to Ricky at the hospital. A get-well present."

"Ricky, oh yeah, sorry about that. You know how it is." Tom shrugged. "Make yourself a drink."

"Thanks, I will. I can see you've had a few already."

"A couple. Want a pop? They're over there." Tom gestured toward the cutlery drawer.

"No, thanks. I've only got a few minutes, got to get to the hospital. Those nurses are damn strict about visiting hours." Albury poured himself three fingers of Bourbon.

Tom fished a gold lighter from his jeans pocket and lit a cigarette. "I'm glad you finally came to your senses, bubba. Tomorrow we deal and it's all over—no hard feelings. I get my square groupers, you get your money, Manolo gets off my ass, and everybody goes home happy."

"Right." Albury toasted Tom and drained the whiskey.

"It's too bad things went so wrong," said Tom, "but I want you to know that we—me and Manolo—don't bear any grudge. And next time somethin' special comes along, somethin' we need a really good captain for, we'll give you a call."

"Thanks. By the way, I hear Manolo's out of town."

"That's right, bubba. It's my show till he gets back."

"No offense, Tom, but are you sure you'll have the money tomorrow?"

"Shit. It's peanuts. I've got more than that on me right now. We're a big-time operation, Breeze, really first-class. I tell you what: I'll throw in a coupla extra thousand for the boy's medical bills, how's that?"

"That'd be fine, Tom."

Albury's fingertips showed white against the conch. He was surprised he hadn't broken it. He looked at his watch. Another few minutes.

"Let's do the trade up around Ramrod Key," said Tom. "I've got it all figured out."

"That's fine, Tom. Only one problem—you're not paying enough. I want more money. Maybe we should wait till Manolo gets back."

Tom pushed himself upright on the sofa.

"What kind of shit is this? First all the hassle with the rip, and now you're trying to fuck me over money, too?"

"Hassles, Tom? No hassles, just business."

"Jesus! Don't you ever learn? Keep up with this shit, Albury, and I'll break your fuckin' kid's head the next time."

"Does Manolo know how cheap you're trying to be?"

"Manolo has nothin' to do with this. Nothin', goddamnit!"

"All the same, I think we should wait till he gets back."

"No!" Tom was roaring now. "You stole my load and you're goin' to give it back to me tomorrow, the way I told you."

"That's not how it's goin' down," Albury said quietly.

Crystal's timing was perfect. Tom was scrabbling on the floor for the pistol when the CB radio above the driver's seat burst to life.

"Ajax, this is Neptune. I have an urgent message from Thor. Do you copy?" Tom glanced reflexively at the radio. He was Ajax. Manolo was Thor.

Almost casually, Albury kicked the gun from Tom's hand. He came out of the chair with the controlled fury of a jungle cat. Tom had no chance.

Albury leaned against the bar to catch his breath, and Tom wailed up at him from the floor.

"Jesus! My arm, you broke my fucking arm."

Albury watched, impassive.

"I'll take my money now, Tom."

"No."

"The money or the other arm."

"OK, OK. The money. Oh, Christ, it hurts."

"Where is it?"

"In the closet . . . a false panel on the floor. There's a

suitcase . . . Take the money and get me to a doctor, OK, Breeze? For Chrissakes."

"Show me the money."

Albury followed Tom toward the sleeping area of the camper's rear. From the corner of his eye, he saw a bulky shadow and whirled to confront it. He jerked open the glass door of the shower stall and Drake Boone fell out.

Albury looked at the corpse.

"My, Tom, you have been busy."

"Look, just take your money and go, OK? This is not your business. You didn't see anything. OK? You're right, I was tryin' to cheat you on the money. Take what you want and we'll call it square."

Clutching his arm, Tom pointed at the closet. Albury grunted at the weight of the suitcase. He dumped it onto the bed, more money than he had ever seen. It smelled like wet dirt.

Albury eyed the cash speculatively. Tom lay half on the bed, his feet on the floor, babbling. It would be so easy: there for the taking. Albury sighed.

"I figure you owe me fifty-three thousand dollars, Tom— fifty for the Colombians and another three for my traps. Count it out."

"My arm . . . I can't."

"Count, and I'll get you something for your arm."

Albury walked back into the camper's living area and rummaged through the cutlery area. Returning, he tossed four plastic bottles onto the bed. Tom wrenched the child-proof cap off one of them with his teeth and swallowed a handful of fuse-shaped capsules.

"Keep counting," Albury commanded.

Tom moaned. He sniveled. He cried. With painful, jerky movements, he labored to assemble a pile of pills on the edge of the bed.

"There," he said at last. "Take it."

Albury distributed the money among his pockets. He saw

the pills ignite in Tom's eyes and watched with scorn as Tom began shoveling the large pile of remaining bills into the suitcase.

Albury went forward and started the camper engine. He maneuvered the boxlike vehicle until it pointed down the concrete promenade. Sunset had emptied the dock. The few passersby on the still night stared incuriously as Albury drove along the seawall until the Winnebago was about seventy-five feet from the end.

"Where we goin', Breeze? What're you doin'?" Tom whimpered.

"I get out here, Tom. Where you go is up to you. You get a fighting chance. That's more than you gave Ricky."

In belated alarm, Tom rolled off the bed in a shower of stinking money. He wriggled toward Albury, dragging his twisted arm.

Albury jammed the queen conch shell between the accelerator and the brake pedal. The engine raced. He slipped the camper into gear and jumped lightly from the cab. He walked away without looking back, ignoring the shout of alarm from the carrot-cake lady as she dove from the Winnebago's path. Albury was already lost in the shadows of the Old Town when he heard the splash.

CHAPTER **22**

PEG ALBURY fortified herself with three cups of black coffee from the hospital cafeteria. Customarily, she was not up and around like this at nine in the morning, but she had not slept well. She inserted a stick of spearmint gum in her mouth, adjusted her hair with trembling fingers, and bravely made her way to the nurse's station on the third floor.

"Richard Albury's room, please."

A lovely Jamaican nurse picked up the telephone, smiled, and turned her back on Peg Albury. Moments later a starched, pinch-faced man appeared. He introduced himself as Mr. Jenks, the administrator.

Peg Albury groped for a chair. "My God. Not Ricky," she murmured. "Not Ricky, too. Is he dead?"

"You're Ricky's mother?"

Peg nodded.

"He's not here," Jenks said with an irritated sigh. "Mr. Albury removed him from the hospital about thirty minutes ago. *Against* doctor's orders, and against my orders. I told him the boy was not ready to travel. The arm needs another two days of traction."

"Breeze got him?" Peg held her straw hat to her breasts. She chewed on her lower lip, deep in thought.

"Where is your husband?" Jenks asked sternly.

"He's my former husband, and I'll be damned if I know. I had to find out about Ricky's accident from the shortstop on his team. Think of that, mister."

"You must find Mr. Albury. A person cannot just waltz into this hospital and snatch a patient out of a room and waltz out again. There are rules, Mrs. Albury, and laws. One of our orderlies is down in the emergency room at this moment, having his face sewn up. I suppose it's my fault. I told him to stop your husband down in the lobby. Apparently Mr. Albury was not of a mind to be stopped."

Peg nodded absently. "He's a contrary sonofabitch, all right." She fitted the hat back on her head. "Did he say where they were going?"

"He did not," Jenks replied. "He asked what his son's bill was, and of course he wouldn't wait while we added it up. He simply handed me five thousand dollars in cash and headed for the door. Just like that."

"Too bad," Peg Albury said, rising. "Ain't that enough? Five grand ain't enough?"

"It would have been, yes," Jenks said caustically, "if your husband had not helped himself to one of our ambulances."

Peg Albury aimed herself toward the elevator. *"Former,"* she clucked. "Former, former, former. Good morning, Mr. Jinx."

It was Huge Barnett himself who supervised the recovery of the Winnebago. He lined up two tow trucks, side by side, wheels chocked, near the end of the pier. He badgered a young mate from one of the tourist boats into diving through the clear green water to fasten the lines. A growing crowd watched in macabre silence from the seawall around the square.

"Together now," Barnett bawled.

The trucks strained. The Winnebago lurched. A large bubble of air broke the surface, and in another minute, bits of debris floated up, swirling in the current.

They looked like rumpled bits of paper. By the time anyone realized what they were, hundreds of them floated around the docks.

"Holy shit, that's money," came a shout from the crowd.

People stripped on the seawall. They dove into the water the way Conch kids of Barnett's era once dove for nickels thrown by tourists. Word raced through Old Town. In ten minutes, there were nearly three hundred people in the water, thrashing, yelling, punching, clutching for the bills. One woman almost drowned.

Huge Barnett lost his famous cool. Slack-jawed, he stomped furiously on the pier. Then he hit on a solution that would again earn him time on the evening news. One anchorman would report it wryly as the "Great Key West Swim-in."

"That's evidence," Barnett howled through his bullhorn. "Evidence in a crime. It must be handed over to the police. So don't move, anybody!"

The ambulance barreled along Truman Avenue with lights flashing, but no siren. Ricky had agreed that a siren would be overdoing it. Through a Demerol fog, he watched his father at the wheel, weaving through the morning traffic with a sleepy, serene look on his face.

"How's the arm?"

"Feels like a bus backed over it."

Albury reached across and squeezed Ricky's good hand. "We're almost there."

Teal had tied the skiff at the old Navy docks. He was sitting on a creosote stump, reading the morning *Citizen,* when the ambulance pulled up. Albury gingerly led Ricky to the bonefish skiff. Together he and Teal extricated the boy from his hospital gown and re-dressed him in a pair of jeans and a modified, one-armed rain jacket.

The skiff nosed into the northwest channel. Albury sat aft with an arm around his son.

As they passed Mallory Docks, Teal saw people leaping from the seawall into the channel. Others hovered above them, pointing, and one shirtless fellow slapped clumsily at the water with a long-handled shrimp net. The harbor was full of bobbing heads.

"Look at the fruitcakes," Teal said.

Albury paid close attention to the chaos. He saw three city police cars, two wreckers, and the corpulent profile of Huge Barnett at the forefront of the gathering. Somewhere on the bottom of the roiling channel was the nicest Winnebago in town.

"Let's go," Albury said.

Teal's keen eyes fanned the water. "God, Breeze, it's money! That's what they're swimming after." He pointed in the current, and Albury watched a soggy wad of hundreds float by.

"Use the landing net," Ricky urged giddily.

"No, son."

"It's fuckin' everywhere, Breeze. Must be thousands in here," Teal said. "No wonder the crazies are jumping in." He leaned over the side and scooped two fifty-dollar bills from a clump of kelp. "Look at this!"

"Let's stop, dad. See what we can get."

"No! Teal, we got work to do."

At Mallory Docks, Huge Barnett decreed a search of all people leaving the water. A few were frisked, and two men—a gay couple from Los Angeles—were actually arrested as an example to other scavengers, most of whom simply trod water until Barnett's deputies were occupied elsewhere. Then the swimmers thrashed to the seawall and handed fistfuls of money to accomplices on shore. It took all morning to restore order.

Huge Barnett carried to lunch with him seven thousand sodden dollars and a feeling of dread. He had recognized the submerged camper instantly. A pasty-faced coroner later had shown him the bullet holes in the corpse of Drake Boone, Esquire. Of Winnebago Tom Cruz there was no sign.

After a third night on the Mud Keys, Jimmy Cantrell had reached his limit of insects, isolation, and body stench. He proposed to take the *Diamond Cutter* inshore and find out what had happened to Albury.

"No way," Augie replied. "Breeze said we head north, up the Keys."

"And just leave him down here? Forget about him?"

"Settle down, *chico*. They got telephones in Marathon, too. We'll find out what happened." Augie rocked on the gunwale, dangling his brown feet in the milt-colored water of the creek. A pair of transluscent needlefish crisscrossed the creek, their gemstone eyes searching for minnows.

Behind him, Augie heard Jimmy climb to the pilothouse. "What are you doing?"

"I'm going to call my wife on the radio."

"The hell you are!"

Jimmy poised the microphone in his hand. "This is the vessel *Black Star* calling the marine operator in Key West."

"Go ahead, *Black Star,* this is Key West."

"I need a land line, number seven-four-two, six-one-three-six. Same area code."

"We copy, *Black Star;* what are your call numbers, please?"

Jimmy hesitated, and before he could invent a number, Augie snatched the microphone and silenced the radio.

"Do you want every asshole in Key West to hear your phone call?"

"Augie, for Chrissakes, she's pregnant." Jimmy's voice cracked. "She's probably worried to death."

Augie nodded grimly. "Get the anchor up." The vessel *Black Star,* he thought sourly, what next? He peeled off his T-shirt and surrendered to the noon sun, raw in a cloudless sky.

Jimmy was right about one thing: another miserable day in the mangroves would be unendurable. Augie punched the ignition and the *Diamond Cutter*'s diesel coughed to life. The young Cuban deftly backed the crawfish boat from its berth in the swamp, wheeled her 180 degrees in the current, and aimed the prow toward open water, the Gulf of Mexico.

"What about the dope boat?" Jimmy yelled from the bow. Augie shrugged. It felt good to be moving, to be free of the whining colonies of mosquitoes and horseflies.

After stowing the anchor, Jimmy joined Augie in the wheelhouse and offered him a warm Pepsi. The *Diamond Cutter* had been out of ice for a day and a half.

"I'm sorry about all that," Jimmy said. "But I really need to talk to Kathy. I was s'posed to take her up to Miami this weekend."

"Sure, we'll get you to a phone. There's a fish camp up on Ramrod Key. I've known the guy all my life, and he won't say shit to anybody. A quiet man. The best kind."

Satisfied, Jimmy retired to the stern and stretched out to watch the Mud Keys melt on the horizon.

It was then that he saw the charcoal column of smoke, rising from the mangroves in fierce billows and smeared by the wind across the pastel sky. Jimmy knew where the fire came from. Augie had spotted it, too. He stood in the pilothouse, his back to the wheel, transfixed by the incineration of five tons of marijuana. He flinched at the explosion that wooshed across the Gulf when the flames engulfed the gas tanks of the pirated crawfish boat.

"Jesus," Augie murmured and opened the *Diamond Cutter* to full throttle.

"Let's go," Jimmy cried, pointing to the distant speck of a speedboat racing from the Mud Keys. The saboteurs were now dead on a course for the *Diamond Cutter*. The profile of the big lobster boat rode high on the calm seas. There could be no hiding this time, Augie knew.

Jimmy bounded to the wheelhouse, panting, the Remington on his shoulder; a shirtless, fuzz-faced Johnny Reb. "You see what they did to the other boat?" he said. "Looked like a fucking atom bomb. Augie, don't slow down now."

The Cuban was smiling, his arms folded. His coffee-brown eyes were fixed on the chase boat, drawing closer, its V-shaped hull slicing the afternoon chop.

Jimmy had added binoculars to his uniform. "Looks like three of them," he said, peering, "and two of us."

Augie smiled broadly and killed the engine. "Looks like a bonefish boat to me."

The mayhem along Mallory Docks had prompted one of Huge Barnett's epic fits of perspiration. Every pore had been a geyser. He smelled like a goat and knew it.

As he changed clothes, even the apparition of Laurie Ravenel bouncing on top of him failed to brighten or elevate him. It had been a catastrophic day for law enforcement in Key West: Tom Cruz was missing, the water was full of freaks, and the island's most reknowned lawyer had been murdered. Murdered—shit, Barnett fumed, his police department had no homicide experts. Murder didn't happen that often. When it did, it was usually a domestic quarrel or a bar fight among the shrimpers on Caroline Street. A knife in the gut, a bullet in the heart, an act of contrition later. Witnesses galore. Made a policeman's job downright easy.

Barnett elbowed his way into a crisply pressed Western shirt, Arizona cactus plants on each shoulder. He stepped into his trousers and belted them high, above his navel.

Drake Boone certainly had ruined the day. This was one

that they'd want solved. There would be newspaper reporters all the way from Miami, and inquiries of an official nature. No medals from the Governor on this one, damnit.

Barnett wedged his pale, sockless feet into a new pair of Tony Llama boots. He arranged the Stetson and walked out to the Chrysler, grunting with each step.

He could hear Freed, the buttfucker, harping away at the next city council meeting. *Any suspects, chief?* Suspects? Boone had more enemies than a barracuda has fangs. When word of his murder got out, a cheer had gone up in the cell blocks at the county stockade—half the guys in there had been screwed by Boone's courtroom incompetence. Suspects?

Still, it was one nasty little murder that would not go away. Barnett knew that he would soon have to announce a suspect. A *prime* suspect. Breeze Albury would do, he reckoned, as long as he stayed gone.

Barnett double-parked in front of the Cowrie and honked three times. When Laurie got in, the chief broke into a wide, brown-toothed grin.

"You look a sight," he said. "And you wore them jeans."

"Let's go," she said in a worried tone. "As it is, everybody in the restaurant's gonna talk."

"You know faggots, they got to gossip."

Barnett took Truman Avenue to U.S. 1, up the island past Stock Island. As soon as they were out of Key West, Laurie scooted over next to him.

"Well, well."

Her perfume was arousing. A sideways glance told the police chief that his radiant date was not wearing a bra.

"I write a little poetry," Laurie said, placing a casual hand on Barnett's right leg. "Don't you think the names of these islands would make wonderful poetry? Boca Chica. Big Coppitt. Little Torch Key."

"Hadn't really thought about it."

"Ramrod. Sugarloaf. The Saddlebunch."

"Yeah. Ramrod, Sugarloaf. Those are good ones." Barnett winked. "I like those."

"Oh, stop it. Watch the road." Laurie patted his leg.

"You haven't told me where you want to go. There's a place up on Summerland we can stop for a drink—"

"No, it's too risky. Breeze knows everybody down here. Someone would tell him as soon as he got back. I know it." Laurie softened her voice. "I couldn't hurt him like that. You understand, don't you?"

"So where do you want to go?"

"Ever heard of the Tarpon Inn?"

Barnett shifted behind the wheel. "Darlin', that's a long goddamn drive."

"I know, chief, but it's got a sweet little bar. And the rooms are nice." Laurie manufactured her cutest giggle. "King-sized beds."

Huge Barnett roared his approval with a laugh that issued tremors through his belly. "The Tarpon Inn it is," he declared, gunning the Chrysler around a poky school bus pell-mell down the wrong side of the most dangerous highway in America.

Laurie Ravenel shut her eyes tightly and prayed that it soon would be over.

The gas station man parked his pickup on a bleached spit of dredged-up rock that formed a jetty into Spanish Harbor. He rolled down the windows, punched a Jackson Browne cassette into the tape deck, and tried to relax.

The message from the post office had been brief, almost too brief. When the gas station man had asked for more details, he had been curtly directed to "follow instructions."

Crystal was in his usual cautious mood.

The gas station man had waited in the truck only seven minutes before the skiff appeared, boring straight for the jetty across two miles of grassy shallows. When it was fifty yards away, the driver cut back and let the skiff glide to the rocks. He was of medium height, dressed in the khaki short-sleeved uniform of charter boat captains; his bare arms and legs were like polished walnut. He picked up the package and heaved it from the boat to the jetty.

"You know what to do, right?"

The gas station man struggled with the package. "Christ, this is heavy."

"Fifty-five pounds," said Teal. He turned the ignition key, and the big outboard came to life. "Your place is how far?"

The gas station man half-threw, half-pushed the package into the flatbed. "Just up the road, maybe a half-mile at the most."

"Good. The radio says they're right on schedule."

"God, I hope so," the gas station man said.

"Good luck." Teal gave a wave as the bonefish skiff planed off, skimming across the flats for deep water and the straight, ocean-going run back to Key West.

"Should I call you chief, or what?"

"Anything you want, darlin'." Huge Barnett was steering left-handed. His right hand, crablike, was exploring Laurie's blouse. She pushed it away, but not too firmly.

"Can I call you Clare?"

Barnett reddened. "No," he snapped. "What is it, your faggot boss went snooping around the city personnel records? That how you found out?"

"Oh, stop, it's not so bad." Laurie moved Barnett's hand to her thigh. "Where I come from, that's a perfectly fine name. Clare Barnett."

"Well, down here it's a pussy name, so just call me chief."

"Don't pout," Laurie said crossly.

"I'm not, damnit. It's this goddamn traffic."

A semitractor rig had lurched into the road ahead of them on Summerland Key. Barnett had been trying to pass it for five miles. Every time he swung the Chrysler into the left lane, the semi had sped up. Barnett had become so enraged that he had lost his erection.

"It'll be morning before we get to fucking Marathon," he howled. "I'm going to try one more time."

The truck weaved into the left lane, then cut erratically back to the right.

"God," Laurie whispered.

Back and forth, the truck snaked down the Overseas Highway, gaining speed as it seemed to lose control.

"Do something!" Laurie said.

"Fucker's drunk," Barnett grumbled. He mashed a switch on the dashboard panel, and the blue light on top of the Chrysler began to flash. Still, the big truck did not yield. Next, Barnett tried the siren.

"He's going to kill somebody," Laurie cried. "What are you doing now?"

"I'm backin' off, darling, because you're right. He is going to kill somebody, and that somebody isn't going to be me." Barnett reached for his police radio. "Think I'll call ahead for a state trooper."

At that moment, the brake lights of the semitractor winked twice. Ahead, the truck was slowing, lumbering off the highway into a roadside gas stop. A flaking billboard announced it as the Big Pine Exxon.

In a cloud of dust and gravel, the semitractor gasped to a stop. Barnett parked the Chrysler off to the side, near the gas pumps.

"This won't take long," he told Laurie.

"I'm going in the grocery store for a beer," she said.

Barnett snatched his Stetson from the backseat and lurched out of the squad car. Clumsily, he tried to hoist himself to the running board of the truck; failing that, he stood below the cab, shouting obscenities up at the driver.

The man was lean and smooth-faced. He wore a red Budweiser cap. "I'm very sorry, officer," he said weakly.

"Get your ass down here," Barnett shouted.

"In a second, please." The driver held up a small brown pharmacy bottle for Barnett to see. "I'm waiting for my pills to work."

"Get down here!"

"It's angina," the driver said through gritted teeth. "These are heart pills. I was having an attack back there on the highway—"

"Gimme your license," Barnett said. A conspiracy, that's what it was; a man can't even get laid anymore. Murders, riots, pansy lunatic truck drivers. A conspiracy.

The truck driver handed down his driver's license.

"Your name is Calvin Mo . . . Mo-something here."

"Moriel."

"Whatever," Barnett said impatiently. "Calvin, I'm not going to give you a ticket, but I'm ordering you to stay off the fucking highway with your bad heart. You're gonna kill some taxpayer, the way you drive."

"I had an attack. I'm sorry, officer, really. I'm feeling better now." Calvin inhaled deeply, as if testing his chest for pain. "I'll call the company and have them send another driver down from Miami."

"Excellent," muttered Huge Barnett, stomping back toward the squad car.

"Chief! Come here." It was Laurie, calling from the doorway of a small convenience store that adjoined the service station.

"It's gettin' late, darlin'."

"Just for a second, come here," Laurie implored.

The Exxon attendant stopped Barnett on his way across the parking lot. "Want me to fill it up, chief?"

"Just give me ten bucks of high test and check the radiator. Make it fast, too."

Barnett found Laurie in the aisle where the cosmetics were displayed. She pulled him close and pointed to a small lavender bottle. "I'm going to buy this," she said mischievously. "For us."

"What is it?"

Laurie removed the cap and held the bottle to his nose. Barnett winced.

"Oh, come on," she said. "It's cranberry oil."

"Yeah?"

"It's a lotion."

"What kind of lotion?"

Laurie smiled shyly. "You know . . ."

Barnett suddenly realized that the back of his Western shirt was drenched. He shivered in the air conditioning.

"You use that stuff? Really?"

"It tastes wonderful. Very sensual," she said. "You can spread it all over." She felt his ham-sized hand drop heavily from her waist to her buttocks.

"Well, then," Barnett said. "All right."

Outside, the gas station man worked swiftly. He lifted the hood of the police car and pulled the radiator cap. Then he crouched down, out of view of the grocery store, and crabbed to the driver's side of the car. In a matter of seconds, the keys were out of the ignition and the trunk was open.

Inside the grocery, Huge Barnett pulled a Michelob from the six-pack under his arm and cracked it open.

"Three bottles of Venetian Cranberry Oil," remarked the cashier, a red-haired girl of high school age. "I don't think we've ever had anybody buy three bottles."

"A little's got to go a long way," Barnett said with a leer. "Now, how much do we owe you?"

Barnett jammed a ten-dollar bill into the gas station man's hand and squeezed his bulk into the Chrysler.

"Where'd that damn truck go off to?"

"Who cares?" Laurie said, moving close. "Let's just go."

Barnett acceded with a grunt and wheeled back on the Overseas Highway, heading east toward Marathon. At the Exxon, the gas station man went to his CB radio and passed a brief message.

As the police car crossed the Bahia Honda bridge, Laurie pressed a soft hand to Barnett's crotch.

"You're sweet to buy me that lotion."

"It's for both of us, right?"

Laurie smiled. "My, my. This must be how you got your nickname." She played with Barnett's cowboy shirt until it came out of his pants. She struggled to unhitch the belt buckle, a brass star with his name embossed in the center.

"What are you doing, darlin'?"

"Don't mind me."

"I'm trying to drive here . . . Lord!"

Laurie rubbed Barnett's marbled belly with both hands. She leaned over and traced circles with her tongue, lower and lower on his midriff. With one hand she unzipped his trousers.

"Lord Jesus!"

Laurie sat up. "You want me to stop?"

"No, honey. Don't stop." Barnett hooked her around the neck with his arm and pulled her back down, but not before Laurie got a glimpse of the sign which announced the Seven Mile Bridge.

Huge Barnett's head spun euphorically; he felt himself grow achingly hard as Laurie kneaded him gently. The disasters of the day—Boone's murder, Tom's disappearance—dissolved with his own tumescence. Barnett kept one meaty hand on the wheel, the other on the back of Laurie's neck, guiding, encouraging. Her tongue tickled and teased, but would not go where he wanted.

Barnett navigated the narrow, pitted bridge with only half a mind to the task. Campers, tanker trucks, and tourist cars flew at him, a hairbreadth away. Barnett's squad car domineered the roadway, listing to port, weaving as he throbbed. The occasional horn of a terrified southbound car barely disturbed his trance. Twenty feet below, a stippled carpet of water stretched out to all horizons.

"Be careful, hon," Laurie whispered from the folds of Barnett's trousers, realizing all that lay between certain orgasm and certain death were the peeling, corroded railroad ties which constituted the sole guardrail. Laurie fought back her revulsion. It wouldn't be long now.

"Come on, darling," Barnett urged huskily. "I think he wants to come out and play now."

Three miles ahead, in the bridge tender's house a friend of Councilman Bobby Freed received a radio call. From his perch, the bridge tender could see a lobster boat in Moser Channel, waiting to pass from the Gulf side to the Atlantic. He pressed a button and bells rang along the Seven Mile Bridge; two sets of red-and-white barrier gates descended on each side of the turntable bridge. Slowly, the cumbersome iron span began to pivot. The bridge tender looked toward the line of traffic approaching from the south. The lead car was a big white Chrysler with a bubble on top. It appeared to be carrying only one person.

Hugh Barnett watched the gates come down through half-closed eyes. Laurie heard the warning bells and sat up, brushing the hair from her face.

"Oh, no," the police chief groaned. "Don't stop now, it's just the bridge."

The Chrysler stopped three feet from the red-and-white gate. A green sign said: Mile Marker 45. Barnett clutched himself and started to rub.

"Chief, look," Laurie said anxiously. Her eyes flashed toward the rearview mirror. "You better stop."

Barnett gave an irritated glance at the mirror, and his houndlike eyes turned cold. Directly behind the Chrysler was a gray-over-black Chevrolet Blazer. On its roof was a blue police light, flashing at the precise rate of one per second.

"What's going on?" Barnett mumbled, to no one in particular. He retrieved his lust-dented Stetson off the floor but made no move to get out of his car.

Until he heard the siren.

"What the fuck!" With an anguished roar, Huge Barnett uncorked himself from the driver's seat and swung onto the pavement.

At the side of the Blazer stood Mark Haller in his crisp Marine Patrol uniform and black cap. He wore a pair of amber Polaroids that made him look like a tomcat when he smiled.

"How's it goin, bubba?" Haller said pleasantly.

"What's with the fucking light and siren?" Barnett demanded.

"Chief, why don't you, ah, *arrange* yourself a little bit. There's a church bus from Macon about three cars back, and I got a feeling they didn't come all the way down the Keys just to see your skinny dick."

Barnett said, "Jesus Christ." He spun away from the long line of traffic and tucked his flaccid organ out of sight. He hoped that Haller hadn't noticed the drip spots on his trousers. In front of Barnett, the turntable bridge now was fully open, and the wobbling antenna of the crawfish boat marked its passage under the span.

"Chief, I'm going to ask you to open the trunk of your car," Haller said smoothly.

"What the hell for, Haller?"

"Please."

"You got a goddamn warrant?"

Haller patted his pockets. "Yep, right here. And I also got a crowbar."

"Fuck you." Barnett produced the key. "This is gonna cost you your phony little job, Haller. Ride around in a fucking motorboat all day catching crawfish thieves and poachers. A real fucking Eliot Ness, you are."

"Bubba, you best open the trunk. Now."

Barnett scowled. "OK, Mr. Grouper Trooper."

The Chrysler's trunk contained a peculiar inventory: two

spare blackwall tires (the left side always seemed to blow out in tandem), an AR-15 semiautomatic rifle; five pornographic video cassettes; a scarlet bikini; a two-pound box of chocolate cookies; a deep-sea fishing rod; fifty feet of nylon rope; a shoebox with approximately three thousand dollars inside; and, finally, a large rectangular package, wrapped neatly in brown paper and postal twine.

The package was the only item Barnett had not expected to see. It was the only item in which Mark Haller expressed an interest.

"What is it?"

"Never saw it before."

"Never?"

"Somebody put it there." Barnett was sweating from a thousand nervous little faucets. "Somebody must have put it there."

"I see." Haller wrestled the parcel out of the trunk and lay it on the pavement of the bridge. Passengers and children from the other cars had emerged to form a curious half-circle around the little ceremony.

The crawfish boat was now safely through the channel. Barnett wondered why somebody didn't close the bridge.

Mark Haller pointed the toe of his boot to the lettering on the brown paper. "Who is Rella P. Barnett?"

The chief said, "My mother."

"And does your mother happen to live at Four-seven-seven Sailfish Drive in Homestead, F-L-A?"

Barnett leaned over and examined the address. "So help me, I have no idea what the hell this is, or how it got in—"

"Let's see." Haller smoothly ran a pocketknife down the length of the package. He inserted both hands in the wound and held the pungent contents up for Huge Barnett to smell.

"Your momma like to smoke, does she?"

"Fuck you, Haller."

"She knows her blend, that's for sure."

A few persons in the crowd began to laugh. A man with

stork legs and a "Southernmost Sunset" T-shirt stepped forward to snap a picture with his Instamatic.

"Get back in your fucking cars!" Barnett yelled. The tourists retreated, eyeing the police chief as if he were rabid.

"You on your way to Homestead?"

"No, damnit. I was just going up to Marathon for a drink. Ask the lady." Barnett waved his Stetson at the car.

Haller peered. "What lady is that, chief?"

The Chrysler was empty. Barnett surveyed his squad car with a simple, disbelieving expression.

"She *was* here," he offered faintly.

With a screech, the turntable bridge finally began to close again. Across the chasm, near the bridge tender's house, southbound cars had begun to honk. Huge Barnett had nowhere to run.

"Chief, would you please turn around?"

"Fuck you."

Haller went to his Blazer and withdrew a small short-barreled shotgun. He walked back to Barnett, pulled the hammer, and held the gun to the chief's cascading midsection.

"Spread your cheeks, bubba."

Barnett felt dizzy. He turned and fastened his chalky hands to one of the railroad ties. It was scalding to the touch, but he did not flinch. He felt Haller's hands patting him down in the coarse, perfunctory way of veteran cops. Barnett's ears filled with the pounding of his own bloody rage. Somewhere in the stalled traffic, the children on the church bus from Macon sang "Michael Row the Boat Ashore" in rounds.

"You have the right to remain silent," Mark Haller recited.

Barnett leaned with all his might on the guardrail, grinding his teeth. Before him, stretched out in alternating aqua and indigo hues, was the Atlantic. It was serene and empty to the horizon, except for the crawfish boat, which had slowed in the channel not far from the Seven Mile Bridge.

"If you can't afford a lawyer," Haller was saying, "one will be appointed for you. However"—then the handcuffs, sharp on the wristbones—"I suspect you can afford a lawyer, chief."

Barnett was hearing, but not listening. Something about the lobster boat had seized his attention. He blinked several times to make sure he was not imagining it: the vision of a woman, buxom and statuesque, her dark hair slick, her blouse damp and clinging. She stood on the deck of the boat, dabbing at her face with a towel.

As the boat's big diesel came to life and the bow swung around to meet the Atlantic, Huge Barnett swallowed the dry ashes of his fury. The dying sun caught the boat perfectly in its coral light, and the name seemed to glow from the stern.

"Let's go, chief, we're blocking the bridge," Mark Haller said, steering him by the elbows. "Time to go back to the Rock."

CHAPTER  23

IT WAS a good hotel overlooking the ocean on Miami Beach, not tasteful perhaps, but less plastic than most. The dark businessman in the corner suite on the eighth floor was a prime tipper, so the waiter was careful to include a newspaper each morning with breakfast.

That day a headline midway down the front page caught the businessman's eyes:

KEYS "SWIM-IN" COP
JAILED AS POT SMUGGLER

It took the businessman only one phone call then to arrange the rest of his life.

"I'd like a first-class seat on this afternoon's flight to Paris."

"Certainly, sir."

"One-way, please."

"And are you an American citizen?"

"My passport is Canadian."

Before he left the hotel, Manolo used a razor blade to meticulously clip the newspaper article. He would carry it in his wallet as vaccination against ever going back.

"What a beautiful morning!" Bobby Freed signaled for another piece of Key Lime pie and smiled at Laurie, who sat before the remains of a gargantuan brunch.

"We did it," she said.

"The reign of King Barnett is over. He's finished; humiliated, even if he doesn't go to jail. The rest of them will be easier. Will you help me get them, Laurie?"

"Yes, Bob, I will."

All night she had been manic, laughing at the memory of Barnett's jostling rolls of fat as he tried to zipper his pants before hundreds of gawking motorists. Then, unaccountably, she had wept. For Albury, Freed knew.

"Let's take a walk," he urged. "I like this town again."

They walked arm in arm, paralleling the water. Some of the passersby in tight jeans and manicured chests looked slyly at Freed. He would be back, their glances seemed to say. Freed doubted it—but then, two weeks ago, who could have predicted this? He'd stopped trying to figure it out—he was just going to enjoy it. The stares didn't bother him at all. Once, on impulse, he darted across the street and bought an exquisite conch shell from an old woman in a floppy straw hat.

On Caroline Street, they strolled to the water's edge and clambered out along some rocks. It was a lovely view. The whitewashed island lay before them, with its shops and pale old houses, its unmistakable harbor. Like Key West itself, it was teeming: boats of every description, diving gulls, a small school of striped grunts lazing into the shadows.

"This is what it's really about," Bobby Freed proclaimed. "I love it."

He gestured toward a tall shrimp boat, inward bound, nets streeling like two outstretched webs in the sea.

As the shrimper pushed into the harbor, its steel arms suddenly lifted from the sea, jerking the first fingers of glistening net from the water.

"Beautiful, a poem," Laurie murmured.

"A ballet," said Freed.

The boat was almost abeam now, the arms rising in a long vertical sweep, the net following faster.

"You could almost reach out and touch it," said Freed. "But I'd rather touch you."

He held her before him, his back to the sea, and then watched in a sickening instant as the love in her eyes faded to horror.

Laurie screamed.

From the starboard net, spread-eagled like a snared starfish, the bloated corpse of Winnebago Tom mocked them.

CHAPTER **24**

(From the deposition of Augustin Quintana, taken on the ninth day of October 1982, before Christine Manning, special counsel to the Governor. Also present was court reporter Mary Perdue.)

MISS MANNING: Augie, when was the last time you saw Breeze Albury?

MR. QUINTANA: What's the difference, lady? He's gone.

Q: It's extremely important for this investigation.

A: Oh, really?

Q: Yes, Augie. The Governor expects a final report by the end of this month. There are many, many loose ends. Captain Albury is one. I think you know something about the others, too: the death of Tomas Cruz—

A: A tragic accident.

Q: The murder of Drake Boone, the lawyer—

A: Tom's work, of course.

Q: And there're those six unidentified Colombians in the morgue freezer up at Key Largo.

A: They are known to be terrible drivers.

Q: Augie, I don't have any more time for games. You know where Albury is, and I'm asking you, under oath. Tell me.

A: I don't like games either, lady. This is the second time you hauled me in here, and I still don't see the point. Breeze Albury is gone, and you can tell that to the Governor. I don't see the problem. They sent you down here as a special prosecutor, right? Well, now you got somebody to prosecute. He's fat and he's famous and his name is Barnett, and he's sitting in the Monroe County stockade right this minute. So go prosecute. Forget about Breeze Albury.

Q: Augie, did you know that the federal marine documentation on the fishing vessel *Diamond Cutter* was altered? That the boat is now registered to yourself and James Cantrell, Jr.? The signature of Captain William C. Albury ratifies the transfer of ownership. Would you care to see for yourself? How did that happen?

A: Breeze is a generous man. Me and Jimmy will take damn good care of that boat. It's a fine boat, lady.

Q: All right, Augie, one more time—

A: No. No *one more time*. I'm gonna tell you again. I'm a fisherman, not a goddamn private eye. I don't know where the hell Breeze is, and I don't know why you won't give up on it. I'll tell you about the last time I saw him. It was at the Seven Mile Bridge. I forget the exact night. We were all in the boat; me, Jimmy, Ricky, Breeze, and the girl, Laurie. Just out for a ride. One more run, Breeze said. He took her under the old turntable bridge at half-speed and split the seam between two nasty coral heads. It was sweet the way he ran that boat, lady. He took her straight out about two miles till we got to a line of lobster pots. Then he hopped down out of the pilothouse and turned the wheel over to Jimmy. He said it was time to go. I said, "Where to?" Breeze pointed back toward a little island about two-thirds of the way out, right under the old Seven Mile Bridge. That's where he wanted to go. He told Jimmy to take the *Diamond Cutter* up close and let him and Ricky off there. Breeze said it was the perfect spot for him, and we all laughed our asses off. The name of the island is Pigeon Key.

Q: And you haven't seen him since?

A: Or heard from him. I wouldn't bother sending out a search party, either. He's just one Conch fisherman who made up his mind to get off the Rock. I know you want to find him, but I won't help. Forget about Captain Albury yourself. And now I gotta go, lady.

Q: If you should hear from Breeze—

EPILOGUE

CHRISTINE MANNING stared at the telephone. These past few weeks, it hadn't stopped ringing. Groggily, she reached across the pillow and grabbed it.

"Christine! You've done a wonderful job."

"Thank you, Governor."

"Seventeen indictments. But what's this I hear about you leaving?"

"In a week or two, sir. Just as soon as I get the files in shape for the new prosecutor."

"You can't be serious. This is one of the biggest cases we've ever had. The police chief, six officers—my God, it's a damn miracle. Barnett's yakking his head off. Seventeen indictments in Key West!"

"Nobodies, sir. The big one got away."

"You mean the fisherman?"

"No, not him. I mean the one who ran the Machine, the one they call Manolo."

Yes, I mean the fisherman.

"Somebody always slips through the cracks," the Governor said. "That's no reason to be discouraged, Christine. We need you on our side when we go to court with these guys. Don't quit now."

"I'm sorry."

"For God's sake, it's an election year. Stick with it. Please. After November, I'll have a slot for a new deputy attorney general. What a homecoming to Tallahassee that would be, huh?"

"Well, thank you, but a quiet private practice seems very attractive. I've heard from a couple of good firms."

"In Florida? They can wait. I'll speak to them. . . ."

"No, one is in Chicago, the other in Boston."

The best surgeons were in Boston. That was what he had said the second night, their last night, as they embraced under a waning moon on the roof of her old Conch house. Boston, he had said.

"Dad, when you were in the Navy, was it integrated?"

Breeze Albury had been staring out the window. Beyond the city lay the busy harbor. He had found the fishing port without trouble, between the Navy yard and a marina for pleasure boats. They were trawlers, bluff, rough-cut boats that looked as though they could take whatever the sea demanded. The men who ran them would be of the same breed.

"Integrated? Sure, I guess so. Why?"

"You told me back on the Rock that this doctor was the brother of a guy you were in the Navy with. I don't remember you ever mentioning any black sailors, that's all."

"Did I ever tell you I told you everything?"

Ricky laughed, a big, tanned, and rawboned kid about to

become a man. He looked good, except for the cast on his arm. He had been thrilled by his first plane ride and the appraising attentions of a couple of young stewardesses. The hotel and its indoor swimming pool had equally impressed him. First-class, all the way to the World Series, Albury had promised him.

"Doctor will see you now."

The surgeon's handshake was dry and firm. Albury liked him instantly. He cut off the cast and spent a long time examining Ricky's arm.

"Exactly how did this happen?" The question caught Albury unaware. The doctor seemed angry.

"Well, I was riding my bike . . ." Ricky began.

"No, Rick, I'll tell him."

Aubury told him the truth. The doctor ran a palm across his forehead.

"Had to be something like that. There's damage to the rotator cuff and the whole shoulder, as well as to the lower arm itself."

Then he turned to Ricky.

"You're a fastball pitcher, son?"

"Yeah."

"His slider is real good, too," Albury interjected.

"I hate fastball pitchers."

Ricky looked at the doctor in alarm. The doctor smiled.

"Two reasons. One is that I never could hit a real fastball. Second reason I hate 'em is that the Red Sox never seem to have any. The pitching is pitiful, year after year."

"Ricky's going to pitch for the Orioles," Albury said.

"If I thought that was true, I'd say let's cut the damn thing off now and save us all a lot of grief later."

Ricky laughed delightedly. He sobered when the doctor told him he would have to have an operation, spend several days in the hospital, and then begin lengthy therapy.

"Do it," Albury commanded.

"Tomorrow morning," the doctor said.

A nurse came and, over Ricky's protest, installed him firmly in a wheelchair. Albury turned to leave as well, but the doctor called him back.

"Mr. Albury . . ."

"If it's about money, don't worry. I can give you a big deposit."

"No, it's not that. I just would like to know a little more about your son. For example, how important is baseball to him?"

"It's his life."

"I see." The doctor seemed unsure how to proceed. "In that case, I think it's important that you understand that the injury is acute. I think we can confidently say he will recover the use of his arm. Even full use. But as for pitching . . ."

"Ricky will pitch again."

"I hope so; we'll have to see." The doctor said it in a way that meant it might never happen.

"Look," Albury insisted. "You're the best in the country, aren't you? They told me you were the best."

The doctor studied Albury levelly through quick black eyes.

"I'll do the surgery. Then I can refer you to some good people in Miami to supervise the therapy and rehabilitation. It will be expensive."

"Forget Florida. We'll be living here from now on. You're all the doctor Ricky is going to need. And a few years from now, on Opening Day, you and I will go together to watch him pitch."

"But do you have a place to live . . . a job?"

"Not yet." The money would last until he found something. He still remembered how to tie a Windsor.

"I would like to work with your son. I really would; it might make a difference. And I have some friends down at the wharf."

"Fishing?" Albury laughed. "Why would you suggest that?"

"Well . . ." The doctor seemed embarrassed. "The accident happened on a fishing boat, didn't it? You're tanned, your hands are calloused . . . you look like you just came off the docks. I guess I just assumed . . ."

"I don't know a damn thing about fishing," Breeze Albury said quietly.

"Oh. Sorry."

Carl Hiaasen and William D. Montalbano
Powder Burn £4.99

Tens of billions of dollars of cocaine money seeps through the veins of Southern Florida every single year. At that price, even the most innocent people are going to get hurt . . .

As the drug war escalates, Chris Meadows watches a friend and her daughter die – victims of the vicious gang war spilling on to the streets. He couldn't turn his back. Now Meadows is the next target. Dangled on a hook by the friendly Florida cops – and live bait for cowboys who'll do anything to save their trade . . .

A fast and furious thriller involving murder and retribution in Florida's murky waters, *Powder Burn* is the *original* Carl Hiaasen. And life without it would be a pale imitation.

Carl Hiaasen
Tourist Season £4.99

Nobody took any notice of the first victim. He was from out of town, probably took a dip when he was drunk. All that he left was a fez, washed up on the Miami beach. The second victim did make waves. The head of the city's chamber of commerce found in a suitcase with a toy rubber alligator lodged in his throat. Now that *was* headline-hitting, bizarre even.

In Carl Hiaasen's violently funny first caper, reporters, cops, politicians, and a very hungry crocodile do a *danse macabre* round the Everglades that makes *Miami Vice* look like *Play School* . . .

'Better than literature' P. J. O'ROURKE

'Read him; he's the best new American writer since I don't know when' TIME OUT

'Fiendish suspense and wicked black humor . . . a rollicking, exciting, exceptional book' JOHN KATZENBACH

'A remarkable example of what talented writers are doing these days with the mystery novel . . . wonderful'
NEW YORK TIMES BOOK REVIEW

'He may well be the funniest writer working in America today'
INDEPENDENT

Carl Hiaasen
Double Whammy £4.99

Dennis Gault, tycoon and fishing fanatic, was only the first of Private Eye R. J. Decker's problems. Hired by Gault to investigate cheating on the Florida bass-fishing circuit, Decker found himself surrounded by murder, obsession, and a plethora of characters from beyond the fringe, to whom catching bass was more fun than sex. Pretty soon, Decker's own neck is on the line as he discovers that fishing in Florida doesn't involve killing just bass . . .

'Sharp humour, energetic action, and a supporting cast of well-drawn weirdos make this one of the most imaginative, zippy, and fun to read capers of the year' THE TIMES

'A careful reading of *Double Whammy* will do more to damage the Florida tourist trade than anything except an actual visit to Florida' P. J. O'ROURKE

'I went for *Double Whammy* hook, line and sinker, and I think you will too' WASHINGTON POST

'An outrageously entertaining high-protein experience' CHRISTOPHER WORDSWORTH, OBSERVER

'A savagely funny crime adventure . . . *Double Whammy* bristles all over' MIAMI HERALD

Carl Hiaasen
Skin Tight £4.99

Somebody wants Mick Stranahan dead. He knows because he's just had to spear an intruder with a stuffed marlin's head. And that wasn't the first time. There was the plastic surgeon with extremely shaky hands ... the personal-injury lawyer with the beaming billboard face ... the vanity-crazed star of TV's *In Your Face* ... and the high-stepping hit man with the moonscape skin. Not to mention the barracuda.

The whole thing is downright *harrowing*. It's Hiaasen at his best. And life without him would be a pale imitation ...

'Better than literature' P. J. O'ROURKE

'Slick, swift, and gloriously funny' SUNDAY TELEGRAPH

'A wonderful indictment of the American obsession with beauty and success ... probably the funniest book of its kind that you will come across all year' FINANCIAL TIMES

'The action flames, the wit's tinder-dry. For snappy prose alone, not to say neat plot, it's a classic thriller' MAIL ON SUNDAY

'Hiaasen brings classic farce to the modern thriller. There is little humour darker than his, and little funnier' EVENING STANDARD

'Hiaasen is seriously funny, and highly recommended' IRISH TIMES

'Taut, fast-paced action. The story jumps. The dialogue is crisp and hot ... his style has racing stripes'
NEW YORK TIMES BOOK REVIEW

Carl Hiaasen
Native Tongue £4.99

PR man Joe Winder didn't *believe* the theft of the last two blue-tongued voles on earth from a billionaire's Florida theme park. He just wrote the story. Asking questions later was his biggest mistake. Before he could say Robbie Raccoon, he was hiding out in the Everglades with a one-eyed wild man and gun-toting granny in pink curlers – and ready to put the skids on the greatest crime rollercoaster in the history of the state . . .

Welcome to the Amazing Kingdom of Thrills! It's the new Carl Hiaasen. And life without him would be a pale imitation.

All Pan Books are available at your local bookshop or newsagent, or can be ordered direct from the publisher. Indicate the number of copies required and fill in the form below.

Send to: Pan C. S. Dept
                Macmillan Distribution Ltd
                Houndmills Basingstoke RG21 2XS
or phone: 0256 29242, quoting title, author and Credit Card number.

Please enclose a remittance* to the value of the cover price plus £1.00 for the first book plus 50p per copy for each additional book ordered.

*Payment may be made in sterling by UK personal cheque, postal order, sterling draft or international money order, made payable to Pan Books Ltd.

Alternatively by Barclaycard/Access/Amex/Diners

Card No.

Expiry Date

_____

Signature

Applicable only in the UK and BFPO addresses.

While every effort is made to keep prices low, it is sometimes necessary to increase prices at short notice. Pan Books reserve the right to show on covers and charge new retail prices which may differ from those advertised in the text or elsewhere.

NAME AND ADDRESS IN BLOCK LETTERS PLEASE

....

Name _____

Address_____

_____

_____

_____

3/87